Sunset Summer

STEPHANIE J. SCOTT

Contents

Author's Note   V

1. Chapter One   1

2. Chapter Two   20

3. Chapter Three   30

4. Chapter Four   40

5. Chapter Five   48

6. Chapter Six   58

7. Chapter Seven   67

8. Chapter Eight   76

9. Chapter Nine   88

10. Chapter Ten   100

11. Chapter Eleven   113

12. Chapter Twelve   127

13. Chapter Thirteen   135

14. Chapter Fourteen   145

15. Chapter Fifteen   159

16. Chapter Sixteen   168

17. Chapter Seventeen   181

18. Chapter Eighteen   194

19. Chapter Nineteen   203

20. Chapter Twenty   213

21. Chapter Twenty-one   226

22. Chapter Twenty-two   235

23. Chapter Twenty-three   241

24. Chapter Twenty-four   248

25. Chapter Twenty-five   262

26. Epilogue   268

What's Next   275

Big Wild Summer   277

Acknowledgments   287

Also by Stephanie J. Scott   289

About the Author   291

Author's Note

♥

Each book in the Love on Summer Break series can be read on its own. Throughout the books, you'll find common characters and settings that take place during different summers.

For bonus content, book release news, and discounts, join my author newsletter at www.stephaniejscott.com

Note: content warning for Sunset Summer involving substance abuse by a sibling, past death of a family member

Chapter One

♥

Following the legacy of a popular sister wasn't easy. In my case, following the legacy of Grace Hayes, *the* Grace Hayes, was like sifting through the wreckage of a wayward party barge.

And that right there proved how much I knew about popularity and parties—I'd just described a party as a barge. I barely knew anything about boats.

For my entire existence, I'd been known as Grace's kid sister. The one with the weird name. Holliday, or Holli for short, which wasn't so weird in my opinion. Even though some kids started a movement in third grade to call me Chris, short for Christmas. You know, because Holliday = holiday = Christmas. Thankfully, that faded by Easter and none of them thought to call me East. Or worse, Eggs.

Grace's notoriety as a capital P Party Girl had spread over the years across town. The Catholic high school kids knew about Grace from the students who'd been sent there after being permanently suspended from our school, West Ginsburg High. Grace had often contributed to their suspension in the first place, sentencing them to finish school under God's watch. Our sister school, East Ginsburg, knew about Grace because she'd dated a Whitman's candy sampler of their football team, hockey team, and baseball team. She left her mark on all three sports seasons.

Even Grace graduating couldn't stop her wreckage from capsizing my life. My summer plans now thoroughly shredded, I faced endless weeks in exile. All Grace's fault.

See, there was this party.

"Holli, wake up," Grandma's voice jolted me awake from the front seat of my grandparents' minivan. In place of the van's comatose digital clock, a wristwatch affixed to the dash blinked eleven-twenty a.m. "We're almost home."

Home. Their home, in Deer Cove. Home to my grandparents and no one else I knew. A tiny beach town along Lake Michigan and a ninety-minute drive from Ginsburg where I lived. Ginsburg, where every plan I'd made for this summer lived.

Out the van window, a laundromat slumped next to a bait and tackle shop. Even the exit to Deer Cove was a blink-and-you'll-miss-it afterthought.

I leaned back against the headrest, my mind drifting back to where I'd resisted the whole ride. To my sister. My last glimpse of Grace as I'd loaded into the van, she'd given me an indifferent nod. Grace with her arm angled into a sling and bandages covering the stitches above her eye. She'd come out of the accident banged up but not beaten down. In fact, she may have had another party lined up that very night. Not that my parents knew.

And stupid me, I still felt bad for her.

Even though she was the very reason for my lockdown with the grans while she remained free back home. Funny, I'd heard firstborn kids were supposed to get the harsher rules and punishments. But she wasn't the one being sent away for summer.

Grandpop turned after the retro Sunset Inn sign on the corner of their property. Grandma considered the sign's cartoonish cursive back in style: the top of the "S" like it was drawn around an egg and the bottom curled under like a cat's tail.

Truth? The sign looked old. Worn. Tired. Like this town.

But my grandparents owned the inn and were proud of it.

We rolled to a stop and I heaved open the van door. I wasn't ready to give up on my summer. Once things cooled down, it should be easy enough to convince my grandparents to let me go home. I just needed to play this right.

I was good at playing the good girl. Intentionally doing bad things risked me breaking into hives. Seriously, that happened *more than once*. I wouldn't wish full body hives on anyone. Even Grace.

Well, maybe Grace. After her arm healed and the stitches came out. Then it was hives ahoy!

Grandpop grabbed for my suitcase, but the weight yanked his arm down. He made an exaggerated face. "Lead boots back in season?"

"Ha-ha," I spoke the laugh. Still, I felt bad he had to carry my baggage. Both literal and figurative. "I've got it." I took the bag and tipped it to the roller wheels.

"Take everything to the sewing room." Grandma nodded toward the other side of a low fence from Sunset Inn's rental cabins. Their pale blue house reflected wide open sky, but the siding was tinged gray with grime. Curtains in the front windows hung half drawn. Paired with the worn front door, the house scowled.

Inside, I found the room where Grace and I always slept. Bolts of fabric and department store sacks with knitting yarn crowded around the lumpy pull-out couch. I opened the door to the small closet. Neatly labeled boxes took up one side from floor to ceiling. Sewing supplies in plastic bins and a pegboard on the back wall covered the rest. No clothes bar or hangers.

This was so not going to work.

I checked my phone for texts as a distraction. My heart dropped. One lone bar of coverage hanging on with a half-hearted flicker. Maybe it was better this way. The post-party damage had already been done.

See, there was this party and...*sigh*.

I'd called my best friend Tala in a panic yesterday as I packed, telling her the news I'd have to delay the movie theater job we'd applied for together until I figured this all out. And I had to ask. "Are people talking? About the party?"

"Like, rumors?" She made a low-key comment in Tagalog, something she did if she needed a couple of extra seconds to regroup. And because she knew I couldn't understand. "There are always rumors."

"About my sister?" About me?

I'd avoided all my online profiles. I'd only texted Tala to say we'd had an accident, but I was okay.

"People always talk about Grace."

They did. And now after this disastrous party, I'd be talked about too. And not in a way I wanted.

Tala knew everything about me. More than my sister did these days. Back in second grade when we met, we'd bonded over ballet (which I wanted to be good at but never was) and our shared obsession with this book series *The Trash Can Alley Kids' Mystery Club*. She was Team Tin-Can Annie, and I was Team Sammy T. Sleuth. Tala always got me. She always saw what I couldn't see in myself.

Grandma appeared in the sewing room doorway. She stood shorter than me with soft brown hair threaded with silver. Freckles and sunspots dotted her white skin from years living steps away from Lake Michigan, the selling point to Sunset Inn. One block from the beach.

"Hey, does the attic still have the daybed?" I peered into the hall to the narrow door at the end leading to the partially finished third floor.

Grandma made an *mmhmm* sound. "It's messy. We can take a look."

Her version of messy varied greatly from my personal definition of a mess. I followed her up the steep stairs to the old attic playroom.

Grandma crossed the room and hefted open a window. "We'll need to air this out. And clean up this clutter."

Sure enough, "messy" and "clutter" to Grandma consisted of two neat stacks of boxes on one end of the room and an old bookcase with some books knocked over on the shelves.

On the other side of the room, my aunt's old dollhouse stood angled in a corner. A daybed and dresser sat in the middle of the room.

The walls sloped to mirror the roof with two windows Grace and I called look outs. We used to imagine the room as our castle.

"I'll take it," I said, trying to sound like an eager buyer. This was definitely not as terminal as the sewing room.

"Let me fetch a box fan from the shed." Grandma looked at me. "I'm glad you're here with us, Holliday. Now wash up and come eat lunch."

Up early this morning and over an hour drive later, it was only lunchtime. On day one.

Downstairs in the kitchen, a grilled cheese sandwich and soup waited for me. The comfort food settled my nerves.

Grandma pointed to a note on the table in the eat-in kitchen. A schedule. "Here are your cleaning shifts."

Just like that, I was now an employee at Sunset Inn. "No interview? That's nepotism for you."

Grandma did not crack a smile at me cracking wise. Then again, I wasn't exactly here on vacation.

I looked over the schedule. This was steady part-time work. Unpaid part-time work. Definitely not like making popcorn at the movie theater sharing a shift with my best friend.

Grandma's ancient cell phone startled awake with a weirdly hyper ring. She answered, talked for a minute, and clicked off the call. "That was the community center. You can enroll today and start your service hours tomorrow."

My skin prickled with heat. "But we just got here. I haven't even had my new employee orientation at the inn."

She still didn't smile at my clearly brilliant wit. "You've been here enough times you know the drill at the inn. If you get an early start on those service hours, you can show the judge you're responsible."

She didn't know it yet, but I wasn't planning on sticking around long enough to enroll anywhere. Tala and the movie theater expected me. The cross-country team expected me. The team I'd just been named co-captain of as an incoming junior.

"I really don't think—"

"Holli." Grandma's voice came sharp. "This isn't your time or place to think anything. We agreed you'd come here and do your community service hours. End of discussion."

I hadn't agreed to anything. I'd been told.

The conversation with my parents rewound in my head. I recalled a lot of yelling and demanding. No actual contract to negotiate. I'd never seen them so mad, and Grace once stayed out all night and came home with a lip ring.

I ate my grilled cheese in silence.

The silence last ten seconds.

"This is very serious, Holli." Grandma rested her elbows on the table and looked me over.

It was mildly terrifying.

"Your sister's blood alcohol level was far above the legal limit. And for a seventeen-year-old, that limit is zero."

Obviously, I knew this, but when Grandma began a lecture, best to wait it out.

"The only thing worse than my oldest granddaughter failing a breathalyzer was discovering my second oldest granddaughter had been the one driving her intoxicated sister. On a *learner's license*."

She wasn't wrong. I'd been the nearly sixteen-year-old (just a few more weeks) who'd done her good girl best by driving her drunk sister home from a party the cops busted. Scratch that—*attempted* to drive her drunk sister home.

I'd crashed the car. My perfect daughter record tarnished.

And I'd hurt Grace. I'd physically hurt her. As much as she infuriated me, she was still my sister. Before she was a mess, she was my hero.

"I raised a better son who raised better girls than what the two of you have been up to lately," Grandma went on. "Well, it stops here. This summer, you clean up your act, Holli. It might be too late for Grace, but it's not too late for you."

Class now dismissed, Grandma rose from the table and headed out the side door and across the lot to the Sunset Inn front office.

I welcomed the alone time. I took care of washing my bowl and plate. I sat back at the table. The silence of the old house echoed louder than her ring tone. The silence served as its own jail sentence.

See, there was this party. I hadn't even wanted to be there, but I went because my sister asked me to. I didn't do well at parties—I tended to stick to the walls—so I followed Grace's lead. Her last request as an outgoing senior.

No party was worth what happened to get here.

After an afternoon sorting through the attic and a self-guided tour of Sunset Inn's cleaning supplies and laundry facilities—both existed in a single, sweltering room connected to the front office—I completed my own orientation and worked my first shift.

Basically, I did what Grandma told me, then took a shower to clean up before dinner.

I was tempted to sulk in the attic, but I liked food too much. Also, my grandparents required me to be seated at the table for dinner. No standing over the sink eating crackers or eating leftovers on the couch.

Following the rules got me closer to going back home.

Maybe I just needed to use my good girl skills to my advantage. I hadn't become the family's reliable daughter by staying quiet. Nope. I excelled at being proactive.

"So, I have a lot going on with the team," I said to my grandparents. "Maybe I can help out this week and then we can look at service hours back in Ginsburg?"

Grandpop didn't blink. "You'll stay here until you see the judge."

I cringed at the word *judge*. The hearing was scheduled weeks from now. Since I'd violated the terms of my learner's permit by driving without a legal adult in the car, I wouldn't be allowed a license until I attended a court hearing. And no guarantees after that either.

That's what the service hours were for. The lawyer my parents talked to the day after the accident said to start early before the sentencing.

I would be *sentenced*. And not in a grammarly way.

I could still skew this my direction. "I have people depending on me. My team, for one, and the job I was hired for."

"What job?" Grandma asked. "Who hired you?"

Almost hired. "The movie theater."

Grandpop sat back. "Good thing we took you when we did. The theater by us is a *Lord of the Flies* situation. I think the general manager is younger than the socks I'm wearing."

"People my age have to work somewhere," I countered.

Grandma pointed at me with her fork. "We discussed this as a family. You're here for the summer."

Away from Grace. The unsaid part.

"But it's not *fair*." The declaration burst out before I could stop myself. "Grace doesn't have to be here and she was the one who was drinking. I didn't drink. *I* was responsible."

"Crashing cars is responsible now?" Grandpop made a show of looking at Grandma. "Well, I'll be. I guess we old-timers are out of touch."

Obviously, that wasn't what I meant.

"That Grace." Grandma shook her head with a look of sadness. "Trouble with the law. Trouble with boys. Bad grades. She hasn't enrolled anywhere for college.

If you're not careful, Holli, you'll end up just like your sister."

If every meal included a lecture, I should get AP credit for this summer.

After dinner, Grandpop left to man the front desk. When they didn't have their part-timer on the clock, the two of them checked in guests and cleaned the rooms. Basically, they did everything to run a small motel.

I looked at my phone again and sent a few texts to Tala. When she didn't respond, I had to assume she was working.

More texts waited unanswered on my phone. The ones I'd ignored the past two days.

What happened at the party?

What happened to Grace?

Is Grace OK? I heard she DIED.

Was your sister arrested?

My teammates only wanted to hear about Grace. I couldn't bring myself to respond. Besides Tala, the only person I'd talked to was Coach. My parents insisted on watching me while I'd called her. Then Dad took the phone to explain why I wouldn't be fulfilling my co-captain's duties.

All of that didn't exactly make me eager to dish gossip about a busted party and how my sister somehow became even more legendary because of it. While I was stuck here. Alone.

The night stretched in front of me all endless and stupid. After watching a terrible game show, I shut the TV off and grabbed a zip-up sweatshirt and my earbuds.

I had my hand on the front door's knob when Grandma called out from the sewing room. "You going somewhere, Holli?"

How had she known? I wasn't in her sight lines. "I thought I'd walk to the shore," I called back. "Maybe run a little. If that's okay."

"All right. Be back by sunset."

Outside, the front walk emptied to a side road wide enough for one car. A dirt walking path ran alongside it. One short half-block and the road ended where the sand swallowed up the concrete. Lake Michigan's own welcome mat. From this view, the lake may as well have been the ocean.

Okay, I was a sucker for a pretty view. I'd always loved coming here to visit.

Key word: visit.

I started a slow jog to get my muscles warmed up. I wanted to lose myself in the familiar in and out of my breath.

I ran and my thoughts wandered. Just days ago I put together a training schedule with the team. The memories came in fragments. The cold shock of sports drinks pouring down my back in celebration of the co-captain title. Cheering and congratulatory chanting. An older-than-fossils jersey sliding over my neck. Who cared if the ceremonial shirt smelled somewhere between worn sweat socks and somebody's garage? That was my moment. Now a hundred miles separated me from the team.

I ran until I reached where the beach turned to rocky shore. Turning back, I crossed the length of beach and headed south to the stretch along town and the public access park.

Eventually, I turned back, slowing to a jog. I walked to cool down.

I headed for a driftwood log parked along the shore. The sun sank lower and shed citrus shades across the water, shifting hues every few minutes.

I sat on the log which was long enough and sturdy enough to work like a bench with room to spare. It was low to the ground, so I stretched my legs in front of me and took in the view.

Closing my eyes, I let the music through my ear-buds wash over. Light atmospheric music from a movie soundtrack I found on my streaming app. It helped me zone out.

Instead of planning how I'd get out of this mess, I let the thoughts go for another time. In ten minutes, the thoughts would come back, but at least I had a break.

Different, not-so-soothing music came from some-where. It sounded underwater. Movement stirred be-side me.

My eyes flew open. I nearly jumped out of my skin. Someone—a guy—just sat on my log.

Well, not *my* log, being a public beach and all.

Still, the whole beach existed and this guy sat right next to me. With some kind of blender-punk blasting from his headphones.

I pulled out an earbud and stared at him. He looked close to my age. Maybe a year or two older. Dressed in a black hoodie, black jeans, black skater shoes. Straight hair settled across his eyebrows, and longer pieces grazed his cheek. He had a fair complexion, almost ruddy, and dyed black hair with lighter roots.

The dude was into black.

He turned, finally noticing me notice him. "Hey. I'm Will. Hope I didn't scare you."

Not scared so much as weirded out. "I'm Holli. Hi."

The music in his headphones stopped. "Are you related to the Hayeses?"

"How did you know?"

"Small town. I saw them drive in and a girl got out of the van."

"Ah." I waved a hand at him. "That would have been me. The van girl."

I cringed. Not at all awkward.

Will showed a hint of a grin. "It's hard not to notice things. I live here."

From what I knew from all my years visiting, the town itself didn't have many kids my age. Lots of vacationers. Besides Sunset Inn, Deer Cove had a bed and breakfast and a campground at the nearby state park. In ten miles either direction, larger beach towns collected the bulk of travelers. Those touring the coast made stops here. They just didn't stay long.

"My family moved here last year from Jackson," Will went on. "It's been...an adjustment." He raised an eyebrow. A pierced eyebrow.

"I'm sorry."

"Sorry for what?"

"That you live here."

"I like it here." He leaned forward with his elbows on his knees. His hands had black X marks on the backs.

"Were you at a show or a club or something?" I asked, pointing to the Xes.

He rubbed a thumb across one. "Tattoos." When my eyes widened, he grinned. "I'm kidding. It's permanent marker."

"Oh, right, sure." My cheeks grew warm. Piercings and hand stamps were Grace's territory. I went to the type of concerts where the tickets required a parent to purchase them on a credit card. A concert my parents then accompanied me to.

Will just sat there, staring across the lake.

"What's it like to live in Deer Cove?" I asked since he wasn't leaving.

"It's what you make of it." He nodded toward the water rolling into shore in a steady rhythm. "There's less going on than back in Jackson, but you can find your trouble if you want."

Great. Just what I didn't need this summer. Some bad boy looking for trouble while I made moves to dig myself out.

If Grace were here, she'd definitely encourage this. She'd tried to set me up so many times. Younger siblings of her friends or randos she met in her extensive network at other schools. At the graduation night party, before things went south, she'd paired me with a guy who'd been kicked out of Ginsburg Catholic and rode a motorcycle. We'd ended up talking GED strategies and I gave him a reference to an affordable tutor.

Grace had been so disappointed.

"What are you into?" Will asked me.

"Into?"

"Yeah. What do you like to do?"

Well, at least this guy acted interested in talking to me about me. If I ignored him, I'd end up playing canasta and cribbage with the grans as my only social outlet.

I relaxed my shoulders and tilted my head the way Grace did when she talked to guys. Like she barely cared. "I run cross-country."

He nodded, seemingly interested. "Have you been on the trails?"

"I haven't. Tonight, I ran on the beach. Do you run?"

"A little."

He didn't look like a runner type, but what did I know? Maybe he ran from the trouble he caused. Like running from cops.

"I'm pretty familiar with the trails around here." His smile blurred the line between confident and cocky. No, not cocky, but confident. "If you want a guide."

"Yeah, if you have a map or something, that would be great."

I thought I heard him laugh, but it came out quiet like a shift in his breath. "I meant I could show you."

Oh. *Oh. Show me the trails.*

I was for sure out of my element here. This guy was magnitudes cooler than me. I mean, I had some pretty fun friends. Tala? Amazing. Plus the cross country team. I had an in with the theater tech crew from when I hadn't made the cut for the stage production. I'd been the assistant to the assistant lighting operator, who happened to be quite an up-and-coming freshman.

Besides that, I lived two houses down from our class president.

Okay, maybe those things landed me short of cool, but I wasn't ashamed of my friends. Not one bit. I liked to make myself friendly to everyone. Even the guy who said he knew Grace and tried to sell me stereo speakers out of his trunk in a Target parking lot. Long story.

Thankfully, my phone buzzed in my pocket, saving me from responding to Will about the trails.

I slipped out my phone, noting my grandparents' image on the screen. I had to answer. "Hello—"

"You've got ten minutes before dark," Grandma said. "I wasn't sure you knew what time the sun set." She ended the call.

"Need to go?" Will asked.

The sun still hovered at the horizon. "I think I'm good." I sighed. "Back home, I kind of come and go whenever. Here—it's going to be different." I hadn't pressed those boundaries too much back in Ginsburg. That was my sister's role.

"Different can be good."

He wasn't wrong, but in my case, different was totally inconvenient. "It's just, I'm not supposed to be here. I have a job back in Ginsburg. The cross-country team to practice with. But I'm here instead."

"You blew it, huh?"

"What?"

"Something must have happened if you're here and not there."

A shot of agitation ran through me. I was that easy to read. Then again, if he looked for trouble—whatever that meant—and I was definitely *in* trouble, he might not see what I did as so bad.

I went for a disaffected vibe. "My parents flipped out on me because I went to a party busted by the cops. Things got pretty crazy."

He raised one dark brow. "Sounds intense."

It had been frightening, absolutely. "Sure. Whatever."

"And you were caught?"

"Yeah—well, sort of. I wasn't drinking." I silently cursed my honesty. Cool kids like Will bragged about drinking at parties. I failed so hard at playing bad. "I was there as my sister's designated driver." An arrangement we definitely hadn't made ahead of time. "It was more after the fact the police became involved, at least for me. Because I don't have a license."

"So, you don't have a driver's license but you were the designated driver. How does that work?"

I sighed. "It doesn't."

Will whistled low. "And now you're doing penance in Deer Cove?"

"Pretty much."

He nodded, taking this in. "I guess you'll have to ride out your summer with the townies."

"Oh. Hey, I didn't mean—"

He raised a hand. "I'm kidding. I get it. Small towns suck. I try to make the best of it."

The sky dimmed as the sun dipped lower. The walk wasn't too far, but I'd better not chance walking in past sunset my first night. "I should go."

Will stood quickly. "Yeah. Of course."

I stood too. "It was nice to meet you."

He looked at the sand, then back to me. "There's a few of us who don't suck who hang out sometimes." He nodded further down the beach. "Maybe see you around?"

I could use a friend out here, even though I didn't plan to stay long. Besides, Will was a bad boy. A finder of trouble. I needed neither of those things in my life.

I glanced up and was struck suddenly by Will's eyes. Brown with flecks of amber.

I was doomed.

Chapter Two

♥

The next morning, my bare feet hit cool wood floor planks, sending a chill through my body. I shook myself awake as I slipped on one of my running tops and added a long-sleeves layer. Not to prep for a run. Nope, I had an early morning date with the community center for my service hours. Early morning this close to the water meant a chill in the air, even in summer.

Grandpop insisted on personally escorting me to my service hours. Was I that big a flight risk? Where else could I go? The bait and tackle shop?

The community center, a one-story brown building two blocks from the inn, looked like a bank instead of somewhere a community gathered for fun. Then again, I doubted *service hours* and *fun* ever joined up in the same sentence.

We checked in at the front desk. "You can go ahead and put this on." The woman at the desk handed me a T-shirt. Green with a leaf logo. "It's sort of the group uniform."

The shirt felt stiff as I switched out my long sleeves and pulled it over my slim-fitting base layer.

"You'll be alright?" Grandpop asked.

I shrugged. Then out of habit, answered anyway. "Yes, Grandpop. Thank you."

The desk staff pointed past the lobby to an open space with a wall of windows facing out to Lake Michigan. "Through the door and out back."

Outside again, a group of eight or so people milled around. I had no idea what a community service group did in Deer Cove, but at least I wore decent shoes. A girl near my age wore cute strappy sandals not good for much besides a stroll through a mall, which I was positive did not exist for at least thirty miles. Plus, she had to be cold out here with the overcast skies.

I wandered to the group, sticking to the edge. A gray-haired guy with sand-toned skin noticed me. He wore a light parka by a pricey brand. "Hi there. You're the Hayeses' girl? Their granddaughter?"

In nodded. My grandparents really did know everyone. "I'm Holli. Glad to be here." Might as well start off in the right with the group leader.

"Ken." He shook my hand like I was an adult. "You should meet this fella here—he's your age." Ken pointed to a guy with a light reddish beard, black-framed glasses, and a messenger bag hanging across his body.

"I'm Chaz." His shirt had a line art picture of a bicycle wheel drawn inside of the outline of the state of Michigan.

"Nice shirt," I said, to be friendly.

"Do you ride?"

"Uh, no. I run."

"I do some light distance training myself. Nothing too fancy. I read a great article on a DIY group hosting

Saturday morning running meetups in cities all over the country. You ever do one of those?"

Okay, this guy was intense. "I'm in high school, so I run with a team."

"Cool, me too. In high school, I mean."

"Really?"

"It's the beard, huh? Makes me look older." He smoothed the side of his well-trimmed facial hair. "So's the group leader."

"The group leader is what?" I looked at Ken.

"Here he is." Ken nodded past me. "Our fearless leader."

The person approaching us wore a black sweatshirt with the hood drawn up. The hood then pushed back to reveal ink black hair. My jaw fell open.

Will.

"Good morning, everyone," Will announced. "We'll get started with attendance first."

I whiplashed to Ken. "*He's* the leader?"

"Someone needs to wrangle us riffraff, am I right?" Ken elbowed Chaz. "He's a good kid. A hard worker."

Will, who looked for trouble, who dressed like color was outlawed, was the guy my family pinned their hopes on to straighten me out?

Will unearthed papers from his cargo shorts pocket. "We've got some new names here." He scanned the list. "Violet?"

A woman in a floppy hat who looked older than my mom but younger than my grandma raised her hand.

"And Holliday." He drew out the syllables in my name like a curiosity. His gaze met mine, practically smoldering. A half smile turned up his mouth. "Nice to see you again."

I nearly melted into puddle.

Okay, so yes it was shocking to see Will again. *Here* specifically. But wow, he was even better looking than I remembered.

I took in the dark hair, eyebrow ring, and sweatshirt with worn cuffs. He looked cool without effort. Confident in front of a group.

Will was *hot*.

And definitely not my type. He was a bad boy. Wait—or was he? Bad boys looking for trouble probably didn't lead community service groups.

"Holli is the Sunset Inn owners' granddaughter," Ken said to Will.

Unable to stop, I stared at Will, confused how someone in high school had been put in charge of a community service group. Was that even legal?

Will continued with the attendance list. "Piper?"

The cute shoes girl waved. She looked dreamy-eyed at Will. Well, that was understandable.

Will nodded at Chaz. "Hey, buddy, glad to have you back."

Will reviewed the group's mission statement which involved caring and communicating with town residents. "Deer Cove may be off the beaten path, but we take care of each other. You all are proof of that." Will looked around at the group, nodding as he met the eyes of a few people. "You make our community better. Now let's make this summer season our best yet."

This did not sound like a boy who looked for trouble. Will was now talking about a street beautifying project involving planting flowers. The Xes on his hands flashed in glimpses as he spoke. A bad boy...gardener?

"Holliday? Would you like to start?" Will watched me, his smile subtle.

"Yes," I answered automatically. "And Holli is fine."

He walked past me to an open shed and pulled out a shovel. "Here you go. We'll be digging right over there."

I probably should have paid attention to what I'd agreed to. A mound of dirt awaited me. Welcome to my summer.

Two hours later, my back felt like it'd been run over by my whole cross-country team. Turning soil and pulling weeds was no joke. We'd been tasked with expanding the community garden on-site at the center. So many residents had signed up in spring for a square plot to do their own planting, word had spread, and the demand was high.

The demand for a square of dirt. I couldn't make this up if I tried.

Will spent the allotted time working with Chaz to extend wire fencing around the garden plots and relocate picnic tables. Not that I'd paid attention.

I tried to blend with the retirees—Ken, Violet, and two others, who knew far more about gardening than I did. They were all here by choice because they liked helping make their town better. At least that's what they'd told me. I didn't tell them the reason I'd ended up here. No one needed to know I'd screwed up my life if I could help it.

"Hey, Hollid—Holli," Will corrected himself as he walked over and shook out his work gloves. "Your city legs working okay out here?"

"These city legs run a six-and-a-half minute mile."

"Fair enough. This kind of work isn't the same as running."

Despite my attempt at a confident smile, he was right. My back muscles weren't used to wielding a loaded shovel. My neck ached. A nurse at the hospital mentioned how whiplash effects from the accident could crop up over the next week. Maybe this was more than aches from digging.

I didn't want him to see me as weak. I tugged at the T-shirt. "Leaf Group isn't so bad, I guess."

"Leaf Group. I like it. So, it looks like you found something to do in Deer Cove after all."

"I'm digging dirt. *So* glamorous."

"Make fun of it all you want, but this is my favorite job I've ever had. Giving back is the best high in life."

My mouth sort of dropped open. "Digging garden plots gives you a high?"

"Different than a drug high." His gaze settled on me like I might understand the difference. Right, because he thought I was a delinquent who fled the police and drove without a license. Which okay, was true, but that wasn't the real me.

I wasn't my sister.

"I like working the land and knowing how to care for it," Will went on. "And how to care for people. Sure beats staying inside playing video games."

The boy was utterly strange. When he said he looked for trouble, I assumed, like, breaking into abandoned houses or joyriding at midnight. Not *working the land.*

He leaned against a lopsided fencepost. "We're free tomorrow—no Leaf Club—if you want to hit the trails. I do odd jobs with the park rangers, so I know my way around."

"Will!" Piper, the girl dressed more for shopping than digging, called over. She walked toward us with an exaggerated limp. "Are we done? My feet are cramping."

Will dismissed the group, instructing everyone to stop by the desk for fresh bottled water. He hung back.

The air shifted. "If you don't want to meet me on the trails, I get it."

"No, it's fine. I'm just..." Confused. Yesterday, I assumed he'd think partying and escaping the cops was cool. Dangerous. Something a bad boy with X marks on his hands from a punk club would respect. Now he was in charge of my community service. "How is it a high schooler is the head of a community service project?"

He let out a short laugh burst. "I showed up one day. Started working with the old leader. When that lady took another job out of town, they asked me." He ran a hand through his hair sliding the longer pieces behind his ear. "Kind of wild, I guess. I'm not allowed to drive the community center van, but beyond that, they just need someone to round up the volunteers and give people direction. Not too hard."

"It sounds like a lot of responsibility." I still wondered why he'd showed up in the first place. Had he been told to? Maybe he'd been given service hours like me, but ended up liking it.

"It's a pretty cool place. There's a food pantry here every first Saturday. Cool if you like meeting different people. A group does home outreach with the older folks around the area who can't get out of the house. We've got a teen night. I know it sounds super lame—believe me, the me from one year ago would totally laugh at anybody inviting me to something called 'teen night.' It's cool, I swear. We do art and we play music and you should totally come."

He sounded nervous. Will, nervous. I was the one who was nervous. "Maybe you could show me around the community center."

Will smiled. Like sunlight peeking through gray skies.

Inside, I followed Will down a narrow hall to a large room with a pool table, an old wrap-around couch, a TV, and a wall of windows facing the lake. Framed art covered the interior walls. Pencil drawings and paintings showed different skill levels.

"We're trying to organize a gallery show," he said. "My friend, Antonio, he drew this."

The sketch was of a young Black man, only half his face was fragmented, as if constructed by puzzle pieces. For a drawing, the look in the guy's eyes appeared so real, so sad. "This is really good."

"I know. Want to see one of mine?" Will pointed to a simple watercolor landscape with splotchy sections of color. The blue sky bled into a beach. Maybe a beach. It was orange at least.

"It's...nice."

"People think a little kid made this." His grin widened. "I'm the worst at painting."

"Well, at least you tried." I couldn't help smiling back.

"I'm into trying new things. Maybe I'll fail. Maybe I won't." He motioned with his hands. "Toss of the dice."

"Is that what your hand thing was? A mimed dice toss?"

He made the gesture again. "Or maybe it's like Yahtzee where the dice are in a shaker?" He tried again pretending to shake a can.

I shook my head laughing. "You are *so* weird."

"Anyway, the group, we hang out here, and we plan stuff. The group rotates ideas, but the point is everyone comes up with something. It doesn't have to be big. We brought in clothes last week for a donation drive. Another time we bought soap and body wash and took it to a shelter the next town over. Stuff like that."

I never would have guessed Will would be so into taking care of the community. I'd totally misjudged him. He looked the part of a bad boy, but my own stereotyping seemed just that.

The clock near the door caught my eye. "I should head out. My grandparents are expecting me." Instantly lame.

We returned to the lobby where people in hiking gear spread out a map on a table.

Will walked me to the front desk. "Make sure you have the front desk sign off for your hours. You know, for the paperwork."

My heart dropped. "Paperwork."

"Yeah. Proof of your community service hours. For your delinquent behavior."

I gasped. Then I saw the look on his face. Teasing. He was teasing me.

Instantly, his grin faded. "Hey, it was a joke. I'm sorry. I didn't mean to offend you."

"Of course. I knew that." I struggled to fix a smile to my face. I swallowed back tightness in my throat and blinked back the threat of tears. *Not now.*

It was stupid to care what Will thought—I'd just met the guy. But knowing what I did now, that he spent his free time helping people and worked a job motivating retirees, I couldn't stop the shame from welling up. In this situation, I was the bad one.

Will didn't understand what I faced. He didn't understand me or what I'd done to overturn everything in my life. More existed to the story than what I'd told him. Than what I'd told anyone.

But I couldn't let myself dwell on that now. If I did, I would crack for sure.

Chapter Three

♥

I pulled out my phone the second I left the community center. The marathon session digging dirt this afternoon gave me time to think. Being stuck in Deer Cove for the summer meant I needed to manage the rumors about the party and the accident.

"Walking and texting is a hazard," Grandma said, appearing in front of me.

I didn't need her to walk me home—a straight shot down Main Street. Yet here she stood. She probably considered me a flight risk. Like I'd steal a car and drive home on a revoked learner's permit.

I stopped walking to scan through the texts. A new message from Christina Gomez, the cross-country team captain, sat at the top.

Dread formed in my stomach with each message. Her texts started with worry followed by shock. Someone must have told her details on the accident since the texts turned panicked. Was I injured? Had I talked to Coach yet? Then demanding. What was I doing at that party, anyway? I needed to talk to Coach. It was crucial I talked to Coach.

I started walking slowly so Grandma didn't snip at me. More texts had come in from my teammates today.

"Holli." Grandma clapped once, loud. "Put the phone down."

I stared at her in horror. My grandmother just *clapped at me* in public. I scanned the area for witnesses. Beyond a few cars driving past, I only saw one family ducking into the library.

"I need to talk to my coach," I told her.

While Dad had told Coach not to count on me, I'd messaged her afterward to say I'd only be gone a few days. A week tops. A little time with my elders would calm everyone down.

The team ran on a schedule, and my coach wanted specifics. Days, times, commitments.

I opened my email on my phone.

Holli: I hope you're resting up with your grandparents. We should discuss the team responsibilities. I can't get an answer when I call your house. Can you meet Friday in my office at school?

Friday. I could do this. Sure, I was almost a hundred miles from home with no way to get there.

"Give me the phone," Grandma demanded.

I yanked it out of her reach. "You don't understand. I left things behind. People need things from me."

"I will not ask you again. Come now, or the phone gets locked away."

Locked away? She couldn't be serious.

I shoved the phone into my bag just in case.

When we reached the house, I stayed outside in the yard. "I have to call Mom."

She waved me off and disappeared inside.

I had the phone at my ear and ringing before the front door closed. The lake down the block drew my focus, with waves rolling into shore coinciding with each ring.

She picked up. "Mom? My coach tried to call. Why didn't you answer?"

"It's been a long few days, Holli. I'm tired."

"Half the time this phone doesn't have a signal out here. I need you to call—"

"You're in no place to demand anything after your reckless driving stunt."

I gritted my teeth. "It wasn't a *stunt*. It was an accident."

"You shouldn't have been driving. You shouldn't have been at a party."

Of course I shouldn't have. I'd told her I was with Tala, only Tala had tickets to a ballet at the Ginsburg Civic Center.

"We've put up with too much with your sister already. I spoke to your coach an hour ago. I told her you'll be staying at your grandparents' through the summer. Apparently, she thought you planned to come home this weekend even though we specifically told her otherwise."

I didn't miss her accusatory tone. "Mom. I *can't stay here*. My team is asking where I am. Tala had that job lined up for me. I'm bailing on them."

"If you think you're bailing on your team, then next time consider the consequences of your actions."

I'd heard this lecture already. Only it hadn't ever been directed at me. I'd only been a bystander to Grace's epic schooling by Mom.

"Your coach and I agreed it's best for you to step down from your team responsibilities. You can still join the team for meets this fall if you continue training."

No. *No, no, no.* So much was happening, so much going on in my brain, my words couldn't keep up. One stupid mistake and everything I'd worked for seemed out of reach.

"Mom, no. I can't just ditch on my life. You don't understand—"

"Work hard this summer. Then come home and be the good girl you are."

Be the good girl.

Being the good girl got me here, in exile from my life.

I settled in upstairs in my attic room after dinner. A few slow-connection clicks and my online social sites popped up on my phone.

On Instagram, I skimmed the list of my sister's friends for pics from the party. A tagged picture of Grace's best friend Kennedy and I decked out in Mardi Gras beads appeared in the feed. I wasn't facing the camera but I still made the caption. *K-money and Little Grace Hayes.*

K-money, a stupid nickname some of Grace's senior friends gave Kennedy, and then me, branded another version of my sister.

But the comments were what did me in:

Grace has a clone. Partying already as a freshman?

I'd just finished sophomore year, but whatever.

Didn't U hear they got in accident? Grace was so drunk. What a waste. Amateur.

OMG IS GRACE OK

Maybe she shouldn't party so hard. Only a problem if you get caught.

Who is Little Grace Hayes and why do I care? O yeah, I don't.

Crazy Grace tragedy on training wheels

I clicked off the phone. The words *Crazy Grace tragedy* repeated in my mind like stamp pressed into my skin. Branded like those Xes on Will's hands.

I'd done everything different than my sister. I didn't drink. I steered clear of parties. I managed good grades. I joined sports every season. None of it mattered to them.

For all the popularity Grace built up over her time in high school, she couldn't escape the haters. People acted like her friend to her face, but behind her back, they talked.

They joked about her. Called her awful names. They didn't respect Grace. They didn't know the Grace I knew, the sister I'd grown up with. Only Kennedy really knew Grace well. The rest was just an act.

The slow creep of sunset drew me to the attic window. From this angle, I couldn't see the driftwood log.

Same log, same time.

Will could be out there. Right now, he was my only friend in Deer Cove.

Because Will ran the community service team, he knew I needed signed-off hours to show to a judge. Already I started with a dirty slate. Maybe it was stupid, but it bothered me.

It bothered me, but not enough to stay inside.

I slipped down the stairs. "Can I walk to the beach?"

Grandpop peered up from a magazine about consumer product ratings. He said something and waved me off.

"What?"

"Ah." He waved me off again. "Someday."

I gathered something about sky and a hand. Maybe about stargazing? Who knew.

On the beach, the driftwood, weathered and husked, waited like a friend. Almost as if it hoped I'd come back. I sat and kicked off my shoes and walked to the water. A shock of cold raced up my toes to my ankles and crept into my bones.

I found a stick and drew lazy shapes in the sand. Water edged up the shore, then retreated, each time edging closer until the waves flattened out and wore the patterns down.

"Hey."

"Yee!" I jumped and placed a hand at my heart. "Don't *do* that."

Will stood two feet from me. "I didn't want to scare you, so I was quiet."

"That makes no sense."

Tonight, Will's hair was styled more but still messy. Cool and edgy. Basically, the opposite of me.

He handed me a take-out coffee cup with a plastic lid. A warm mocha scent drifted out.

"For me?"

"If you hate it, I have coffee, black. You can have mine. It's decaf."

"You were so sure I'd be here you bought me coffee?"

"Let's say I was hoping." He gave me an unreadable look. His shoes now ditched, he rolled his jeans up a few inches, creating a haphazard thick cuff. "Sorry if I made you feel weird earlier. The delinquent comment. I don't think bad of you or anything."

He'd already apologized, but I liked hearing it again to quiet the voices in my head.

"Here's the thing." He let the water wash over his feet and winced at the chill. "It doesn't matter to me why you're here. What you do with your time, and how you move forward is what matters."

"You sure are the dispenser of advice. How old are you, anyway?"

"I'll be a senior this year at Upper Coast High. I'm seventeen. I know I probably look like some loser who has no business telling somebody like you how to live. I only say it because I've been there."

"Someone like me. Which is what?"

"You don't want to be here. Your grandparents set you up for volunteering for the summer—"

"The *whole* summer?" Dangit, they were serious about this whole summer business.

"I guess you really don't want to be here."

I blew out a breath of frustration. "I have stuff going on at home. Anyway, you say you've been there. What does that mean?"

He paced between the driftwood log and where the water sipped the sand. "When I started at the center, it changed me. I'm all about moving forward. Staying positive. Not looking back." He shrugged. "Life is only fulfilling when you give back."

"You sound like a motivational poster." Maybe he'd been through therapy or something. "And you used to get high? Not on volunteering, but like, with drugs?"

He laughed gently. "Yeah. Among other things. I was messed up. Now I want to help people any way I can." He watched me, seeming to wait for a response.

More like waiting for a confession.

"You think I've done drugs?"

"Have you?"

"No. And I've only tried beer. It's not my thing."

"So, I can check substance abuse from the list."

"You have a *list*?"

"Not really. I'm curious about you is all."

"I guess I thought...you said you looked for trouble. So I told you about the trouble I got into."

He scrunched his brow. "I said I look for trouble?"

"Last night. You said there were places to find trouble."

He tipped his head back. "Yeah. Okay. I just meant it in a general way. Like, you can find it if you want. I didn't mean *I* looked for trouble. Those days are behind me."

Color me three shades of embarrassed.

"Hey, don't feel bad," Will said quickly. "I was probably just nervous. It's not often a pretty girl shows up on this beach. This ain't exactly Malibu."

Now I was shaded in blush. Will wasn't sounding so much like the bad boy I'd assumed. He just looked the part. "I thought you'd think the story about the party was cool. It was actually really scary. I crashed my sister's car."

He stilled. "I didn't realize. I'm sorry. You're okay?"

"I am. My sister got hurt. Fractured arm, scratches and bruises."

Will stared at the water. "But she's okay?"

"I'd never describe Grace as okay." Marathon drinker. Serial dater. Prankster of teachers and graduation ceremonies (she wore a hot pink bikini beneath her graduation robe and flashed the commencement audience). "I don't think the accident shook her like it did me. Grace sort of rolls with what life gives her. I need more time."

This felt like a lot to dump on someone I didn't know. I walked to the log and sat.

Will sat beside me. "Whatever happened, maybe today's the day you start looking forward. Do you ever think about what you could be better at?"

"All the time. I got into AP English and AP Chemistry, and I'm going to have to really work at it."

He looked about to laugh but didn't. "I meant stuff apart from school. Life stuff."

"Oh, right." He stumped me there. "You know, most of the guys I've seen who look like you talk about bands or skating or snowboarding."

"Maybe I'm not most guys."

"I guess that wasn't fair."

"We can talk about bands if it's easier."

I could say I came down to the beach for the sun or the peaceful lapping waves. I could say that, but I'd be lying.

Since he point-blank asked me about life and I had nowhere else to be, maybe I needed to figure this out. I took a breath. "The accident—it was my fault. It's why I'm here."

His expression shifted more serious. "Sorry to hear. Car accidents...those can be rough."

I could practically feel weight slide off me. "Yeah, it has been rough. When the police showed up at the party, it was a free-for-all. Everyone for themselves, and then my sister—she was crying. *Sobbing.* I had to get her out of there. I had to take care of her."

My throat dried up and the rest of whatever I thought I'd say fell away.

Will moved a hand toward me but didn't actually touch. "When did this happen?"

I wrapped my arms around myself. "A few days ago."

"Days?" He shook his head. "You're probably in shock."

That sounded accurate. "The car is gone. I only had a level one license. I still had learning hours to do under supervision. That's pending full suspension."

He breathed out, like air released slowly from a balloon. "Suspended license. Court stuff. But your sister's good?"

"Besides the injuries, she's exactly the same. I wanted to help her, but I made everything worse."

"But you have your sister," he said, this time more insistent. "She can't stay mad about her car forever."

"I can't stand being compared to my sister, but I'd do anything for her. I'm always trying to make things right between us. It never works."

"Trying is better than nothing. Think how many people don't try. They let things happen and don't do anything. You tried."

Will didn't press me further. He didn't leave either. He sat beside me, watching the water, either in solidarity, or lost in his own thoughts.

Either way, he was here. Right now, that was enough.

Chapter Four

♥

Talking with Will last night made me feel like at least somebody sort of understood me. Except now, checking off my list of chores at the inn, all I could think was how Grace hadn't talked to me since I left. No texts, no calls. I could call her myself, but I wasn't sure what to say.

As Will said, no community service hours for today. The program ran three days a week with different service activities on weekends. If I could manage one of these days off to get back to Ginsburg, I could meet up with the team. I could still make this summer work.

But my day didn't leave me much time for scheming.

I prepped a room at the inn with Grandma's oversight, waiting on a family with a reservation. I was surprised only half the rooms were booked. This was summer. My grandparents always said summer was their busy season. It was why they never visited us in Ginsburg May through September. We'd always had to come here and squeeze in time.

I also hadn't seen their part-timer around. Just Grandma and Grandpop running all the check-ins and preparing the rooms. Which left me and Grandma to run the loads of towels and sheets in the utility room at the inn. We stuffed welcome baskets with local hand-made soaps and assorted teas.

After dinner, I'd planned to run to keep on my training schedule but ended up passing out asleep on the daybed in the attic. My legs ached in weird places. Probably from the digging and crouching in the garden during service hours.

I woke a good hour before sunset. Will. He'd probably be out there at the log.

Grabbing my favorite hoodie and my lip gloss, I headed downstairs.

Grandpop looked up from reading the newspaper on his favorite recliner. He was a slim man, all angles with softer creases around his eyes.

"I'm meeting one of the volunteers on the beach," I told him. "The head of the service hours, actually." A responsible, dyed-black-haired cute high school senior, but he didn't need to know that. "Is it all right if I'm out past sunset?"

"You better run that by your grandmother."

Which was a no. Bummer.

Grandma moved into the room. "Stay on the beach. Be back before curfew."

Sunset must be my curfew. Small towns were *very* weird.

Still, I took this as permission to get some time in with the under-sixty crowd.

"Take a flashlight," Grandpop called out. "And say hi to Will for us."

I whirled around. "You know Will?"

"We know everyone."

I grabbed a flashlight from the hall coat tree and left out the front door. Of course my grandparents knew everyone. The whole town was a hundred people.

Okay, surely more than a hundred people made up Deer Cove, but what did I know about small town populations?

Ahead, waves tumbled into shore in a predictable rhythm. I breathed a little easier and started toward the log.

Both times, I'd shown up first. Maybe Will watched for me. Where did he live? I didn't know much about him.

Adding on lip gloss, I smoothed back my hair. This wasn't a date exactly, but it felt like *something*.

My first boyfriend, Erik, I'd met through honors society earlier sophomore year. We'd done a fundraising blood drive at the school where he and I passed out juice and cookies to the donors. Our relationship mainly involved study dates at the library or at his house in his family's kitchen. After two months, he called it off. Erik liked making out with a girl named Madison more than he liked studying with me.

As I waited for Will, I thought of Grace's attempts to funnel me into her social circle. Her friend Kennedy was another version of Grace, each of them feeding off each other for who could skip the most classes.

Not all of Grace's friends thrilled themselves with the delinquent life. Lila and her bestie Natalie were nice to me and didn't do reckless things with their free time. Lila treated me like more than Grace's dorky little sister. I'd even gone to a party with them at a lake house. Of course, my sister had been there and hogged all the attention. The cops busted that party too, but we'd gotten lucky and it all blew over. Something about lake town politics.

One close call with the law had been all I'd needed to keep things on the straight and narrow. Figured Grace hadn't learned. She looked for opportunities to get caught.

Where was Will? I didn't have his number to text him.

Maybe I assumed too much here. He probably had a life outside of meeting me by a log at dusk.

I decided to walk the beach since I wasn't due back yet. I headed across the beach along town where dim lights from Main Street reached through the trees. I passed dog walkers and couples, then ended up at a residential area. A posted sign marked it as private property.

Turning back, a voice called over. "Hey!"

I squinted. A guy in a baseball cap stood by a campfire. Another guy and two girls surrounded him. They looked close to my age.

I gave a tentative wave. "What's up?"

"Just hanging out."

The cap guy's shorter friend opened a beer. "Want one?" He nodded toward a cooler partly covered by a beach towel. "Cops never come out here."

Grace would have already cracked open the cooler by now. "No thanks. I should get going."

"You don't have to drink," a girl with long black hair said. "Are you staying in one of the hotels?"

"Um, yeah. At Sunset Inn." Not a total lie, just not exactly true either. So, a lie. "Actually, my grandparents own it. I'm staying with them. They're uh, probably expecting me."

"*Oooh,*" the cap guy taunted. "You're gonna get in trouble from Grandma?"

The girl scoffed. "Ignore him. I usually do."

The short guy looked past me. "Uh-oh, party's busted."

Crap. This was exactly what I didn't need. To be *near* a party about to be busted.

Only when I turned, I didn't see a police officer or a ranting property owner.

It was Will.

"'Sup guys," Will said to the others as he walked closer. His lips drew tight. Between his expression and the looks the two guys exchanged, an entire invisible conversation played out in front of me.

Will nodded at me. "Holli. Hey. Sorry I was late."

So he *had* planned to meet me.

"I was just passing through," Will said to the others. "Maybe see you around."

"Me too," I said. "I mean, passing through." I couldn't stay here.

"We're all good," the cap guy said, smirking at Will. "We like our impurities out here. Impurities forever!" He and the short guy bumped fists and laughed.

Whatever *that* was all about. I looked at Will. "Let's go."

Will watched me for a beat. He nodded for me to go first and followed behind toward our end of the beach, by our driftwood. Laughter carried over from the fire, like a final good riddance.

Will scowled. "You didn't need to leave on my account. I'm fine walking alone."

"I didn't want to be there. I waited for you, but then I wasn't sure if you'd be by the log. I mean, we don't have a schedule or anything."

I wouldn't mind a schedule, but it felt pretty nerdy to mention.

"Those guys are jerks," Will said. "They only care about themselves."

We walked a few paces in silence. I started to say more, but Will seemed upset, and I didn't know what to tell him to make it better. We didn't know each other all that well.

We reached the log. He folded his arms and looked over the water.

"You just moved here last year, right? It must not be easy to make new friends."

He made a noise of agreement and kicked his foot against a flat rock half-buried by wet sand. Gone was the laid-back easy smile.

"Are you okay?"

Will turned. "Your sister and the accident. That's why she's all banged up?"

"Yeah."

He shook his head. "Something doesn't add up. How do you just crash a car if you're the designated driver?"

"The roads were slippery. I was inexperienced." I hated admitting this. "I only have a learner's license, remember?"

Will stepped toward me. "You're not being honest. Not with me, and not with yourself."

And just like that, whatever connection I thought Will and I had been building severed. "What are you talking about?"

"You were drunk. You crashed your sister's car, and you feel guilty. That's why you're so miserable."

I almost laughed, but his face fell more serious. "No. I told you I don't drink."

"Admit it—you drank at the party."

"*No.* I didn't. The accident was just that—an accident." Where was this coming from?

"The only reason you left their beach party back there is you have to work for me and report your service hours. You were *caught*."

Hot tears sprung behind my eyes, but I forced them back. "I wasn't drinking at the party. If you don't believe me, it's your problem. My sister got hurt. If I could've fixed it—all I wanted was to help."

His arms locked tighter across his chest. "It's poison, you know."

"What?"

"Alcohol."

Okay, this was definitely going to a weird place. I didn't have stand here and take this. "I'm leaving." I started up the beach toward the access point to my grandparents' street.

"Holli, wait." Will reached for me with a light touch at my arm. "I'm sorry. It's just, I can't stand those guys. All they do is get wasted and then drive around like every-thing's cool. They don't care about risking people's lives.

I can't respect people who abuse their bodies. Especially if it might hurt somebody else."

"You mean abuse their bodies like when you did drugs?"

His face fell. "Yeah. Exactly like that."

He acted pretty self-righteous for someone with his own checkered past. "Your life is not the same as mine. Don't accuse me of things you don't know anything about." If I wanted a lecture I'd sign up for an online class or just go home and sit in front of Grandma for long enough.

"I'm sorry." Will's voice came softer now. "I'll walk you back."

"I'll be fine. I can basically see the house from here."

"Holli—"

"I'm not my sister." I looked him in the eye.

He looked back.

That look. It was like he saw through me. Right through to everything. Down to my darkest secret. The one I feared I'd let slip.

I turned and walked off, leaving Will, and the night, behind.

Chapter Five

♥

I stared head-on into a toilet bowl.

The bowl nearly sparkled, but I couldn't seem to pull myself away from scrubbing.

The last time I knelt this close over a toilet came after one of Grace's epic binges. It happened a few months ago, and it wasn't the first time she'd stumbled home in the middle of the night on a weeknight.

Usually, she'd tiptoe past my door with only the soft thud of her door closing to signal her presence. Our house was perfect for sneaking into since the stairs led up to a loft overlooking the family room with halls leading in one direction to my parents' bedroom, and the other direction to our rooms.

All I'd wanted was sleep, but she woke me up to talk about ditching college to travel. She wanted to cross the United States. She'd camp or stay with family and randos she knew from the internet. She'd call herself Betty or Esther or something old-fashioned. A terrible plan.

And then she'd asked if I'd go with her.

Obviously, her rambling came from drinking, so I rolled over to ignore her. I'd never be the one to run off with her, shirking responsibilities at home. I wished I knew why she wanted to run away so badly. Why she wanted to disappear by becoming someone else.

And then she proceeded to get sick all over my bedroom.

A hot flash pulsed through me as the memory faded. I always helped Grace clean up. I rested my cheek against the lid on the clean toilet. If only bleach could scrub the memories I didn't want to hang onto.

A throat cleared behind me. "There's clean and there's rest-your-face clean. We'll settle for clean."

I shot up from my toilet hugging. "I..." I had no excuse for hugging a toilet.

"Let me show you check-ins at the desk."

I followed her for the short walk across the parking lot to the inn's office. Inside, a sandwich waited for me on the desk by the window with a strawberry carbonated drink next to it. They always bought the same strawberry pop for Grace and me when we visited.

"Did I ever tell you about when we first moved here?" Grandpop asked from behind the desk. "This office was only half the size. We built on to it and made the desk. Your father helped me run the electrical."

I ate while he explained the remodeling in detail. I didn't really care so much, but it was sweet how pumped he got when talking about the inn. He was so proud of it.

Grandma fished out a room number from the collection of silver keys in the cabinet below the desk. She explained the check-in log and showed me the computer registration system. "Here's the policy manual."

Again, the pride over a glossy binder. It was sweet. I wondered if Tala's boss showed off a policy manual like a firstborn child.

"How about giving the desk a test run?" Grandpop waited on my answer.

I looked between them. Grandma already had her hand on the door prepping to leave. "Like, now?"

"We don't have a check-in scheduled until after three," she said, opening the door and actually stepping outside. "It's mostly babysitting the desk in case anyone calls or walks in the door."

"Or if one of the guests need something." Grandpop moved to the door too. "Best way to learn is to dive in head first."

Sink or swim? Beautiful. Just beware of rocks below the surface.

Okay, we were talking running rental rooms, not a murky lake. Besides, I'd grown up visiting them. I knew more than a first day part-timer. "Sure. Go on." It wasn't like I had other plans.

Grandpop clapped his hands together. "Excellent." He took out his phone and tapped at it. "Jim? I'll be over in a jiffy. Yup. We got Holli to run the desk. Should have had the grandkids come out for the summer ages ago."

With Grandma already gone to who knew where and Grandpop making friends with this Jim guy, I was on my own.

I texted Tala.

The phone rang in my hand. I answered.

"Hey girl," Tala said through the line. "I'm off today. What's up?"

"Tell me everything going on in your life. I don't want to talk about mine."

"Sure. I smell like popcorn and hot dogs. And fake cheese. Don't freak, but I'm sorta kinda seeing this guy at work."

"Oh my gosh! What's his name? What's he like?"

"I said no freaking. We went out twice with the other closers. With these hours at the theater, I swear the only people I see are people I work with."

I slumped back in the office chair. As she filled me in, Tala's adventures temporarily became mine.

"Okay," Tala said. "Speaking of guys, I know you said you don't want to talk about your life, but you texted about Will. I need details."

"Nothing to say. He got weird."

"What happened?"

"Grace happened," I said before I could stop myself.

"She's not even there, Holli."

I squeezed my eyes shut. "It doesn't matter. It feels like her shadow chased me here." I told her about the partiers on the beach and what I'd told Will. "Anyway, I just want to do my thing and get out of here."

"You're coming back soon?"

I wished. "I'm working on it." Except I wasn't.

She quieted. Tala always gave me space to think without it getting awkward. "Hey, if you don't want to answer this, I get it," she started, her voice edging into careful territory. "Some of those rumors from the party. I don't really know what to think."

"What are they saying?"

"The fight Grace got into. That it was about way more than what it seemed, for starters."

What everyone saw was drunk Grace being her dramatic self. "Yeah. There's usually more to Grace's issues."

"People are saying she hooked up with somebody's boyfriend."

My sister was an attention hog, a drama queen, a starter of drinking games. She wasn't a boyfriend-stealer. "A lot happened at the party. People get confused."

"At first I heard she hooked up with Kennedy's boyfriend, but then they said Maria Chavez—her guy."

"Grace would never hurt Kennedy. I don't know Maria, but well, people were drunk." Which was precisely why I stayed away from parties and drinking. Nothing good came from any of it.

"That's what I was thinking." She cleared her throat. "It's just, apparently Kennedy and her boyfriend just broke up, and Kennedy went on some kind of binge."

"What kind of binge?"

"This girl who works at the theater lives next door to Kennedy's family. They saw an ambulance there last night. My coworker says the family is acting strange about the details. They think Kennedy tried to OD or something."

"What?" I shot up from chair. "Does Grace know?"

"You know more about your sister than anyone. No one's seen her since the accident. How she's doing? How are *you* doing?"

Maybe my parents actually locked her down. They'd never been very successful at keeping Grace under lockdown, but she also no longer had a car to escape in.

"Are you sure about those rumors? I need to talk to Grace, but if she doesn't know—" I almost said I didn't want to upset her. Screw it. I'd upset her. Maybe she was upset already, back home.

"I'm sure about the Kennedy stuff. And for real, how are you?"

I imagined myself telling her exactly how I was, and exactly what happened. This was Tala. The one friend who knew my secrets, because I'd never really had any. Good girls who followed rules could easily confide in their best friend when nothing needed to stay hidden.

Until now.

Tala wouldn't understand. I wanted her to, but she wouldn't understand how I chose Grace when Grace never chose me. I didn't always understand it myself.

"I'm okay." I told her. "I'm doing what I'm supposed to."

After we hung up, I pulled up my social profiles for updates. Pictures of my teammates on a hilltop posed at the end of a run. A bunch of girls crammed into a booth at a breakfast place. A gap existed next to Christina where I should have been.

Life went on in Ginsburg without me. As much as I didn't want to be known solely as Grace's little sister, a deeper thought nagged. What if no one remembered me at all?

My grandparents hadn't offered a time when they'd be back, so I faced theoretical hours at a dead-as-dust front desk in a sleepy beach town. The most excitement so far happened when cabin six needed directions to the state park. We had plenty of maps in our rickety brochure holder by the door.

Time inched by. At the same time, my mind raced. I needed answers.

I called my sister.

"Grace," I said in a rush when she answered. "When did you last talk to Kennedy?"

Never mind this was the first I'd talked to my sister since I left for Deer Cove. She hadn't even said goodbye.

"Kennedy's not my friend."

"What?" So, they'd really fought at the party. I hated rewinding through that night, but I needed to make sense of this. "Since when? Since graduation night?"

"What do you care?"

Why did she have to be so difficult? "Tala told me people are saying you hooked up with someone's boyfriend."

"People are always going to say things. Those people just happen to be liars."

"Kennedy got taken away in an ambulance last night. Tala knows someone who lives by her who saw it."

"Maybe it was her dad. He had a heart thing once."

"They said Kennedy. She might have taken pills and—"

"You don't know that. Now you're the one spreading rumors."

"I'm only telling you what Tala said."

The line went quiet. "That's messed up. I'm sure it's not like what it seems. People are always trying to start stuff. They're always trying to bring me down. I wouldn't hook up with my friends' boyfriends. Is this why you really called? To verify gossip?"

She had me there. I didn't usually care. Asking about gossip meant taking on all the emotions along with it. And worry. I really hated to hear bad stuff about my sister.

She was right; there was more to this call. I needed to ask. I needed to know.

"Do you remember?"

"Remember what? I need more direction, Holli."

I kept my voice light. "Tell me what you remember from that night."

"The party got crazy. It happens. Maybe not in your world, but that's how it is."

"Grace. I'm for real. Tell me." *I need to you to remember. I need you to tell me you remember.*

"Kennedy was mad at me. I swear, it wasn't my fault. Whatever people are saying, it's not true. You know, it was probably Kendra and Sonia. They start stuff because they're jealous."

Entire conversations were being glossed over. She wasn't mentioning any of what was important. "The car, Grace. Do you—"

"I don't care about the car, Hol. I mean, it sucks. And my arm fracture is a drag. Other than that, I don't remember anything after the party. Or leaving the party."

My heartbeat rose. "What's the last you remember?"

"Fighting with Kennedy. Then I went outside. I don't know what else. It's like there's a big, fat blank spot, and then I woke up in a hospital."

My insides hardened to stone. She didn't remember. The sobbing, the begging, her drunken determination. She didn't remember any of it.

I could barely breathe. "How do you think we got home, Grace?"

"From the party? You said you drove."

Rushing water sounded in my ears, but the office remained silent. My throat dried up. "Yeah. I said I drove. That's what I said."

A long beat of silence followed. "*Holli.*" Grace's tone came across like a warning. "What are you saying?"

I couldn't say it. I wanted Grace to say it so I didn't have to.

"Holli, are you sure you weren't drinking? I won't tell. I just need to know because you're not making sense."

The room blurred and it had nothing to do with intoxication. "Everything was so chaotic with people running out of the house. You grabbed the keys. You seemed like you knew what you were doing. I was scared."

Only when we crashed, it was too late to realize Grace was anything but in control.

"You pushed me into the passenger seat," I went on. "You cried so hard, I just thought you were upset."

"Let me get this straight." Ice coated Grace's tone. "You're saying it was me. You're saying I was the one driving."

The tears came. They rolled down my cheeks in silent streams.

"Why would you *lie* for me?" Grace burst out. "Do you have any idea what this means?"

I did. It meant I didn't really need to do service hours. That I could go back home and join my team again. Back to my life in Ginsburg.

For Grace, it meant a more serious violation. This time driving drunk, not just in possession of alcohol. She'd face serious repercussions for multiple violations.

My record was clean. My parents never expected the worst from me when they definitely expected the worst from Grace.

I'd lied because I loved my sister. I'd lied to help Grace. To save Grace.

Only I'd only made everything worse.

I said I drove because I could make the situation better.

I said I drove, but now we both knew I hadn't.

Chapter Six

♥

I didn't know what I expected from telling Grace I covered for her the night of the accident in the biggest I-Owe-You in history.

The lie made more sense than the truth. The ugly, awful truth churning my stomach. How else would I explain to the officer, or to Mom and Dad, to our grandparents, how I knew Grace had been drunk and I still let her drive? I'd wanted to believe she could so much I forced myself to believe it, against my better judgment.

It wasn't like I hadn't tried to stop her. Everything had happened in a rush.

In a single second, the party changed from loud music and laughing to cops pounding on the door. Kids made a run for it. Grace, my usually headstrong sister, had been a crying mess over drama I didn't care about.

I'd gotten her out of the house. I had her keys and told her I'd get us out of there. Grace snatched the car keys from my hand. She'd forced me into the passenger seat. The rest came back as a blur of panic and heart pounding and terror over being caught.

Fleeing from the scene, I'd done what my sister asked. I'd done what I was told, like I always did.

After my grandparents finally decided to come back and relieve me of desk duties, we ate a dinner of takeout from the next town over. All through dinner, my shoulders grew tight and my stomach flipped. I tried to appear normal, but it had to be obvious I was shaken.

"Holli," Grandma said after Grandpop shuffled back to the Sunset Inn office. "You seem unwell. How are you feeling?"

Like a terrible granddaughter. An awful sister. A bad daughter. "I'm just thinking about Grace. And what happened." I had to talk about this in some way or I'd burst.

"Your sister is sick." She tapped her head. "I've been saying it for years. She's struggling against something. I think it's depression."

Grace rarely acted depressed. She wasn't a mopey type of person. "I don't think so."

"Depression comes in a lot of forms. It isn't just feeling sad. I'm going to talk to your father about having her come out here. I think it would be good for her."

Grace would hate that. One thing Grace hated was feeling trapped.

I could go back to Ginsburg, but the damage had been done. What good would spilling the truth do now? Now that Grace knew, maybe she'd think twice about how much she drank. It wasn't just slippery roads. It wasn't an inexperienced driver without a license.

It was her.

I didn't go to the beach for sunset. I didn't want to see Will tonight. My emotions felt too messy. We'd left on an odd note, with him accusing me of driving drunk. I didn't know what he'd make of the truth.

I watched the sun go down from the open attic window. And maybe I checked for a figure in a hoodie.

The next day, I walked into the community center with my guard up.

"Hey, Holli." Will's voice came across even, his expression blank.

"Hi." I smiled, pleasant, kind. The type of smile you gave your group leader to seem harmless.

I moved over by Chaz who helped the retiree bunch fill bags with beach trash.

"So, you're here for the summer, right?" Chaz asked me.

"Yeah. Looks like it." I smiled, trying not to sound like a bummer. It wasn't his fault my life was a wreck.

Chaz rambled about historical trivia while we de-cobwebbed picnic tables pulled from storage. He knew a lot of Deer Cove history.

Chaz was delightfully dorky in a way I enjoyed. He didn't act ashamed of geeking out over town lore.

Later when cleaning up with a garden hose, flinging the last of the cobweb gunk from my sleeve, Will found me. "Listen, I'm sorry about the other night—"

"No worries." I had my Everything's Great smile ready.

"No, I owe you an apology. I accused you of something and it wasn't fair. It's my fault, and I own it."

Will definitely sounded like he'd been through a round of therapy. "Thanks. Apology accepted."

Will sighed and a smile emerged. A hopeful smile. "So, uh, do you have plans? We're all caught up here, and I said I'd show you the park trails. For being a volunteer, you already get a free state park pass."

I looked for an out. Piper stared at us with narrowed eyes. Yeesh. "Um, is Piper not cool with you talking to me."

Will swung around.

"*Hey*," I said through my teeth. Boys were *so* obvious.

Except Will seemed to be communicating something to Piper through elaborate miming. She didn't gesture back, but instead mouthed back words.

I pointed toward Main Street. "I'm going to get going."

"Holli, wait." Will turned back to me, his eyes doing some serious puppy dog pleading. "See, I've got a problem." He picked at a leather cuff on his wrist. "I'm pretty helpless right now if I'm gonna run a 5k in a few weeks. I could really use a trainer."

"When did you start running?"

"Last week."

I nearly slapped my palm to my forehead. "And already you're doing a 5k?"

"It's a charity run." He shrugged. "Chaz asked me, and I said yes since it's for a good cause. Except I'm sort of an idiot with stuff like sports and running and don't know what I'm doing."

"So, it's not just you showing me the trails. It's me showing you how to run."

"Yeah. Pretty lame, huh?"

Except it wasn't, really. I felt flattered. "Not lame. Running down the street is different than running a timed distance race. You don't want to hurt yourself."

I only pushed Will away because of my own drama. He seemed genuinely sorry for accusing me. What was my alternative, anyway? I needed to keep training for when I joined the team again.

"I could go out to the trail with you," I said. "I actually don't like running alone."

"Yeah? If you're cool with it, I'd really like your help."

I liked hearing him say he wanted my help. I liked feeling needed. "Go ahead and change, and then we can meet back here."

"Change?" He looked over his T-shirt, cargo shorts, and skate shoes. "I'm good."

"Those aren't running shoes."

"They're all I've got."

I opened my mouth to explain the crucial importance of a properly fitted running shoe but decided against it. "We'll take it slow. But I'm going back for my other shoes."

He nodded. "I'll pick you up in a few. It's faster to drive in through the front park entrance."

Fifteen minutes later, a car pulled into Sunset Inn's gravel lot. The car looked like any other aging black sedan except for the zillion stickers plastered to the back bumper and window.

A dark-haired head popped out from the driver's side as I crossed over to his car. "Hey, so I changed after all. I found this other shirt in my trunk."

The only difference? The shirt was black with a band name on it. He still wore the cargo shorts and skate shoes.

The inside of Will's car smelled like a mix of fresh pine and artificial car freshener pine.

I closed my side's door and immediately sensed the closeness. Will's personal space. His very personal car space.

For a moment, I imagined his hand crossing over to mine. My cheeks heated.

After a short drive, we reached the park.

Will joked with the guy running the gate like old friends. He continued on toward a parking lot where hikers geared up beside open trunks.

We got out and Will led me toward a picnic area where the trees parted for a wide view of Lake Michigan. This part of the park was farther uphill; I just hadn't realized it during the drive in.

Will raised his hands over his head in a quick stretch. "So, Miss Marathon, how should we get started?"

"Let's do a lap around the area to warm up."

"I can do a 5k in these shoes, no problem." Will ran in place with knees high for emphasis.

I couldn't help laughing at his exaggerated moves. "I meant walk first. You know, if you're planning to run the whole race, we should come up with a running schedule."

"Does this mean you'll be here the whole summer?"

I internally squashed my frustration and started walking our lap. "Something like that."

"Well, don't look to be let off easy. Right now, I'm at about a twenty-minute mile."

"*Twenty minutes?*"

He offered a shrug, but the smirk gave him away. I burst out laughing. Will couldn't hide anything. Even when teasing, he let his feelings broadcast on his face.

"A training schedule will help you focus without overexerting yourself," I said. "You increase distance incrementally. You don't want to get hurt running too much too fast. There are strength-training exercises for your off-days. Some days you'll go for endurance—what?"

Will stared at me, blinking.

"Too much?"

He smiled. "Naw, I was just trying to make you think that. I couldn't find a better trainer unless I hired one for real money."

I shoved him. Not hard, but enough to make me regret making contact with his lean arm. Probably lean from working the land. I pictured his muscles flexing from digging—not a bad visual.

My thoughts went to Will shoveling at the community center. Then shoveling with a tighter shirt. *Stop it, Holli!*

Will picked up his pace to keep up. "You don't have to be my personal trainer if you don't want. I get annoying sometimes, just jumping onto ideas. Sometimes I want to do everything. I don't want to say no to life."

"I'd like to help you," I said, meaning it. "I'm working on my own running schedule to match up with what my team is doing back home. I'll be going out in the mornings. If you want, you can join me."

"Cool, Okay. Except I work at nine."

I waited for the rest. "So?"

"Nine. In the morning."

"I run at seven. In the morning."

He gave an exaggerated sneer. "*Why?*"

"Mornings are cool—no blaring sun. Running wakes me up, and then I can focus on the rest of the day knowing I got my training in."

"I figured we could run after work, see. For that whole sleeping in thing."

"The problem with evenings is my grandparents are all about eating dinner together and doing household chores."

"I guess I can manage getting up earlier than I would even for *school.*" He emphasized the L in school. "I can manage to meet you at seven. *A.M.*"

I quickened my walking pace again. "There you go. I'm helping you become a morning person."

"I'll never be a morning person. Believe me, you'll find out."

We headed toward a trail marker across a picnic area clearing. Will cracked his knuckles. "Since you're still around, tonight is teen group at the center. Maybe you want to come? We'd really like to have you."

"We?"

"Oh, me and Piper. We talked about it earlier."

Will and Piper. Of course.

"Chaz comes too, when he's not working. And Antonio, who drew the art I showed you. It's like you know half the group already."

"And I'm already your trainer. Sure, I could come. Why not make some new friends, right?"

His grin ignited. "Awesome."

Will appeared so much more smiley than I expected for someone who frequently wore all black.

We reached the trail head. Will watched how I stretched and followed the same motions. "The program director, she likes to lecture me about stuff. Like I haven't proved my reliability a hundred times over."

"Hopefully she lectured you on those shoes."

"Oh yeah, we chat regularly about footwear. Usually over tea."

I wished I had something to toss at him, but instead I stuck out my tongue. Sure, I turned sixteen soon. Sixteen going on seven.

"She was lecturing me about you, actually."

I released my stretch. "What?"

"The whole, watch out for cute girls in the program, blah blah blah."

I'd been warned about? "What did you say?"

Will windmilled his arms. "It's not like I'm the one actually signing off on your hours. Only a director can. I guess because I'm in a leadership position, she thinks it makes me different. I don't know."

Huh. "I'm not used to being the girl who's warned about."

"That's more your sister, right?"

I adjusted my ponytail and looked ahead to the trail. "We should get going before those clouds come in. Looks like rain."

"I guess you don't want to talk about your sister, then."

"Try to keep up," I called back as I began a slow jog. Ahead, the trail laid out before us, flat and even. The trail wouldn't demand answers. Trails never talked back.

Chapter Seven

♥

After a shower and dinner, I returned to the community center for tonight's teen group. Thankfully, my grandparents were cool with me going out. I'd be staying in town, and they knew everybody anyway.

A guy with a fuzzy black afro stood in the community center lobby. "All right—fresh blood." He rubbed his hands together, a wicked grin pointed my direction.

"Blood?"

Will shot out from the hall. "Holli. Hey. Welcome. Never mind Antonio." He jabbed his friend with an elbow. "Quit freaking her out."

"Did you bring a guitar?" Antonio asked me.

"Was I supposed to?"

Will shoved Antonio toward the hall. "Piper's bringing the guitar."

Just then, Piper from Leaf Group walked in carrying a black leather instrument case. The image made me blink twice. She didn't strike me as the guitar playing type. Then again, I'd been wrong about a lot lately.

"'Sup everybody." Her gaze lingered on Will, then moved to me. "Hey, Holli."

"Hi." I watched for any indication of annoyance about me being here. She clearly liked Will. "So, you play guitar?"

She nodded. "I'm taking lessons. I'd like to find a band to play with, but so far I haven't found anyone good enough."

Antonio placed a hand at his heart. "Your words are like daggers, my lady." Then he air-guitared and sprinted toward the back room, his cackles echoing from the corridor.

"Please don't leave," Will said to me, giving me an apologetic look. "I swear, the rest of us are semi-normal."

"You, normal?" Piper hip-checked Will and sauntered off. Her golden highlighted hair swished along her back.

"Hey." Will rubbed his palms against his cargo shorts pockets. "It's cool that you came."

"Watching Tom Selleck as a cop on TV with my grandparents is your competition."

"Who's Tom Selleck?"

"The guy with the mustache."

"I'm supposed to know one single actor defined by a mustache? And I'm the weird one?"

"It's a very distinguished mustache. Never mind." This was not going well.

Will started walking the way Piper disappeared. "Let me introduce you to everybody."

In the activity room, three younger girls, probably freshmen, crammed together on a worn couch. Chaz waved from his spot in front of the TV watching an extreme sports reality competition with two other guys.

"So, who's the leader?" I asked.

"You're looking at him."

"What don't you do in this town?"

"The library wouldn't hire him," Antonio said, popping up from behind Will. "They have a no piercings policy."

"*Anyways.*" Will's hand went to the silver ring at his eyebrow. "Our group has a sponsor who's over twenty-one, but he doesn't come to all our meetings. Just when we need permission to use the building for events. The front desk has a breathing adult staffed at all times for liability."

Antonio slapped a hand on Will's shoulder. "Everything else? All this dude."

For the next hour, we ate snacks and mapped out service projects. Half the kids had summer jobs or babysitting responsibilities, but they spent their free time hosting food drives and planned a community art gallery event. One of the freshman girls had single-handedly organized a mobile pet service where she and two other volunteers visited a nursing home in a neighboring town and brought their dogs. She said she started it because she liked animals but knew not everyone could have them. Her parents drove her to gigs.

Will asked each person for ideas, until everyone in the group contributed. Even me.

He clasped his hands together. "All right. Ready to roll out?"

Everyone hopped up. Antonio and Chaz pulled blankets and folding chairs out of the open closet door.

Will caught up to me. "We hang around and build a fire outside if you're cool with sticking around."

"Sounds fun." I took two chairs and followed the group out the sliding glass doors to the fire pit behind the center. It was still pretty light out, but I had curfew by dark. Maybe the other kids did too.

Piper overturned a bag onto a blanket spread between a couple of the chairs by the fire. Everything needed for roasting marshmallows and s'mores. I couldn't help a small squeal.

"Are they your favorite too?" Piper asked. "It's not summer without them."

Tala's family had a fire pit in their backyard. S'mores-making was our number one first order of summer. Except this summer.

I wiped my eye. Go figure the mention of a marshmallow would get me all sad and whiny.

Will took a pokey stick and held one end over the fire. "How do you take your marshmallows, Holli? Wait—let me guess. Charred on the outside, gooey center."

"Kind of like your personality," Antonio said to Will and snatched the stick.

"Dude, shut up."

"Come on. Holli needs to know you're a big softie. Right here." Antonio thumped his chest.

"No way. I'm hardcore." Will grimaced and held up a fist, showing off a studded leather wrist cuff.

"Aw," Piper said all syrupy-sweet. "Will's growling at Holli."

Antonio squinted at us. "I think he's trying to woo her."

Okay, changing the subject. *Fast*. I passed the marshmallow to Antonio who loaded it onto the stolen stick. "Very lightly toasted."

Will kicked at the sand. "Nobody likes marshmallows the way I do."

"See what I mean?" Antonio ruffled Will's hair. "Such a gooey center, this guy."

Will waved him off and took back the stick. Just then, Piper reached across for the chocolate. Her long waves grazed against Will's arm.

I blinked. "So, um, lightly toasted can be tricky. It's like barely any time over the flame. Just a hover near the embers there, but not too close or it catches on fire."

Will finished roasting, and I assembled, then tackled, the s'more. Chaz sat on the other side of me and explained how a vendor in another beach town made artisan sugar puffs, which were marshmallows that cost four dollars each.

Piper picked up her guitar and sat by the fire. The group counted off into teams.

"Campfire Shuffle," Will told me. He sat close and very much in my space, which I didn't hate. "The person with the guitar plays part of a song, and the first to name the song and artist wins a point for their team. Get ready, because some of us play dirty."

Antonio made a crass joke, and Will shoved him. I could swear Will's face reddened.

He and I ended up on opposing teams. All the better for me to observe him. The game began with short bursts of songs. I won a point and then another. Chaz high-fived me after each win.

Will threw up his hands after I won two more points in a row. "How are you getting these so fast?"

"How do you *not* know these songs?" I shot back, laughing.

"Ha!" Antonio pointed at Will. "So much for never listening to popular music."

Antonio was also on my team but hadn't won us a single point.

"My music is popular," Will said with forced hurt. "In certain circles."

We played until a few kids bowed out to catch rides home. Finally, my team ended up victorious. The prize was not having to clean up.

The sun slowly made its way toward the horizon. The group thinned out. Those who lost the shuffle game put away the chairs.

"It's almost sunset," Will said to me as he closed the activity room. "Log?"

I glanced to Piper. "I should probably get back home."

Will noticed where I looked. "Are you sure? It's not a problem."

"Piper, is she a...friend?"

"Of course. There's not, I mean she's not—she's just watching out for me, is all."

Why Will needed Piper to look out for him drew my curiosity more than I wanted to admit.

Piper waved to Will. "See ya. You too, Holli." Her smile had a mischievous, knowing look. Like maybe she wasn't into Will at all, but knew Will was into someone else.

"Ready?" Will asked me.

I took the lead toward the driftwood, hoping he wouldn't see my fierce blush. I could not control my cheeks. My own personal embarrassment alert system.

We reached the log after a quiet walk across the sand.

"Did you have fun tonight?" Will asked.

"I didn't expect to find friends here."

"I didn't expect to not hate this place, either. Surprised me, too." He sat on the driftwood. "How's everything with your family?"

I settled on my end of the log and zipped my hoodie higher. "Fine. Great."

"Great? Really?"

"Okay, maybe not great."

Silence snaked its way between us. Loud, stifling silence.

"Things kind of suck right now," I said.

"Could've fooled me. I figured you wanted to push dirt around all summer in a town with one stoplight."

Everything with Grace and the party and the lies weighed heavy again.

"Oh, here's the running schedule." I took out a folded piece of paper. "I know you only have a few weeks until the 5k. There's some speed work and conditioning in there. You should be fine by July fourth."

Will looked over my hand-drawn calendar with instructions written into each day. "Does this mean you won't train me?"

"If you can wake up at seven. *A.M.*"

"I'll do my best." He carefully folded the paper and slid it into his shorts pocket. "Did you hear Antonio mention the show in Muskegon? A bunch of bands. This Saturday."

"So you can get more Xes on your hands?"

"Something like that. It's all ages. Are you in?"

"Teen group down the street is one thing. I doubt my grandparents will let me leave town. This summer is a punishment after all."

One danger of having any fun this summer was to forget why I was really here. It didn't take long for reminders to crop up.

"Muskegon isn't too far down the coast. You can tell your grandparents it's part of your service hours. A service project *event*. They'll have to go for it."

"Do you have a calendar? I can point out how they weren't born yesterday."

"Ha—nice one." Will stood and found a rock to skip across the darkening water. "Maybe you can just ask them?"

A super good-looking boy with piercings wants to take me to a concert. I promise I won't be the one driving.

"Maybe." Probably not, though. "You said your family moved here last year?" I asked instead of leaving.

"My aunt and uncle live in town. My mom wanted to be closer to them. After my brother died."

My eyes fell shut. "I didn't know. I'm sorry."

"I wanted to tell you before, but you were pretty shook about your accident. It never felt like the right time to bring it up. Also, it leads to questions I'm sometimes not in the mood to answer."

I didn't know what it was like to lose anyone so close, especially a sibling. Though I understood the need to constantly explain about a sibling. "You don't have to tell me if you don't want."

Will made eye contact. His brown eyes had a sadness to them. "I want to tell you. He was set to go to University of Michigan last fall. Had all the papers turned in and everything." His voice had an even tone again. A little hollow.

"What's his name?"

Will stared.

My chest froze. If I could take the words back, I would. "Sorry, I shouldn't have—"

"No." He reached for me. One slight move, and then he retracted his hand. "People never ask his name. They want to know how it happened." His shoulders eased. "His name is Adam. Adam Jerome. Jerome is my grandfather's name, which is butt-awful, so thank God he only got it as a middle name."

I reflected back his own smile.

Silence returned, only this time it softened around us like a warm blanket. No wonder Will was sometimes on edge. He was still dealing with the loss of his brother.

The lake fed waves into the shore, the water black with night except for the glassy strip illuminated by moonlight. I should go back to the house. I should.

"You should tell me about him," I said. "Your good memories and favorite stories. I mean, if you want to."

Will smoothed his fingers along the rough surface of the log. His expression moved from contemplative to a slight grin. "I do."

And then he did.

Chapter Eight

I slipped inside minutes after sunset, fearing the whole way back to my grandparents' house I'd be reprimanded.

Instead, both of them nodded as I passed through the front living room to the bathroom to wash up.

It wasn't too late, but I wanted to get a good night's sleep for tomorrow's run. Seven in the morning. Will. And a trail I'd never been on.

It was a date.

The next morning, I waited in front of Sunset Inn for Will. At ten after seven, I texted, just as he rolled up on a bike.

He skidded into the lot. "Hey. Sorry I'm running late. It's *really* early."

"Wouldn't you rather run when it's cooler?"

He dismounted from the bike and leaned it against the side of the front office. "I'd rather not run at all."

Color me confused. "But you're running a 5k race. You asked me to be a trainer."

I noticed what Will wore. Black T-shirt, cargo shorts, and the skate shoes. Again.

"You really don't have running shoes?"

Will kicked his heels against the gravel drive. "I said I liked to try new things, remember? I don't always have the funds to buy equipment for every new thing. The race, I didn't think it was a big deal. I thought these shoes would be fine."

"How are your feet from the other day running at the park?"

"Good except for the blisters. But that's what bandages are for."

Even running shoes needed breaking-in time. "Fair enough. You ready to show me this new trail?"

Will watched me a second, like he'd been expecting me to say something else. Maybe an offer to go to the diner for breakfast instead.

"Uh, yeah. I thought we'd do the walking path through town. It circles through the park on the other side of town away from the lake."

"Oh sure. The one by the fountain and the kiddie park?"

Will scrunched his nose. "Fountain yes. Kiddie park no. Maybe things have changed since you last visited."

That was probably true. I hadn't spent as much time in Deer Cove with the grans in recent years. Holidays yes, a few summer weekends, but we usually took day trips to some of the other beach towns or coordinated time with other family for a family celebration. I hadn't explored Deer Cove in ages.

"Let's walk first."

I let Will lead. He played town tour guide by pointing out businesses with anything noteworthy. Will's version of noteworthy was worth its own note.

"That's where Chaz lost his lunch after meeting a girl," he said about an order-up hot dog and burger stand. "By lost his lunch, I mean spewed his potatoes."

"Gross."

"Yes. Remember that. Chaz is gross." He winked. "Over there is where my cousin Ryder burned out on his dirt bike in front of an outdoor yoga class. And there's the bank where my mom works."

Finally, useful intel. "Is she there now?"

"You want to meet my mom?"

"Is she punk like you? Black hair and spiky cuffs?"

He laughed. "She's not there yet. *Too early.*"

He'd never give up razzing me about the morning thing.

"All right. Ready to start at a slow jog?" I asked. "We can always go back to a walk if you get a side cramp or something. How about we run until we reach the fountain." I could see it in the distance and it wasn't too far.

"You're on."

For the next thirty minutes, we took turns picking a marker to jog to, then slowed to a walk for two minutes before finding a new landmark. Will told me about the town. He told me about Adam. Stories like how he and Adam and their dad built a skateboard ramp and kids from the neighborhood came to do work on stunts. The family fished on a small fishing lake back where they'd lived and his mom always caught the most fish.

We jogged past the neighborhood where Will lived, off the inland side of Main Street. The houses seemed to each be a different color and style with flowers in window boxes and bikes left out in the yard.

Circling back to the inn, Will tumbled into the grass beneath a shady tree near the Sunset Inn sign.

"Don't forget to stretch or your legs will cramp." I sat beside him on the grass with my legs pointed out in front of me.

Will lay all the way on his back. "I'm never running again."

So much for the 5k. "If you hate running, you don't have to do the race."

He propped himself up with his elbows. "I made a commitment. Chaz is going. I said I'd go."

"Chaz does regular meet-ups with other runners," I reminded him. "You could always walk the 5k."

"No way. I'm all or nothing. Right now...I'm nothing."

I finished my cool down, urging Will to at least do some calf stretches.

"I can't believe I have to go to work after this," Will moaned. "It's only eight in the morning and I'm wiped."

I felt a teensy bit bad, but the most challenging part to any new routine was to start in the first place. "You'll be at the community center today?"

"Yeah, but I'll actually be at the state park. I'm on loan there for ranger duty. Meaning I do whatever the rangers want me to fetch or haul."

No wonder he dreaded more work. "We'll do a shorter run next time."

"Too soon. I can't think about next time." He looked at me, taking in my whole face. "Didn't you say you had a summer birthday?"

"Yeah. It's actually...tomorrow."

"Shut up." Will smacked the ground. "Holliday. You kept your birthday from me? What other secrets do you have?"

My smile fried to my face. "Secrets? I don't have secrets."

I swore he could see right through me. He saw those darkened corners.

"You didn't want me to know about your birthday or you would have said. Birthdays deserve attention."

"That's sweet, but remember, I can't go anywhere. I'm grounded. But thanks for the offer."

Will was already standing. He held his hand out for me to take and pulled me up. "You're turning sixteen."

"And? You're already seventeen."

"Yeah, but sixteen is a good age."

Not when you had no promise of a driver's license. Okay, I was shortchanging myself. This summer wasn't what I expected, but it didn't have to be a total bummer.

"Don't you stress," he told me. "I'll plan something."

That's what I was afraid of.

Will was coming for dinner.

Not just any dinner but a birthday dinner. *My* birthday dinner. At my grandparents' house.

All of this had been arranged behind my back by Will and my grandparents. While I'd been knee-deep in rotating bed sheets through the laundry in the Sunset Inn utility room, Will had chatted up Grandpop in the front office. I'd had no idea.

Grandpop, being his friendly self, immediately invited Will for dinner for the following night. Which of course happened to be my birthday. Which of course Will knew.

Will hadn't said a word about dinner while we worked at the community center together earlier in the day. Here I'd thought the balloons and assortment of vending machine snacks at Leaf Group had been the big surprise. The retirees even bought me a salted caramel mocha from the shop down the block.

Then we got to pulling weeds behind the bait and tackle shop as part of our Main Street Beautification Project. A little birthday magic to brighten my service hours.

But nope, that hadn't been it. When I'd arrived home, Grandma broke the news. My birthday dinner included a guest.

Turned out, Will was looking for trouble after all.

He arrived right before six-thirty. I opened the door to Will's patented grin. "Surprise." He handed me a small bouquet of daisies. "Happy birthday."

A hundred sensations hit at once. He'd brought me flowers. I'd never been gifted flowers by anyone, let alone a guy. Let alone a guy like Will. His hair looked freshly clipped around the back and hung shorter in the front. He wore a black button-down shirt tucked into gray pants. No cargo pockets in sight. His leather cuff and skate shoes, gone. No markings on his hands.

"How dare you."

He grinned wider. "Do I clean up okay?"

"You look great, and still somehow like you."

"I'm going to assume that's not an insult." He hadn't moved from the doorstep. "Wow, Holli. You look amazing."

"Oh. Thanks." I smoothed my hands down the flowy skirt grazing my knees. I had on a light tank top with beading around the collar and a long chain necklace Tala bought me. My honey brown hair lightly curled to rest along my shoulders.

He still sort of gawked, which made sense since last he saw me I had dirt streaked across my face with my hair pulled back and stuffed under a Central Michigan University cap courtesy of Grandpop, his alma mater.

I stepped aside to let him into the house.

"Check it out. New shoes." He turned a foot showing off gray leather boots.

"Nice. Did you pick up running shoes too?"

"By new, I meant borrowed from Antonio. The shirt is his too."

So, no shopping spree. I didn't mind. Will put in effort to clean up for my family. They would have welcomed him in a T-shirt with the hand Xes too, I was sure of it, but this extra work showed Will wanted to set a good impression.

"William?" Grandma came over to the door. "So nice to have you tonight."

William. My heart.

"Thanks. Oh—I brought this." He handed her a small glass jar with a crafty-type ribbon around the lid. "It's jam. Homemade. My mom cans it herself."

"How wonderful. Thank you." She herded him toward the living room and suggested he make himself at home.

Will sat on the couch. I perched on the edge of a wingback chair usually reserved for looking nice in the corner.

This all felt totally surreal. Like first date nerves plus meet-the-parents rolled into one.

Was this a date? Dates typically required first being asked out. I distinctly did not recall being asked. Not that I minded the idea of being asked out by Will. I just didn't know what to make of this. Or whether dates should involve Grandma's good dishware.

Grandpop joined us wearing a collared shirt and clean khakis, so Grandma definitely had a hand in attire choices for the night. "Welcome, Will. Good to see you again. Ready to eat?"

We sat at the table, where Grandma unveiled a glass pan of lasagna, a side salad in a bowl, and garlic bread.

Will's eyes widened. "Wow, you really pulled out all the stops. Is this your favorite meal, Holli?"

"I heard you say at Leaf Group you liked Italian, so I suggested it."

Will sat back. "But it's your birthday. You should pick."

"I like lasagna just fine. It's especially good when I'm training because I burn off those carbs with distance runs." I cleared my throat sensing the heat of my grandparents' attention on me. "I helped with the sauce."

"No jar sauce in this family," Grandma added. "Jarred tomatoes maybe, but I like to add my own spices."

Jarred tomatoes and spices, really? *Please, somebody airlift me out of here.*

I checked for Will's reaction and he seemed fine, even content with the conversation. "My folks started a garden this spring. We're growing tomatoes, basil, and peppers. Basically a pizza in plant form."

Oh my word. Will channeled the chatty just like he did with the retirees at Leaf Group. Now he had Grandpop on a roll about composting.

"I'm sorry to hear you lost your brother Adam," Grandma said after a stretch of silence.

Will stopped chewing. I flashed Grandma an urgent *cease and desist!* look, but she wasn't paying attention. Probably on purpose. What was she thinking making such a personal remark?

Will grabbed a napkin to wipe his mouth. "Thanks. Adam was an amazing person. I just want to do half as much as he did."

Grandpop nodded solemnly. "For a parent to lose a child must be incredibly painful. And for you."

"A tremendous loss," Grandma added.

They both said this so matter-of-fact, not at all dancing around the subject like I would.

I cycled through options to shift the subject, but all I could come up with was more talk about vegetables. How we planted herbs at the community center garden. How my thumb made contact with a worm and I hadn't even freaked out.

"I've been talking to Holli about my brother," Will said. "It's been nice. At first, I didn't talk because it was too hard. I feel ready to remember him again. The memories don't just make me feel sad."

The conversation ended up shifting on its own. Will never broke a sweat.

"We'd usually have a cake for Holli," Grandma said, "but I hear you have a plan, Will."

I looked at Will. "You do?"

He grinned. "I told you birthdays deserve attention. We have something set up over at the center."

He'd said *we*, so he'd enlisted help.

I was very afraid.

My grandparents shooed us away—no dish duty tonight. I grabbed a cardigan and sandals and left the house out the front to follow Will to the rest of what waited for me.

I felt like I could breathe again in the fresh air. "First of all, I am so sorry my grandparents asked about your brother. Out of nowhere."

"It's all good. I was surprised your grandmother remembered Adam's name. It's not like she ever met him. My mom must have told her about Adam when they met. She's not real shy about him or what happened."

"I'm glad you weren't too uncomfortable. Then again, you did invite yourself over, so you only have yourself to blame."

"Hey, my only goal was to get permission to have you over to the center tonight. Your grandfather brought up dinner. I have a standing rule to never pass up free food."

"But then you kept it a secret all day!"

"Birthdays are for surprises."

"Are they, Will? Are they?"

We turned the corner onto Main. "Your grandparents are nice. Besides, now they're buttered up for you to ask about going to the show in Muskegon."

Huh. Even if he had been strategizing, he'd intended to win me some freedom this weekend.

We reached the end of the block about to cross when Will stopped. "Hold up. Let me see if they're ready."

I should have been more vocal about not liking surprises. Knowing something was planned but having no idea about the plan stressed me out.

"Okay, let's go."

Will and I walked around the center building to the back. In front of us, balloons and a small crowd appeared. "Surprise!"

Each person held two lit sparklers. It wasn't actually dark yet, but the effect was still great, especially with the blue lake behind them.

Bright green and white checked cloth covered a picnic table with a three-tiered cake set in the middle.

Piper rushed over and handed me both sparklers. Then she took a silver plastic crown from the bag over her shoulder and placed it on my head.

"Happy birthday, Holli!"

My smile was so big it hurt my face. "Thank you, everyone. I've never had a surprise party before."

"I know it's not a *total* surprise," Will said beside me. "With having to get permission and all and me basically telling you I had a plan. I'm kind of bad at secrets."

Definitely a good thing, since one of us had a big one.

Chaz stood beside a petite but stocky girl I didn't recognize. She had dark hair that reached the middle of her back. "Hi, I'm Carmen," she said. "I guess I'm crashing your party."

"I'm crashing my own party." I laughed. "This cake looks delicious." I moved closer to the picnic table. The frosting was bright green with leaf cutouts stuck to the side. "Aw, it's like Leaf Group."

"We made the cake," Will said. "By we, I mean mostly Piper and Antonio. I did those leaf cut-outs with a cookie cutter."

On closer inspection, the bottom layer shifted part way off the plate and the top bit had a smashed corner, but color me impressed anyway. "This is great. Thank you all so much."

We dug into the cake and cracked open the chips and cans of pop on the other end of the table. I had a message from Tala waiting on my phone I took a quick peek at. The message filled up my whole screen with emojis and a dancing cat with a party hat.

We hung out for an hour before Piper and Chaz had to take off.

Antonio got a small fire going in the pit, so he, Will, Carmen and I stayed to talk and burn through the rest of the sparklers.

My oddest birthday yet. With my stress long forgotten and my cares cast aside, it might have even been my best.

Chapter Nine

♥

It was a Hayes family miracle. My grandparents allowed me to go to the concert in Muskegon with Will and the teen group.

Or maybe not a miracle. Will's butter-up strategy actually worked. Ever since his appearance at my birthday dinner, Grandma and Grandpop raved about Will and his maturity and work ethic.

Will was my ticket to summer freedom.

At six o'clock, after a few quick text exchanges with Tala about my night's plans, I walked to the community center. Will rolled up in his sticker-coated car. The stickers piled on top of each other in a frantic war to be seen.

"No wonder you lost at Campfire Shuffle," I told him when he emerged. His hair was styled extra messy, but in an artful way. "I've never heard of any of these bands."

"Popularity doesn't equal quality." He tapped a fading sticker with a skull on it, only hearts filled in for the eye sockets. "This band charges ten bucks for tickets at every venue, no matter where they play. They stay after shows to talk and donate a portion of their sales to a suicide hotline. I'd say they have a more meaningful following than artists with millions of YouTube views."

While I chewed on that thought, two more cars pulled in. One a full-sized van, also covered in stickers on the back. But the side of the van was what got me. An airbrushed, mountainous landscape with a wolf howling at a dragon.

Will was talking, but I couldn't take my eyes off the fire-breathing dragon. The wingspan alone took up half the side panel.

"It's amazing, right?" Will's face lit up. "The van is Antonio's. Can you believe he bought it like this?"

"Private seller," Antonio said as he approached. He wore a dragon T-shirt to complete the theme. "I call it the Dragon Wagon. The guy who sold it said he'd paint over the art, but I said no way."

Behind him, Piper transferred a bag and jacket to the van.

"We're driving *that* to Muskegon?" My comment landed with a decidedly awkward thud. "Sorry, I didn't mean to sound..." *so horrible.*

Will knocked his fist against the van. "The dragon is a fierce protector on the road."

"The A/C works," Antonio added. "And Chaz helped me install a killer stereo."

"I just saw this article online about car audio competitions," Chaz explained. "The cars only have to be drivable for something like ten feet. The rest of the car's non-essentials are removed to fit audio components for making the sound as loud as possible."

Antonio slung a brown-toned arm over Chaz's pale shoulder. "We like to say Chaz knows a little bit about a lot of stuff nobody cares about. It's a special gift."

Piper had shed her trendy fashionista look for an all-black ensemble. She wore a nose ring hoop and electric pink lipstick. "Holli, I've been *dying* for another girl to join teen group since I started. Girls besides the freshmen, I mean."

"What about Carmen? From my party?"

"Carmen doesn't come around too often. She's kind of a wild card."

It felt good to be seen, to be needed, but I couldn't help the sensation I stuck out around them. In a group of interesting people full of flavor, I was the plain toast.

We piled in the van to head out. Now knowing Will and Piper were just friends, I didn't feel the tension anymore. A dumb tension anyway since Will didn't belong to me.

Everyone talked about the bands we'd see at the show. As the miles passed, my worries faded.

Except the second we filed in line at the weathered brick theater in Muskegon, I couldn't shake the distinct feeling I didn't belong.

All around us I saw worn leather coats, black band T-shirts, piercings, rainbow-dyed hair. Every look was punk, metal, emo, or whatever. My outfit would score a "cute" comment from my mom, but not from this crowd. I thought I'd gone mature with frosty eye shadow and darker lip gloss. My look was a kid playing dress-up compared to the heavy black liner across every gender.

It was more than the clothes. The girls reminded me of Grace.

We reached the front of the line. Will nudged me forward. "Hold out your hand."

The person working the door drew an X on the top of my hand with permanent marker.

Will leaned close when he joined me through the door. "Now you're one of us."

Inside the theater, the seats were gutted for standing room only. Every surface was coated black—the stage, the floor, the ceiling. The walls too, but those had peeling band posters with newer posters layered on top.

As we moved through the growing crowd, my shoes stuck with each step. Nearer to the stage, bodies gathered in a restless mass, waiting for the music to start.

Will added a light hand at my back. "Is this spot good?"

A sweaty, sour stench drifted past, like a locker room littered with empty beer cans.

"This is great!" I just needed to get used to all this.

Antonio and Chaz split off to find a place nearer to the stage. Will drew closer. So close one breath would press our arms together. Something I wanted to feel and felt scared to want all at once.

Piper squished into the spot between me and the wall. "So Holli, what kind of music do you like?"

"Oh, probably stuff you all wouldn't care about."

She crossed her arms. "In case you forgot, I played all those Campfire Shuffle songs by memory. I'm equal opportunity with music—I like everything."

"Everything?" Will opened his eyes extra wide. "You like banjo funk fusion? Dubstep opera?"

"Dubstep opera is not a *thing*." Piper narrowed her eyes. "Anyway, I only know the first band playing tonight. The rest of these groups are new to me. We can experience them together."

She joined her arm with mine, so easily like we'd been friends for ages.

The first band took the stage. A white woman dressed in faded red leather picked up a guitar, followed by a blond wearing a skirt with shredded tights and a band tee. The third was an Asian woman with a black mohawk who positioned herself behind a drum kit. I turned to Piper with my mouth half open. She shot back a smile. Will gave me a thumbs up.

The red leather woman strummed once against her guitar. The note hung in the air, distorted with some kind of effect.

The blonde stepped to the microphone. "Hey. We're What About Caitlin. Thanks for coming. One two, one two three four!"

And then they were off. The music roared fast and loud. Like a train barreling down the tracks at top speed.

When the song ended, the crowd broke into cheers. All I could do was stare and numbly clap before the music started again.

"Holli is like Knives Chau from *Scott Pilgrim*!" Piper shouted to Will.

I finally took my eyes from the stage. "What does that mean?"

"She was really into Scott's band," Piper explained. "The comic and the movie."

This time I didn't feel like a dork for saying I hadn't seen the movie they referenced. Instead, I made plans with them to watch it.

The band continued with eight more songs, keeping my attention the whole time. I followed a lot of female singers on my music app, but mainly listened to pop stars who played stadiums and awards shows. Not music like this.

I wanted to listen to this band when I ran. Especially for the last mile when it was time to pick up my pace and close in on the finish line.

Their set ended, and the band changed over.

"I can't tell if you're stunned or horrified," said Will once we could hear each other again.

"You are looking a little windblown," Piper added.

I smiled. The roots of my hair vibrated from the loud volume. "I loved it."

Will held up his fist and I bumped it. "I was so hoping you'd be into them. Their lyrics are all about taking control and being dedicated, and that's so your deal."

Will paid enough attention to me he thought he knew my *deal*. My heart soared.

"See," he went on, "You're super motivated. Like, with your running. You could say screw it, my summer sucks, I'm not doing anything. You're not. Even at the center when we're working, you take the lead with some of the volunteers."

"I'm just doing what I'm supposed to."

"Exactly. You have no idea what it's like to keep people motivated who work for free. If they don't show up, they don't have to. Then we've still got a dirty beach and a community center full of people wondering where to go and why stuff is broken. Like the retirees. Good people, but they sure like to talk. You keep them on task."

"Oh. Well, you're welcome."

Suddenly, I lurched forward into Will. I was like a sweat-drenched towel splatting against Will's chest.

He caught me and moved his hands to my shoulders. "Are you okay?" He looked beyond me. "Hey buddy—watch it."

I shook my leg out. "I'll be fine."

"These shows get rough sometimes," Will said. "I'll block any jerks from bumping into you."

He moved behind me, a solid and secure presence. Thank goodness it was dark—my face flamed.

Without meaning to, I replayed the feeling of my body against his. Every nerve awakened. As if my nerves hadn't already shot awake from the last band. Now it was like someone stuck my limbs into a socket.

Another band played, this one less a speeding train. The singer growled into the microphone. Not really my thing.

Maybe it was cheesy how I enjoyed Will's protection, but I did.

Between sets, Will pointed toward the door. "Wanna get out for a minute?"

I nodded, and we made our way to the front with Piper following. We passed a table with shirts and CDs and vinyl for sale. A What About Caitlin shirt hung on the wall above the table.

I pulled out money from my pocket and detoured to the line, pulling Piper with me. The drummer from the band sat at the table.

"Thanks for supporting us," she said after handing over my size shirt. Her black mohawk looked even more pointy up close. "Here's a flyer with our upcoming shows and links where you can download our music. We also sell CDs."

I thanked her, and Piper and I squeezed our way past the growing line to the doors leading out front.

Outside, cool night air smoothed over my hot skin.

Will waited by the exit. "Oh good, there you are. Did you buy a shirt? Lemme see."

I held up the shirt.

"Awesome. We'll turn you into a growling punk any day now."

"Or not," Piper said. "Quit it, you, with all the growling."

We walked a ways from the exit where space allowed us to talk. I expected Will and his friends to pull out e-cigs, like Grace did anytime we found ourselves outside without our parents. No one lingering on the sidewalk smoked. Only one older guy farther down the walk flicked a lighter against a cigarette.

Will noticed where I looked. "Sometimes I crave it. I'm clean though. Eight months."

"Smoking is *so* nasty." Piper turned her mouth down in a disgusted expression. "I'm glad I never started."

"So, you quit smoking?" I asked Will. "That must have been hard."

"I only miss it if I smell it." He shrugged. "I don't know, it's a thing."

"Will's hardcore though." Antonio appeared. He and Chaz snapped a picture of themselves making stupid faces. "He's no smoking, no drugs, no alcohol. No *hanky-panky*." He punched Will on the arm.

Will deflected the punch. "I would never say the words hanky-panky. Besides, it's no impurities. Substances, not people."

"Girls are total impurities, man." Antonio pulled up a picture on his phone and showed it to me. On the screen, a dark-haired girl in a low-cut tank top made a pouty face.

"Antonio got dumped," Chaz explained. "Hard."

"Sorry to hear," I told him.

"Seriously, though. Why are girls so complicated?" Antonio threw up his hands. "I did everything for that girl. I listened to her. I even babysat her little brother for free. And what do I get? She's with some other joker because of his ride. Like my van is some kind of problem."

No one rushed to defend the van. "It sounds like she didn't appreciate you," I said. "Maybe you were so busy being what she needed, you didn't think to ask her to be what you needed." I pressed my lips shut. Where had that come from? "Sorry, I didn't mean—"

Antonio shook his hhead. "No, don't be sorry, Holli." He turned the phone over in his hands, then slipped it into his pocket. "What you just said took me to a different place. I'm gonna need to think on it."

"That was deep," Chaz agreed, stroking his beard. "It reminds me of this podcast I listened to about the changing nature of relationships in the new era of social media."

Music cued up, and the sidewalk crowd funneled back inside. Our group cleared out. All but Will and me.

"You okay?" he asked.

Will frequently asked me whether I was okay. And I tended to hover on the edge of not being okay. "Yeah. I was dumped this past year too."

"Oh, dang. How long ago was your break-up?"

"A couple months ago."

"No wonder things feel like crap for you right now."

We leaned back against the old brick. I slid down to sit, the pavement cool through my jeans.

Will sat next to me. We both looked at the sky as it shifted into night.

"Hey—sunset," Will said, just when I said, "Same time, different place." We looked at each other and laughed.

Will's fingers walked toward mine, which lay flat against the sidewalk next to me. "I'm glad I met you."

Warm pulses like a reverse shiver coursed through me. "Me too."

Will touched my hand. He wasn't holding it, but sort of making it known he was there. "When I lost my brother, it changed everything."

"Is the accident why you stopped smoking and drinking?"

"I had to. I was the worst person."

"I'm sure that's not true."

"No, I was. I didn't care about anything. My grades were all Ds and I didn't care. I got in fights—didn't care. My mom tried to get our family to go to some church counseling thing, and I blew her off. All I wanted was to drink and party and numb myself."

He picked a stray weed wrangling through the pavement cracks and shredded it into green confetti.

"It's not even like my life was bad," he said. "My parents are normal enough, I guess. But I was never going to be like Adam. You know, until I had to be."

His story sounded eerily similar to my own sibling situation.

"It was a drunk driver," he said. "Some dude was so down about his life he was wasted at six in the evening on a Tuesday. He crossed right through a median and smashed into my brother's car. In an instant, Adam was gone."

My body numbed. *A drunk driver.*

"It shouldn't have been Adam." His words came so quiet, I wasn't sure I'd heard them at all. "We were both in the car. If someone had to die, it shouldn't have been my brother."

My hand retracted before I realized I'd done it. I couldn't breathe. I couldn't swallow. I wanted to repel this information like water from a raincoat. "You can't mean that. No one should have died."

"But someone did. My brother. He's gone, forever, all because of a reckless drunk."

Reckless.

"I knew then, alcohol was poison," Will said. "It's a sick, horrible poison that numbs you to life. I'd been fooled by it. Being the one who lived—" He paused, struggling with the word. "I couldn't be like the guy who killed my brother. It's why I quit, and why I don't have room for people who actively poison themselves."

I stared at my hands.

"The charity run I'm doing is for a substance abuse clinic. I started a chapter at my school for Students Against Drunk Driving. A community center event with them is where I met these guys." Will gestured toward the door, where his friends disappeared. "That's what these mean." He showed me the back of his hands, where Xes marked each one. "We're all about clean living and being positive."

It was so much to take in. Will bared his heart and more, and I could only think of Grace. Partying so often, so addicted to the rush, and the attention.

I stood. "They're probably wondering where we are. We should get back."

My words came too fast. I needed to get back inside the theater where the noise could drown my thoughts. Where the music would numb me, like a drug.

Chapter Ten

♥

For the ride back, I curled up with an old blanket in Antonio's van, pretending to be tired.

Will reached for my hand in our cozy situation in the middle seats of the van. I moved my hand, pretending to yawn. He wouldn't want me to hold his hand if he knew the truth about my family. The ugly, reckless truth.

Grace could have died. She could have *killed* someone. A blameless and innocent someone like Will's brother. And it could have happened because of me.

I was exactly what he despised. I made excuses for someone who poisoned their life.

Antonio dropped me off at the inn. Super nice of him and not too much of a detour.

Will hopped out as I gathered my things. He walked me to the door at the house. "I'm glad you came."

"Yeah." My smile felt fake. It *was* fake.

The usual light in his eyes dimmed. Maybe he was tired like me. Maybe he knew I had horrible secrets.

"Thanks for everything," I told him. I really was grateful, even though this would be the end of what we'd started.

Will opened his mouth like he wanted to say more but didn't. Instead, he nodded and took off back to the van.

The next morning, I dragged myself up. For fleeting moment, I saw my bedroom at home and imagined Grace down the hall. Sleeping in later than me. But my view shifted to the sloping attic walls. The dusty scent mixed with a lake breeze coming in from the screened window.

Last night. The concert.

Will.

I sank back against my pillow. Will's expression when he declared alcohol was poison played through my mind. Disgusted. Angry.

He blamed alcohol and the people who abused it for losing his brother. And he wasn't wrong. That was exactly what happened.

Grace—she'd been lucky she hadn't crashed into a person. The only casualty of our accident was a ditched bike in someone's front yard.

My phone buzzed on the table beside the daybed.

Will: *Please tell me Sundays are holy days and we get a break from running.*

I smiled. I liked Will. I wanted to keep liking Will.

Me: *No run today. Sleep in.*

It was on the schedule I'd given him. No run Sundays or sub in strength training.

Maybe Will just wanted to talk to me.

I could still go for a run. I needed to clear my head.

Making my way into the kitchen, Grandma held out the blocky cordless phone she insisted on keeping in case their cell phones spontaneously shorted out. "Your mother is on the line."

I took the phone. "Hey."

"I have an update about your case. The attorney will make a personal visit. Be ready with any questions."

"They're coming here? Are you coming too?"

A beat passed. "Your father and I have to work, Holli. This attorney is expensive. I can't take off in the middle of the week to drive nearly two hours each way."

So, that would be a no.

Mom yammered on about things at home, but I didn't absorb much.

"I love you, Holli," she said and hung up.

Grandma took the handset and placed it back on the...thingy where those handsets charged.

She squeezed my shoulder. "We'll be right there with you. No lawyer is talking to my grandbaby without me and your Grandpop."

I left for my run and took a route through town the opposite direction from the community center. My head didn't really feel cleared up, but I'd done four miles and felt pretty good otherwise.

Back at the inn, the day stretched ahead.

"Holli, why don't you stock the rooms with tea and bottled water?" Grandma nodded toward the supply cabinet behind the front desk.

Filling a basket of supplies, I left the office and crossed the gravel lot to the cabins.

Sunset Inn was an L-shaped row of rooms, each with a kitchenette, a dining table with two to four chairs, and a pot belly stove beyond the standard bed, dresser and bathroom. Little cabins with rustic, weathered sides and firewood piled up beside the doors.

I reached Cabin 4. This was where Grace and I held our sleepovers. Once Grace turned twelve, so long as business was slow and we stayed relatively quiet, we could sleep overnight in the cabin. Of course, this cabin was the one most clearly viewed from the house so our parents could check if we'd left the light on too late.

This bunkbed nook made Cabin 4 our favorite. A round window positioned along the top bunk provided a glimpse of Main Street. Grace usually won top bunk, but sometimes we'd squeezed up there together to watch for action on the street.

I could almost see twelve-year-old Grace sitting on the top bunk with her legs hanging down.

My mind rewound to our phone conversation. Grace had to change now that she knew the truth about the accident. She'd blacked out with no memory of driving us away from the party. The truth had to be a wake-up call. If Grace promised to never drink again, then we could leave this in the past. I could move forward with Will. I just needed to know Grace would promise.

I sent her a text. *Can we talk?*

Straightening up the kitchen supplies, I waited for her answer. Only a reply never came.

Grandma had more work for me, so I closed up with one glance back at the top bunk. One more reminder how my sister wasn't always the way she was now.

I couldn't avoid Will forever. The truth was, I didn't want to avoid him. I just needed to get my act together.

Hustle up, Holli, Coach would say.

Back at the community center for service hours the next day, I slipped in just as the group started.

"All right, everyone," Will said to the volunteers. "This week we have special projects with the state park. I'll go through the list of what they need and we'll divide into groups."

I tuned out the details. I'd go where needed and stick near the retirees who reliably talked about weather, nature, and their grandchildren. Or grand-furbies in the case of Violet whose daughter worked as a veterinarian.

We piled into a white van with the community center leaf logo on the side. Squeezing into the middle seat reminded me of riding in Antonio's dragon wolf wagon. Only this time Will rode shotgun beside one of the center staff.

At the park, everyone split into their pre-determined groups. Will pointed my way. "Holli, you're with me."

I nodded toward the older volunteers. "I'm good with Violet and Ken." I wanted to hear how their garden tour went with the seniors group. That would be senior citizens, not high school seniors.

Will reached for me. "Hang back a sec, 'kay?"

I sighed. "I'm sorry, Will. It's not you." How could I say what I couldn't dare say? "I think things are starting to stress me out."

Will's dark hair fell around his eyes like his own armored protection. Only nothing could mask his face. His eyes broadcast everything. I'd hurt him.

"Knowing what happened to my brother changes things, doesn't it?" Will stuffed his hands into his shorts pockets. "People don't know how to act around someone who lost the star of their family. When they find out I live straight—clean—it gets more weird. Like I've made myself an even bigger outcast."

Hearing about his brother and his views on alcohol *had* changed things between us. But the changes between us weren't his fault. I didn't know how to tell him those things without telling him everything. And I wasn't ready.

I looked around at the other volunteers. The groups had their trash pokers and collection bags out, already getting to work around the parking lot perimeter. No one paid attention to us.

Maybe a little honesty would help. "You said alcohol is poison. It got me thinking about a lot of things." I took a breath. "My sister. She's really messed up right now."

"What kind of messed up?"

"She parties a lot. I think it's worse than I realized." I knew it was worse. Obviously, Grace didn't have a handle on her partying if she blacked out part of the night. "We had a fight on the phone the other day. She's not talking to her best friend. I tried talking to her about it, but it was like she didn't care. It's hard because I'm not there. I just don't know what to do. I'm worried about Grace."

He thought this over. "She's your sister. You'd probably do anything for her. Like drive her drunk self home from a party when you don't even have a driver's license."

I felt my insides crack. If only that were the truth. I laughed to cover my nerves. "Our court case is coming up. I'm hoping the judge knocks sense into her. To have someone else tell her she needs to change."

Will looked past me. "Let's walk."

I joined him and we moved toward a picnic table. "Your sister," Will said, "if she has a drinking problem, the change needs to come from inside. You can't have someone tell you to change. For me, it took losing Adam. That was my turning point."

I wanted a turning point for Grace. It was the whole *you can't have someone tell you to change* part that was the problem.

"Antonio and Piper both have families affected by drugs or substances," Will said. "They had to learn a different way exists. They're making choices now to live in a new way. I want the same for the people I care about. I get passionate about it. I hope she gets help."

"Thanks. I've never said out loud that my sister has a drinking problem, but I think you're right."

"Every day, I try to make up for what happened in the accident. Every day I feel this...this feeling I don't deserve to be here. I have to do something to prove myself. Does that make sense?"

"I guess so, but it's not true. It was a tragic accident. You don't have to prove anything."

"I'm not used to doing the right thing. Not like you. I have to be deliberate and I need rules. I need structure."

Guilt wedged the cracking divide inside me wider. He thought I always did the right thing. Not even close to true. I'd let my sister drive that night and risked other people's lives. I should have gotten myself together enough to stop her. I should have told my parents what happened. I was still lying to them. I was lying to too many people.

Will clasped his hands together. "Let's get to work. We aren't going to solve everyone's problems today, so we'll work out our frustration gathering brush and tilling some soil."

The worst companion to my guilt—hope—lingered in his eyes.

We headed to the ranger's station where Will checked in at the desk. He returned with a small keyring and a box. "Do want to know where we're going?"

I shrugged. The less I said, the better right now.

"Come on. Be hard on yourself later. For now, pretend none of that stuff is your life. Guess where we're going. *Guess.*"

His smile held such delight, I hated to disappoint him. "Leaf duty, in the forest."

"You think we need to rake around here? The leaves are part of the show." He gestured toward a parked golf cart.

I pointed to the bumper. "Needs more band stickers."

He slid in the driver's seat and started up the cart. "I knew you couldn't stay mad at me for long."

"I wasn't mad at you, Will. I'm mad at..." Myself. Life. "Just, let's forget about it for now."

"No worries. One more guess at what we're doing. It rhymes with shirt."

I hung onto the cart's side handle as Will veered onto a road designated Maintenance Only. "Dirt? We're shoveling more dirt?"

"Good guess, but no. It also rhymes with dirt." He slowed to round a corner by a sign with an image of a campsite. We passed a checkpoint where Will waved to a park worker manning a brown, shingled booth.

What else could we be doing that rhymed with—and then I saw the sign with an icon of a hut. The word "Yurt" written underneath. I burst out laughing. "*Yurt*? That's a thing?"

Will hooked the cart right and pulled up to a round structure with a wood porch extending from the door. "The first time I heard of a yurt, I had the same reaction. It's like we're not even in Michigan anymore. These things are amazing."

Will's enthusiasm appeared genuine. I could tell because he spoke fast and his eyes sort of sparkled. It's how he looked when he talked about the music he liked and helping people.

It was how he looked at me sometimes.

"So, it's like a cabin?"

"Yeah. They're a type of dwelling going back to ancient Mongolia. I mean, I *had* to look it up."

"Chaz probably knows all about yurts."

"He does. Chaz is awesome."

I followed Will to the first structure in the grouping. "Are these new? I feel like my grandparents would have mentioned yurt camping."

"I think a few years old is all." He removed crinkled papers from his shorts pocket and unearthed a copper-colored key from the keyring. "We're taking inventory of the vacant yurts with these maintenance lists."

He opened the door, then ducked to clear the frame. I walked right under.

Inside, wood lattice climbed the walls. A bunk bed took up one side, custom-made for the round structure, unlike my grandparents' store-bought Sunset Inn beds. A table and chairs sized for a take-out dinner sat along the opposite side of the room. In back, a futon.

"Not too bad for camping." I touched a lamp. "At least there's electricity."

"The glamping crowd is pretty into these. Glam-camping," he said before I could ask. "I wish I didn't know glamping was an actual term people say, but I do and I can't have that ignorance back."

I laughed. "This is the only way I could get my family to camp. And that's a strong maybe."

A framed cross-stitch picture by the door read *Home Sweet Yurt*.

"What's the rest of your family like?" Will asked.

My throat tightened. Even when I tried to forget, my family was always one thought away.

"Sorry," Will said. "I told you we wouldn't think about family and then I asked. I just want to know more about you."

He shouldn't have to apologize. "My family are the hotel and pool type of vacationers. The closest I've been to camping is staying at Sunset Inn's cabins. Those have little kitchens in them, so it's more, I don't know, upgraded than these. Though *upgraded* probably isn't the right word." I sat at the small table and pulled out my water bottle. "I can't say I ever thought I'd be taking a water break in an ancient Mongolian dwelling. In the woods."

He looked over the inventory list. "Life is weird, huh? Have you ever slept outside? Just you and a sleeping bag under the stars?"

"Alone? No way. There are bears out here."

"The beach is pretty safe. Maybe not alone, but with friends."

"Sounds cold." Though the waves hitting the shore helped put me to sleep every night from the open window in the attic. The one thing other than my grandparents I'd miss about this place when I went back home.

I looked up at Will across the yurt. Okay, maybe I'd miss more than Lake Michigan.

Will tested a flashlight for battery power. I joined him, looking over the list to see what I could help with.

"Adam was really into camping," Will said as we each took a window to make sure it opened, closed, and latched shut. "He'd take off with just a sleeping bag and a backpack. We'd go together sometimes."

"Sounds fun. I could see Grace—" I stopped myself.

He set down the clipboard and propped an elbow against the top bunkbed. "You know, meeting you, it's brought back a lot of memories about Adam and the accident."

"I don't know if I should apologize or say you're welcome."

"No, wait. That sounded bad. I saw a counselor after I moved. She said new things would trigger the grief. It's not bad, it just is. I take my progress and draw from that. I keep moving forward."

This seemed like an important conversation, so I sat down on the lower bunk. Will sat beside me, sinking the mattress lower. "Before Adam died, I never had to care about money. Or insurance. Not until we had to pay for Adam's funeral. Did you know coffins cost thousands of dollars? And they call them caskets. You pick out the fabric color inside and everything. Something changes in you when you're sitting in a funeral home decorated like somebody's grandparents' house, being asked to fork over all your money to bury somebody you just lost."

A pressure built in my chest. "That's terrible."

"When Adam turned sixteen, he got to choose what to do with the money my parents saved for him. Not like it was much. He could save for college or buy a car junior year and get a job. He chose the car."

We both knew what happened to the car.

Will snapped and unsnapped the leather cuff on his wrist. "I wanted to use my savings money for the funeral. My parents wouldn't let me. I *begged*, and they said no way. My aunt and uncle loaned us the money. It's why we're here. Dad's working with my uncle. Mom's working over at the bank. We're almost all squared up. I've got a job and can pay them back some too. They really pulled together for us."

"Family is super important." My own words sounded empty.

"Knowing my aunt, she'll find a way to use the money for me anyway."

Time ticked, so we left to go through the rest of the yurts.

I told him about my grandparents and the inn while we checked off inventory lists. The more I talked, the more I could try to convince Will I was a good person too. The more I could try to convince myself.

Chapter Eleven

♥

Back home after my service hours, I met Grandma out front by the Sunset Inn sign where she added composted dirt for fertilizer around her flowers. All stuff I knew from working with the volunteers at the center.

"The lawyer will be here tomorrow morning. Ten a. m."

My blood pumped thick and hot. A day and a time made it real.

"Your father's driving in," Grandma said. "Your mother's working."

She didn't mention Grace at all.

It was strange how so much of why I was here came as a direct result of my sister and yet we hardly discussed her by name. Funny, it should have been exactly what I wanted. No longer in Grace's shadow. None of my new friends knew about Grace unless I told them.

Grandma looked up at me staring unfocused. "I'll be right beside you. I imagine this is scary. It probably didn't seem like such a serious matter at the time, but I blame your sister for that."

Okay, so Grace made it into our conversation after all. "It's not—"

Grandma held up her hand. "You're young yet and you don't get how vulnerable your situation is. Your sister isn't right in the head. I know I sound harsh and I don't mean it as an insult. She needs help. I've talked to your folks about this until I was blue in the face. It's a miracle they let me have you this summer."

We hadn't talked openly like this. "Um…"

She shook out her garden gloves. "Holliday. I'm your grandmother and I won't let anyone run circles around you. Not some big shot lawyer, not a judge, and certainly not your sister."

Dang. Grandma had my back. "Thank you."

The next day, I dressed for a run, but texted Will not to meet up.

Me: *Sorry I'm being a rotten coach. I need a solo run this morning.*

I didn't get a return text until I came back to the inn.

Will: *This seven a.m. thing is not working out. Totally missed my alarm. Solo run time granted.*

I showered and dressed in the nicest clothes I'd brought with me and returned back downstairs at the same time Dad pulled up to the house.

He came in through the front door. He had on a business suit with a loose tie and jacket hanging open. "Hey, Hol." He got to me first with a hug.

I hadn't realized how much I'd missed him. He and Mom had been so mad at me at the hospital during the aftermath of the accident. So much yelling. So much lecturing.

Dad hugged Grandma, who said she'd pull Grandpop from the front desk before the lawyer arrived.

"This is all routine," Dad told me. "No need to worry."

Right. Routine if you're used to getting citations added to your *existing* record. Grace had been through this already. And Dad led meetings working as a project manager at his company. He did the suit and tie thing and met with higher-ups all the time. The only interview I had experience with was when my school's sports blog questioned me about cross-country meets. Nothing about this situation was routine.

A slick black sedan arrived to the Sunset Inn lot. A Latina-looking woman dressed in white pants and a light blue blazer got out, followed by a younger guy carrying a laptop bag.

I hid in the sewing room pretending to look for something—what? a skein of yarn? *Why yes, so many yarn skeins to choose from.* In the living room, shuffling sounds carried over as the adults assembled and introduced themselves.

"Holli?" Grandma called out.

I squeezed the softest yarn in the pile. For good luck.

If things went well today, carrying around yarn for luck purposes would require explaining.

I wandered out and sat on a footstool parked near the door. In case I needed a hasty exit.

"I'm Miranda," the lawyer said. She wore a heavy gold watch on one hand. "Holli, thank you so much for meeting with me today. It's also a great opportunity for me to get out to the coast for some R and R."

Miranda reviewed a summary of Grace's alcohol violations first. Even though Grace wasn't actually in possession of alcohol, she'd consumed it, and her blood alcohol level at the hospital hit above the legal limit, which was zero for anyone under twenty-one.

"Though Grace herself wasn't driving, the zero-tolerance alcohol violation raises concern. We'll be recommending community service hours, and a standard course for alcohol awareness. Now for Holli." Miranda looked at me. "Tell me about what you've been doing with your summer."

"Um..." My mind went blank as printer paper.

Grandpop shared how I tended to the cabins. "She's enrolled at the community center and made friends the very first day." He sounded almost proud. "I'll let Holli tell you herself."

Now on the spot, I fumbled through telling her about the garden projects, the state park work, beach trash clean-up, and the teen group.

"And you're teaching Will about long distance running ahead of the charity 5k race," Grandma pointed out.

"Who is Will?" Miranda asked without looking up from her legal pad. When she did finally look up, she could probably fill in the rest based on my blush.

"A friend," I added quickly. "He's running the community group even though he's in high school. A legal adult is always on the premises."

Miranda grinned. "No worries from me. I think you have an exceptional reputation, Holliday, and a solid family behind you. We'll make it clear this was a situational lapse in judgment. You were under extreme stress."

Heat crawled up my neck. The night of the party came as both a blur and crisply embedded in my mind. She got it right, my judgment had lapsed. If I could explain it in court, maybe this wouldn't be so bad. My story made the most sense. I'd done what I had to do at the time. Even if it was a bad decision.

"Now we need to review the options the court has for your future." Miranda focused on me like I was one of the adults in the room. "If you have any questions at any time, ask, so I can explain."

She waited until I agreed.

"Once we get inside the courtroom, things will move fast. A lot of court-specific terms will be thrown out there, which you may not understand. Some light reading for you." She patted a clipped stack of papers on her lap.

Reading material. I could handle reading material.

"You're lucky." Miranda's tone shifted to more serious. "This would be a different conversation if one of you girls had been drinking and behind the wheel. Juvenile detention, and higher fines. The state has really cracked down. They take zero tolerance seriously."

The air left the room. One swoosh, gone.

I nodded in frozen fear.

Miranda gestured for her assistant to pull something from the bag. "Likely, Holli, your driving privileges will be restricted a minimum of six months. Given the supervised learner's license status, it could go longer. I hate to say this is a package deal, but you two being sisters and Grace having traffic tickets already in the short span of her driving career, the court could rule a harsher sentence to teach a lesson, so to speak."

She handed papers to Dad. "Wise choice to start these community service hours early. The grandparent angle and separating the girls is another plus."

It hurt to hear how Grace and I being forced apart was a silver lining. I'd covered for her because I'd do anything for her. I'd like to think she'd do the same for me. If it came down to it, I could see Grace taking a bullet for me. Or driving me away from a police invasion.

Miranda explained additional court proceedings. I'd be expected to stand in front of a judge and swear an oath to tell the truth.

Good girls didn't live lives that required lying to the court.

Dad and Miranda discussed details and I couldn't help my mind from wandering. What was clear was I'd lied, I was currently lying, and I'd be lying some more.

After Miranda left, we put together a quick lunch with Dad. I'd only managed a cup of tea this morning—my nerves were too much. My stomach was about to revolt if I didn't eat.

"You did well," Dad told me over soup and a leftover casserole.

He looked tired. I bit at my lip, feeling the guilt instantly that I'd been the reason he'd lost sleep and had to drive all this way today. "I'm sorry," I said.

"We're disappointed Holli, but we'll get through this. Just keep doing what your grandparents say. Keep up with those service hours."

I nodded. "I'm trying."

If it were Grace, he'd tell her to try harder. Because it was me, ever the try-hard, he didn't. "I know." He squeezed my shoulder and managed a small smile.

After lunch, Dad took off. I laid on my bed in the attic for five minutes until I bolted upright. I needed to burn off energy.

I changed into running clothes and spread SPF across my skin. I grabbed a hat and let Grandpop know I was headed out.

Halfway through my route, Will crossed toward me from a beach entry point in town. He had on a light blue shirt—not one of his usual black band shirts or the Leaf Group green. This was fitted, which showed off his lean arms.

"You've got to be kidding me." He threw up his hands. "You're running again?"

I slowed to a stop to catch my breath. "I met with the lawyer today."

Will's grin subsided. "How'd it go?"

"Fine."

He stepped in so close I breathed in the mint scent of his gum. "Fine?"

I shrugged. I couldn't handle lying to him. I focused on the water instead, wondering how far I could swim before my arms gave out.

"I had to meet with an attorney after the accident. He was assigned by the court. The guy who'd hit us—the drunk driver—had a charge against him. They wanted me to testify."

"What happened?"

"That reckless jerk went to jail, is what." His voice hardened to stone. "I helped send him there. I kept it as my only thought the whole time. It was worth it to re-live what happened if it meant sending that killer to jail. And now he's there to rot."

My breath left me. I had no idea what to say.

"Hey." Will reached out to me. The faded X on the back of his hand blurred in my vision. "It'll be alright. I know you're freaked, but everything will work out."

Beyond us, the water stretched to infinite distances, wide and blue and deep. Nothing felt fine. "I'm not a good person."

"What? Holli, no. You're the greatest person. You're so great. You got into an accident. Key word, *accident*. I know it doesn't feel that way, but it's not your fault."

"I should have known better."

"You lost control of the car. It happens. No one died."

The very word *died* sent me in a trance, staring over the choppy waves. He was right, no one died. We'd been lucky. We'd crushed a bike. But what if someone had been riding it? "They could have."

"Hey." Will's voice came low and moved across me like soft cotton. "Hang out with us tonight. Antonio and his new girl are watching movies at his house. You want to come?"

A warm flash ran through me. I did want to go. Very much.

A slow grin spread on his face. "We can have s'mores."

As if he had to entice with me food. "Antonio has a fire pit?"

"No. But we can use the gas stove to roast the marshmallows."

S'mores and movies sounded nice.

"Come on," he said. "It'll be a date."

Later in the evening, Will picked me up in his sticker-mobile. He had music turned low when I entered.

"Is this a sticker band?"

He laughed. "I don't think I've got these guys in sticker form. Here." He handed me his iPod attached by a cord to a jack in the car. "You be the DJ."

I scrolled through the options. "These names are crazy. Solve for X? Murderlation Station? These have to be made up."

"They're real bands, I swear."

I finally landed on a familiar band name and chose a song. The song started with drums and simple guitar with female vocals. No growling.

"You like this one?"

"Yeah." The singer sang about fighting for truth and coming clean.

The truuuth...is all we ha-ave the vocalist belted out.

Well, that sure hit a nerve.

We made it to Antonio's, a nice looking two-story yellow house with bright-colored flowers along the driveway. Will and I entered through the garage. Inside, we took a set of stairs to a lower-level family room. I stopped at the sight of the person in front of me.

"Hey, Holli." Piper had her knees folded over on a comfy-looking couch.

I turned to Will.

"I said Antonio and his new girl." He shrugged.

"He didn't say who, did he?" Piper said. "Figures."

Antonio emerged from the hall and handed us cold cans of pop from a little kitchen area along the back wall. "Yeah, we're kind of a thing. We had the DTR."

I burst out laughing. "I didn't know guys knew about DTRs."

"What's a DTR?" Will asked.

"Define The Relationship," the three of us who were not Will said together.

Will made a face. "Seems like defining a relationship takes out all the fun."

Piper tossed a pillow at Will. "You *would* think that. Ooh, guys look what Antonio and I worked on this afternoon." She grabbed a sheet of paper from the coffee table and handed it over. The paper was squared off into panels with drawings and word bubbles. "I wrote the story and Antonio did the art. It's stupid really."

I read through their homemade comic about a vampire cat joining a school club for undercover ghost hunters. "This is funny. You put this together today?"

Piper looked at Antonio and grinned. "We just brainstormed a bunch of ideas to see what would happen."

"I watch a lot of anime." Antonio glanced to Piper. "We both do. They're always putting together clubs at school in anime so we tried that angle."

It was cool how they collaborated, and sweet how they kept looking at each other.

Antonio clicked a remote toward the TV and pulled up a streaming service. "We should do a whole series."

"Could you enter it to the gallery show?" I asked. "I know you just did this today, but it's good. You're both super talented."

Piper's skin shaded pink. "Thanks. So, about the gallery. My friend just agreed to play live music. She's really good. I think she'll do the event for free."

"What do you think, Holli?" Antonio asked. "Will you be around for the show?"

"Well, I am *here for the summer.*" As soon as I said it, with a sarcastic bent in my tone, I regretted it. "Sorry. I just have some things going on. I'll probably be there."

"Oh good. I'd hate to lose you so soon." Piper smiled.

Similar to how Grace described a big blank space in her mind after the crash, that was how I saw life after the court hearing.

Will breathed quietly next to me. We hadn't planned that far ahead.

We all settled in front of the TV to watch a super-hero movie I'd missed seeing in the theater. Half a couch cushion separated me from Will. The glow from the screen flickered across his face in the dim room. I peeked over. The darkened room gave me the chance to look at him for longer. Covertly, of course.

I imagined us at the community center art show dressed up. Me in a sundress and Will in, well something black, but maybe with a fitted jacket and one of those skinny ties. Maybe a loose jacket. Messy hair.

Will called this a date. I couldn't believe me, dorky Holli, dated someone as cool as Will. Hot, older Will. Why would I want to go back to Ginsburg at all this summer? Things looked pretty good for me in Deer Cove. I had a place here.

Will's gaze connected to mine. I quickly turned back to the TV. Thankfully, the darkness hid my blush.

Halfway through the movie, Antonio hit pause. "I need chips and hot salsa real bad." He and Piper ran upstairs, their steps like a carpeted avalanche tumbling upward.

Will angled himself so his back rested against the armrest. "You think you'll come back after your court hearing?"

He was the only one here besides my grandparents who knew about my court case. "I want to."

It was true. I *wanted* to come back. I wanted to come back to Will.

Only I wasn't being honest with him.

Maybe the court hearing would take care of that annoying feeling. Once everything was sorted, then I wouldn't feel this stress weighing me down.

He reached his hand to mine. "I get you have stuff to get back to at home. But I can't say I'm not pulling for you to come back for the rest of the summer."

My skin grew warm all over. "Really?"

He laughed softly. "Yes, really. If it's not clear, I like you, Holli. I like how you're working through some things. It means you're real. People who pretend they have everything together are fake."

Will didn't see me as fake or a liar. He believed in me. Maybe I needed to believe in myself.

A rumbling sounded overhead, followed by laughter. Antonio and Piper would be busy for a few more minutes, it sounded.

I inched closer to Will.

He moved nearer to me.

We met in the middle of the couch, cross-legged and facing each other.

He smelled minty. His black T-shirt looked soft, maybe even new. I imagined him taking it out of the dryer minutes before leaving the house to come get me. For some reason, my heart swelled. Will cared about me.

Whatever happened in the coming weeks, Will rooted for me. He was on my side, and I wanted to hang on with all I had.

"Holli." He drew so close, his breath tickled my chin. "Can I kiss you?"

At once I shivered and grew warm all over. He wrapped his hands completely around mine. I wanted to climb inside his embrace.

Without over thinking, I leaned toward him. Will made up the distance and our lips met. The mint danced across my tongue, fresh and sweet. Will's touch came gentle and sure at the same time. The kiss was nothing like I expected.

I loved every second.

He deepened the kiss enough to check if I was there with him. I was. I wanted this.

We each pulled back at the same time.

I should have blushed or felt embarrassed, but I wasn't, and I didn't. "I like you, Will."

"I like you too."

I squeezed his hand. Pure giddiness surged through me. Like what I felt around my favorite things. When I crossed a finish line. When I laughed so hard with Tala I shed tears. Trick-or-treating as a kid with my big sister Grace.

We kissed again. I wanted this sealed as a new memory. A new favorite thing.

I'd only kissed two other boys before this. Erik, the short-lived boyfriend, and a boy at sports camp in seventh grade. I couldn't remember a single detail of those kisses. Not when I had Will focusing on me.

A thrill raced through me out to my fingertips. I wanted to kiss Will forever.

Popcorn scents wafted downstairs. Antonio and Piper cascaded down again, sending Will and I apart to our separate cushions.

Antonio cracked a smile. "What were *you two* up to?"

"You first," Will challenged.

"Making popcorn and making out." He shook his shoulders in a dance. "Yeah, yeah we did!"

"No more nachos," Piper said and set down the popcorn bowl on the table in front of us. "And yeah, we were upstairs kissing. No shame."

I reached for Will's hand. No reason to pretend this wasn't happening. This felt comfortable. It felt right.

This was the most sure I'd felt in a long time.

Chapter Twelve

♥

Over the next week, my routine fell into place. Run with Will. Work my service hours—with Will. Meet on the beach at sunset. Also with Will.

There was a whole lot of Will going on.

Still, I had to clean at the inn, help my grandparents with household chores, and report on time for dinner. Business seemed to pick up and for a few nights every cabin was booked. Staying busy helped the days pass in a good rhythm. So long as I followed the schedule, everything stayed in its rightful place.

"Can you help me move this column-thingy?" Antonio called across the community center lobby to Will.

Tonight's teen night involved more gallery event planning. The nearby coastal historical society had dropped off a few podiums and display cases we planned to use for our event.

Piper circled the display pedestal. "This is kind of worn and dusty, but the price was right." She glanced to me. "That price would be free."

"This is going to look professional," I said. "Super impressive."

Piper beamed. "Thanks. It's really coming together. Now we just need more actual artwork. Don't tell Will or he'll get ideas."

"Hey, I heard that." Will gave her a growl, but it honestly just sounded cute. "I've got two more watercolors just begging to be displayed. They're on display at home. On my refrigerator."

"Aw, your mom hung them up?" Piper made her voice sickly sweet.

"Actually, she asked me to take them down. Said I was embarrassing myself."

Antonio elbowed him. "How about stick to lifting heavy stuff."

"Maybe it *is* my calling. Lifting art." Will struck a flex pose.

Was it hot in here? I fanned myself. It definitely felt balmy.

Piper gave me a knowing side-eye. "How about you, Holli? You should do something for the show."

"I'm like Will. I'm just the muscle here." I skipped the flexing. "I wish I could draw."

"It doesn't have to be a drawing. What about a craft, or a poem? It could be anything."

Will finished moving the pedestal to a corner. "I bet you've got artistic talent you don't even know about. You're so busy running marathons and picking up beach trash, you don't have time to find out."

"Probably not."

"Hey, you never know unless you—"

"Or maybe I'm not artistic, okay?" It came out sharp, but I wasn't even sorry. He needed to stop pushing.

"I only meant you're good at a lot of stuff."

He meant well and I knew it. I was just in a funk. I couldn't shake what nagged at me most.

My court date. My very real court date two days from now. My grandparents planned to take me back to Ginsburg tomorrow afternoon and stay overnight. Court would be bright and early at eight in the morning the next day.

Will knew, but we'd avoided talking about specifics. Or at least I had.

After the planning session, a few stragglers set up a fire in the pit out back. Antonio had to leave, taking Piper with him. The freshmen girls left together.

"You can head out," Will said. "I'll stick around and close up."

It felt selfish to be annoyed he had to stay when I wanted him alone for some beach time before the sun set. It was my last night before court. I didn't know what would happen after tomorrow. I didn't dare let my mind go there, even though I'd read through Miranda's materials and everything.

"I'm going to take the slow route back," I told Will.

He kissed me lightly on the lips. "I'll text you before you leave."

I wandered to the water's edge. The sky dimmed as I made my way to the driftwood, closer to home.

Home. Not my home, but funny it felt like home. My little attic nook and dinner with the grans every night. I didn't hate it.

A plastic ball landed at my feet. Not far off, a family chased after their dog. I picked up the ball and hurled it back, only a change in wind sent it sailing toward the water.

"Oh no!" I ran to fetch it. "So sorry!"

"I got it." Will appeared from the other side of the family, crashing into the water up to his shins and plucking out the ball. He swung his arm and the ball sailed back to its owners in a perfect delicate arc. The dog changed direction, heading toward the ball again.

Will trudged through the sand to meet me.

"Your shoes—" I started. But Will didn't have any shoes on.

"I ditched 'em back at the center. Summer nights don't call for shoes."

I laughed. "You say the weirdest things sometimes. With that arm, I'd almost think you play baseball."

"My brother and I used to play, but I'm not much for team sports." He grinned. "That probably doesn't surprise you. Hey, I wanted to say I'm sorry for pressing you about the art thing. I just figured you could try something new."

I slipped off my sandals and let the water wash over my toes each time the waves stretched far enough. "That's what you do. You dive headfirst into anything new or a challenge. I don't work like that."

"You could."

"I don't *want* to."

He stayed quiet. So quiet, I started to question myself. Maybe I should try new things more often. Then again, venturing out to Grace's party had been a disaster.

"I was supposed to start a job this summer at the movie theater," I told him. "A new experience. Now everything is new. It feels like too much sometimes. I'm going back home tomorrow just when I've gotten used to life here. I don't like so much change all at once. All I want is to hang onto what's familiar, but what's familiar keeps changing."

His hand found mine. The heat from his body filled me down through my legs and out into the sand. Like being rooted in place.

I felt safe here in Deer Cove. Wanted. Seen.

Back in Ginsburg, I'd face my team frustrated by how I hadn't been there. My best friend who'd been making her own friends.

"I'm scared," I admitted.

He faced me and moved a strand of hair from my cheek. "Why don't you tell me about it. We can be scared together."

"So you can growl at my fear?"

He grinned. "I might. But really. I might not be good at everything I try, but I'm pretty good at listening."

I clasped his hands and leaned in to kiss him. Will was my constant among change. Will was my safe place.

The next day, I arrived home. To my actual house, in Ginsburg.

I followed my grandparents inside, not quite knowing what to expect. Grandpop had offered to drive me solo so Grandma could stay back and watch the inn, but she'd insisted on supporting me at court. Grandpop then insisted he be there at court too, so they'd called their friend to cover at the inn.

Everything in the house looked the same as I remembered. Only the smell was too artificial from the air conditioning. Back at Grandma and Grandpop's, the windows stayed open all summer taking advantage of the free breeze off the lake. The attic may have been sweltering during the day, but at night, it was perfect.

Mom hugged all of us. "Grace isn't here."

A mix of relief and annoyance hit me at once. "Where is she?" It came out bratty and demanding.

Mom immediately rolled her eyes. So, thirty seconds in and she was done with me. Great.

"She's at work. She got a job walking dogs."

Dog walking didn't sound like a job where you were *at* work so much as out and around with dogs, but I decided to stay mum. Grace probably loved it.

Meanwhile, I scrubbed toilets and tilled soil in the blazing sun.

I headed upstairs to my room.

The ceremonial team captain jersey hung on the back of my desk chair. Somebody probably wanted it back.

I sighed and fell back on my bed. Closing my eyes, I thought of Will.

I rewound our latest kisses. It almost didn't feel real. Being back in my room, every memory in Deer Cove seemed like a dream. I rolled over and checked my phone looking at my last text from him.

Will: *Good luck with the court hearing. You've got this.*

His affirmation struck me deeply. He cared about me. But I was also lying to him.

A knock sounded at my open door. "Holli."

Mom. "You can invite Tala over if you'd like," she said. "You haven't seen her in weeks."

Promising, at least. "Okay."

She hovered in the doorway. "I have an outfit picked out for you for tomorrow."

Inside my open closet, a button-down shirt, black skirt, and a lightweight black cardigan hung facing forward against my other clothes. Altogether, the pieces looked like a school uniform. Maybe Miranda suggested the look. Reform school fashion.

"Your Grandma says you've been doing well. Making friends?"

"Yeah. I am actually."

"Good. I'm glad. Have Tala come over," she said again. "No going out anywhere, but she can come here. Then it's early to bed. Big day tomorrow."

Right, because my big days were now court dates.

Since I had the green light, I texted Tala. She already knew I'd planned to come back, but we hadn't connected on specifics. I'd had no idea if my parents still had Grounding Mode activated. They might have forbidden me to see any friends.

A few minutes later, my phone buzzed with a call.

"I'm super sorry, Hol," Tala said after I answered. "I'm covering a shift tonight at the theater. If I could get out of it I would, but they're desperate. It's opening night for the new *Road Rash*."

"They made another one of those?"

"Yeah, unfortunately. None of the original cast either. This time it's that one action guy's daughter who's in the make-up commercials. And the wrestler, The Hurt. So basically, we're expecting to sell out. Can you come by?"

Looking out the window, I blinked, expecting to see the beach. "I can't. I've got my court thing tomorrow."

"Sorry. Can you meet up tomorrow after?"

"Maybe." For moment, I imagined Tala here in my room with an overnight bag. We'd watch stupid YouTube videos and do face masks.

"You've got a good lawyer, right? Your parents won't let you get screwed. It was an accident, Hol. You tried to do the right thing."

Tried being the key word.

"Call me tomorrow after court. Tell me everything."

Even with the lawyer preparing me for what the hearing would be like, I didn't have any idea what would happen. It was as if the conversation with Miranda never happened since it happened in Deer Cove. Like it happened to another version of myself.

My phone buzzed again.

Will: *Hey. Thinking of you.*

I stared at the text, feeling my two worlds merge. Will was real. He cared about me and had my back.

The one thing I'd needed to hear. The one thing that felt like it fit.

Chapter Thirteen

♥

Later that night, footsteps sounded from the hall and a door shut.

Grace.

I bolted from my bed where I'd half fallen asleep watching a movie on my laptop—blessed high speed internet. In the hall, light sprayed from beneath our shared bathroom door.

A few minutes later, the door opened. Grace stopped at the sight of me.

"Hey," I said. "So, you're walking dogs."

Her hair stuck up in the back and hung matted in spots. Like her hair hadn't been washed recently and she'd rolled in a pile of burrs. I only knew about burrs from working at the state park back in Deer Cove.

"Yeah. Little dachshunds and cockapoos. Small dogs that won't run away from a gimpy girl." She gestured with the arm in the sling. "And one bulldog named Marty."

Despite looking a mess, Grace had a softness in her eyes. It was a weird thing to notice, but something about her seemed small and sad. Not like the giant personality I was used to living beneath.

"Are you okay?" I asked.

Without speaking, she used her good arm to steer me by the shoulder into my room and shut the door.

"Just play it cool. You're doing fine." She stood with her back to the closed door. "Everything's going to work out."

I folded my arms. "For who?"

She sucked in a silent breath. One small flinch gave her away. She wasn't so in control after all.

She circled around me to my bed and sat at the end. "It's better this way. It is. Look, I know I haven't been the greatest. I get it. And you and me, we don't always see things the same. What you did for me—" She swallowed as her attention landed on different points in the room. "You did a big thing for me, Holli. It's big. I'm sorry I lost it that night. I wish I could get the memories back. If you hadn't been there, I don't know what would have happened."

Everything she said was what I'd been desperate to hear for weeks. Things would have been worse had I not been there and done what I had.

Grace *needed* me.

"Did you talk to Kennedy?" I asked.

She picked at a fingernail. Blue polish, chipped on every finger. "A little. She's fine. We aren't really cool with each other."

"What happened?"

She let her head fall to one side. "You know Kennedy. She plays the Ginsburg Game. She did the popularity thing to get what she wanted from high school and now she's done with it. She's already BFFs with her freshman roommate at State. They met at the first orientation of the summer."

"It doesn't mean you're replaced."

"She called me trash. She said I'm destined to be a townie loser. All because I'm not going to college."

This was news to me. "You're not? What did Mom and Dad say?"

Grace rolled her eyes. "*Who cares*. I'm turning eighteen in weeks. Then they can't legally keep me under their thumb."

I truly didn't understand my sister. "What are you going to do? Keep walking dogs?"

"Sure, among other things. It's easy money. I have some house cleaning gigs coming up and a coffee shop job with Chase. Once my arm heals up it will be easier."

"Who is Chase?"

She put on her bored expression. "We hooked up at a party once like, forever ago. I saw him again when I was out and we got to talking. I'm going to live with them once this court case is done."

"Them who?"

"Chase and Bo, his buddy. They've got a rental in the student neighborhood by the loser school."

She meant Ginsburg Community College, sometimes called the commuter school, mainly by people my grandparents' age. Commuter school had morphed into loser school, which I'd heard too many times to count in general conversation. Our high school had one of the highest percentages of four-year college enrollment in the state. It was a big selling point for the school district. The kind of thing you'd see on real estate advertisements trying to lure buyers to our mid-sized Midwest city.

And of course, Grace wanted nothing to do with four-year schools. Or the two-year commuter school. Grace wanted to float through life as if nothing mattered.

But things did matter.

"It's going to be awesome, actually," she rambled on. "I can walk to work at the coffee shop, so who cares about a driver's license. Living blocks from the loser school, the parties will come to us."

A numb chill shook me. I could barely form words.

"What?" Grace looked at me with annoyance.

"I can't believe you." I paced from the door to my closet, then back. "You...you're talking about living with some random guys and having parties come to your door. You just said you don't care if your license gets taken away."

"And?"

"And if you don't care if your license is taken away, then why am I doing any of this? Grace, I'm in deep trouble. The stuff Miranda went over with me—this is serious. I have to tell my side of the story to the judge tomorrow. And right now, you're saying you *don't even care*."

My breath came fast and sharp. I couldn't get enough air.

The walls crept closer to close me in. I wanted my peek of the lake and the beach and the smell of freshwater air. But I was here, back where I supposedly belonged. Trapped.

Grace stood, mild panic in her expression. "I didn't mean it that way. You know me, I say dumb stuff all the time. Of course I care about my license. The whole reason it's not taken yet is because of what you did. You're the one who's helping me. I get to live a normal life because of you."

Grace's version of a normal life meant a careless one where she drifted from random job to intentional party. I'd sacrificed my summer, my reputation, all so she could not even bother to go to community college or plan a future for herself.

I was done with her right now. "You know what? I'm tired. Mom's right. It's a big day tomorrow."

"Holli," Grace had a warning to her tone.

I couldn't tell if she meant a threat or if she was scared.

Even if she was scared, it was for herself, not for me.

I opened my door and held it open. "Goodnight Grace."

Grace took her cue to leave. She paused in the hall before crossing to her room. "Things will be okay, Hol. I promise."

Grace sat beside me outside the courtroom in a navy blue fitted blazer and a white blouse. Both from Mom's closet. She looked like a poster for the Model UN. Me, her junior delegate in the wannabe reform school outfit.

Dad, my grandparents, and the lawyers entered the courtroom first. Miranda paused by the door. "Just a moment and we'll come out for you."

Grace and I waited on a hard bench in the hall. A man in uniform walked by in steady measured steps. Probably a bailiff on patrol to keep order. He was pretty good-looking, maybe in his early twenties, though I was terrible at telling people's age. Grace shot him a smile as he passed. He blinked and kept walking.

I tried to clear my mind of impending doom. I hated everything about today. So long as I stayed calm, everything would be fine.

Right?

Grace scrolled through her phone, looking bored.

I wanted her to tell me everything would be okay again like she had last night. Only to couple that with a speech how she'd reconsidered her life and would never need me to lie for her again. I wanted her to hug me.

She didn't.

The door ahead of us opened. "Ready, girls?" Miranda waited for us to pass before she followed us in.

The room wasn't very big. Definitely not like the large courtrooms on TV with rows of seats for an audience and a jury bench. Two tables faced the judge's stand. A short row of chairs spread across the back wall near the door.

Mom caught my sleeve as I passed her. "Do what the lawyer told you."

No problem. I was good at doing what I was told.

A court official instructed us to sit at one of the plain wooden tables. My limbs felt twice their size. Like moving underwater, slow and heavy.

Miranda had herself set up at the second table. Given this wasn't a case where two parties argued against each other, she was the only lawyer here. This was us against...the law.

Yikes.

The judge entered the room. She reminded me of my eighth-grade music teacher with flecks of gray in a dark, short haircut. Glasses with one of those chains draped around her neck.

The judge began opening remarks and my body went numb. How was this my life? Sitting here in a real live courtroom? Not observing for a school project. The judge was talking about *me*.

I peeked at Grace. She had a pleasant, but not-too-pleasant look. Paying attention with a touch of remorse. Dang, she was good.

Miranda provided responses to something the judge said. The back-and-forth with Miranda went on for a few minutes.

The judge reviewed papers in front of her as Miranda spoke. "I see Grace has a prior traffic violation, but this is Grace's first Minor in Possession violation. I understand this happened at a graduation party?"

"Yes, Your Honor," Miranda answered. "An unsupervised party comprised of a house full of underage drinkers, most of whom left the scene when police arrived. My client here entrusted her sister to drive her home, though as noted, Holliday Hayes had not attained her full status license as she was driving only on a learner's license."

The judge nodded. She looked at my sister. "Grace. How often do you attend parties where alcohol is served?"

"Not often, Your Honor," Grace responded.

My breath stalled in my throat.

"Not often, or not ever?" the judge asked.

Grace didn't miss a beat. "It's hard to avoid alcohol entirely, but it's not something I actively pursue. With our parents working so many hours, and Holli being so involved in school activities, I've been the family's second driver."

My fingers involuntarily clenched into fists. I glanced behind me. Dad's gaze focused firmly on the judge. Mom stared at her hands folded in her lap. My grandparents whispered to each other.

"This is a family who works together," Miranda explained. She went on about my grandparents offering their help. About their family-owned business and the work ethic instilled into my father. The picture she sketched depicted a dutiful daughter all right. A dutiful daughter named Grace.

I wanted to crush something.

With nothing to crush, I tucked my hands under my thighs and gripped the chair seat.

Miranda and the judge took turns speaking. None of this felt real.

Grace jabbed me from the side. I gave her a dirty look. Her eyebrows rose. "Say *yes, Your Honor.*"

"Yes, Your Honor," I spat out on command. A silence followed. What had I agreed to?

The judge removed her glasses. "I understand your nerves. Let me explain further." She discussed Michigan driver laws. "Holliday. Do you agree with the charges presented before you?"

At the next table, Miranda smiled at me with a subtle nod. We'd talked about this. I'd driven outside of my permitted, parental-supervised hours, and then caused an accident. After curfew. I didn't get a chance at a license for another six months at least.

A fire deep down threatened to rise. *The Lie.*

No, I had this. I had the power here, not the lie. Miranda's angle made Grace into the dutiful daughter, even though I'd been the one to save Grace from jail time, license suspension, and thousands of dollars in fines. I called the shots. I only needed to stick to the same story. The one everyone knew and believed.

Everyone stared at me. I still hadn't answered.

A pressure formed over my foot. Grace smashed my toes with her shoe. She gave me a lightning-quick glare. Sweat beaded at her hairline.

I only needed to say what they wanted to hear.

Liar. You're a liar.

My heart raced. This was too much. Way too much.

That drunk is in jail—where he'll rot.

Will's words repeated through my mind. Will. He would be so disappointed to know the truth.

The truth...I pledged an oath when I walked in here. I wasn't supposed to lie. One confession, and the weight could fall off. The truth would be out, and everything could be set right.

The judge's eyes pierced through me, but her voice came out soft. "Is a short break in order?"

Grace smashed my foot again.

"N-no." My voice emerged unsteady. "Sorry, Your Honor. I'm just a little, um. This is new to me."

The judge nodded once. "Understandable. However, we are on a schedule. Do you require additional counsel?"

I ventured a look at Miranda. She appeared reassuring, but her eyes flashed annoyance. She probably had a lunch date with the hot bailiff.

My gaze landed on Grace. A glint appeared in her eyes. I'd seen Grace in every form possible. Happy, drunk, angry, bored, mischievous, disgusted, desperate.

I'd never seen her like this. Grace was filled with fear.

Chapter Fourteen

♥

Finally, it was over.

We left the courtroom for the hall where the air came at me a hundred degrees cooler.

"You did well, Holli." Miranda's practiced smile told me she'd played the part enough times at making people feel better.

I'd almost blown it. I'd frozen in front of the judge. In the end, I'd done what I was told. The version of the truth they all knew worked best for everyone. Grace had her own allotted community service hours for the Minor in Possession violation. Fewer hours than me.

"Let's have lunch," Mom said in a false bright voice. Then again, she'd been chugging courthouse coffee all morning. "I'll call ahead for a table."

Dad started listing places to eat. Grace already had her phone out to ignore everyone. My grandparents chattered to each other. As if all our problems could stay behind after the courtroom doors closed.

Neither Miranda nor the judge pressed for an alcohol prevention program for Grace. Our "supportive family" proved to be enough so intervention wouldn't be required. Instead, the judge issued a stern warning to Grace, assigned her community service, and told her good luck in college.

College. The college Grace didn't plan to go to. Nobody knew that either. Yet another secret I kept for Grace.

All of us headed outside to the parking lot but stopped again outside the doors as my parents discussed more lunch options.

Grandma came up beside me and placed a hand at my shoulder. "You did well, Holliday. I'm sure this was overwhelming."

I sank into her arms. A flood of emotion hit. I wanted to cry and laugh at the same time, though neither of those reactions felt right.

"Grace," Grandma called over to my sister. "I'd like you to work with Holliday, at home with us. I think it would be best for you to get away from here for a bit. Spend some time with your sister and get fresh air by the lake."

Grace's expression flicked from bored to disgust. "No way. I'm not wasting my summer in Deer Crap Cove."

Dad looked up from his own phone where he'd been reserving a table on an online app. "The girls should be home—our home. Now that everything is settled, we can take it from here."

Grandpop shook his head. "I don't think moving Holli back so soon is the right idea. She made friends back with us. She has a set schedule at the community center."

"Like the attorney said," Grandma added, "the teen group can add to those hours since they're doing projects and not just hanging out *wasting their summer.*" She pointed a steely look at my sister.

"I'm sure Holli would rather be here." Mom looked at me to agree.

Home didn't feel like home right now. Home was where I lied. Every day seeing Grace and my parents would remind me of those lies.

But the team existed here. I didn't train nearly as hard in Deer Cove to keep up my pace. Meets this fall would be a disaster unless I got my act together.

Will's face flashed in my mind. The feel of his hand over mine, his lips, his embrace. Sitting on the beach watching the rolling waves at sunset. My head pounded.

Every option I had, something was missing. Deer Cove wasn't home, but it felt like my safe place. Here felt anything but safe, but it was where I'd invested the most with my friends and at school.

In Deer Cove, my grandparents watched out for me. My own parents just wanted to schedule lunch.

"Can I call my friends?" I asked. "I haven't seen anybody since..." I left the rest off. I looked at Grandma and Grandpop. "I think if I see some friends it might help me decide what to do."

Mom laughed without any humor. "Decide? You think you get to decide anything? You go where we tell you."

"No privileges." Dad took out his keys. "At home, you're grounded. No friends. Only community service."

"What about the cross-country team?" My entire reason for staying. To get back to my regular training.

"We can't watch her 24/7," Mom said to Dad, no longer listening to me.

"Come on, Hol," Grace said. "You don't really want to go back to that lame Deer town. They don't even have a real beach with a boardwalk. Besides, those kids are used to people going in and out of their town. They visit, then leave. Nobody actually stays there."

Grandma muttered something I couldn't hear, but I thought I caught the word *ungrateful* in there.

My parents bickered all the way to the car. I followed my grandparents instead, climbing into their old minivan. Inside, a swirl of sand on the worn floor mat reminded me again of Will. Of sitting next to him on the beach. I knew where I'd rather be.

At lunch, the family determined I was allowed to see friends for the afternoon. My grandparents had pushed for it, saying I'd been working hard and could use a break.

Grateful, I texted Tala. She was working, of course. I messaged Christina next from the cross-country team.

Me: *Hey, I have the afternoon free. I miss you all so much!*

Christina: *OMG Holli! Yes totally let's hang out.*

Relief filled me. Her next text said she and some teammates intended to meet up for a movie. Perfect. I could see Tala at the theater too.

Back home, I changed clothes. My closet burst with options. I picked a tank top and my favorite jeans—I had no idea how I'd forgotten these jeans in my packing for Deer Cove.

Soon after, Christina pulled into my driveway. I slipped into the passenger seat and clicked into the seatbelt.

"Hola, girl." Her dark espresso hair was styled in effortlessly trendy waves with bronzed highlights. Her skin glowed an even deeper golden hue from hours running outside.

"Hey. It's so good to be back."

"Yeah. We missed you." The words sounded right, except something about her tone seemed like forced cheerfulness.

Then again, a whole lot had happened we should probably talk through. Or not. Maybe I read into things and just needed a fun day at the movies.

We turned off my street onto a main road. I should set things straight to get past the weirdness. "Listen. I'm sorry about missing out on team stuff. My parents flipped after the party and the accident. Next thing I knew, I was going to my grandparents' house and locked in for the summer. If I was allowed to come back, I would have."

"Ugh. Parents, right?" She made a scoffing sound.

"They don't really get the team responsibility thing."

She told me about her own parents scheduling tutoring sessions for her this summer to prep for SATs. "It's such a drag, Holli. I hate it."

An upbeat pop song by a Latinx artist played out of the car stereo. I liked the song fine, but I suddenly missed Will's ear-splitting, blender-churned punk bands.

A call came through on the wireless connection in her car. Elena, another teammate, needed to be picked up. We detoured to Elena's house.

"Where does she live?" I asked, noting a familiar street sign as she turned into a subdivision.

"She's back by the soccer field where we did that one training event. Remember? From last fall?"

The soccer field mere blocks from the graduation party house. I cringed, seeing the turn-off street come up on the right. The house sat at the end of a cul-de-sac with thick woods behind it. A perfect location for a party all tucked back in the neighborhood. Perfect according to Grace who'd said the police never broke up parties out here.

Christina must have had no idea about the house since she didn't say anything as we drove past. Soon enough, we stopped at a modern two-story home with a red door. Elena popped out with her long reddish-golden hair in a knot at the top of her head.

Once Elena got in, she and Christina dominated the conversation. They talked about a practice run yesterday and how our coach gave the seniors unfair breaks.

I nodded. "Totally—Coach does that."

"And what is *up* with Emily lately?" Elena said and snorted.

"Who's Emily?" I asked. But they'd already moved on to laughing about an in-joke I couldn't make sense of.

We reached the movie theater, where I should have been spending a good chunk of my summer working alongside Tala. If only things had been different.

Get a grip, Holli. Have some fun today.

Jasmine and Deja waited for us outside the theater. They each wore short skirts showing off toned legs. Deja's chestnut skin contrasted against a pale pink tank top. Jasmine had on a cross-country T-shirt knotted at the waist to show skin at her stomach. Three guys clustered around them. One I recognized, the others I didn't.

"Hey, girl!" Deja held her arms out to Elena.

Jasmine hugged Christina, then pulled back and saw me. "Holli. I wasn't sure you'd show up."

She wasn't exactly mean as she said it, but the comment still cut. "Sorry about this summer—"

But she'd already turned to introduce the guys.

Everyone seemed to talk at once. I hung at the edge of the group.

Inside after getting tickets from the automated kiosk, I headed for the concession stand. Tala's high ponytail swished behind her as she turned to fill someone's popcorn.

My heart nearly burst seeing her after so many weeks.

"Holli!" Tala's face brightened when I stepped forward to the counter. "It's *so* good to see you." Nothing about her reaction made me think she acted fake, which came as a huge relief.

"I miss you. How is it going? You're working a ton."

"Yeah. I'm saving up for dance classes. Money is kind of tight at home, so these summer hours will pay off later."

Tala took ballet, and with two younger siblings involved in sports, her parents' money stretched thin to cover team costs and events.

Tala eyed the line behind me. "I don't have a break for a while yet. Sorry, I can't talk much now since we're so busy."

I ordered popcorn and a drink so I'd look like a paying customer if her boss was around. "I get it, I knew you'd be busy. I'm here with the team." I glanced toward the line next over where Christina and the others laughed with the guys. So, they joined our movie group now?

"Everything cool with you all?" Tala took out my favorite boxed candy, even though I hadn't added it to my order.

"Sure. Of course." I passed over cash for the food.

She gave me a look of sympathy. "Come see me after your movie. Or if you want to sneak out of the theater for a break, things will slow down here in about thirty minutes."

She handed back extra coupons with my change. "I charged you the employee rate. We might have an opening for another weekend position if you're still interested. If you're back, I mean."

I could still salvage this summer. I'd have to find a new community service project in Ginsburg, but at least I'd have time to see Tala.

I nodded and promised to sneak out and chat.

The group took turns ordering their food. Elena bought her candy first and joined me waiting for the others.

"So, are you back for training, or what?" Elena sipped her drink.

Elena and blunt were synonyms. "Um, something like that. I think."

She made a humming sound that seemed judgmental, but maybe I was reading into it.

"Isn't Caden's friend cute?" She nodded toward the guys with Christina, Deja, and Jasmine. "He goes to that tennis academy. It's his high school—a whole private school thing where they live on campus and train for tennis every day. I can barely swing team runs on summer break. Can you imagine your whole existence being sports and training?"

"I think they still have to study—"

"I mean, I'm already so bored when I run, I'm like writing stage productions in my head to pass the time."

"Wow, that's impressive. Do you ever write them down?"

Elena's attention remained on our friend group paying for their food. "What am I going to do with a stage play? Act?"

"I...." I almost told her it would be good to have a variety of experiences for her college applications—a very me thing to say. But Will's outlook came to mind. "If you're bored with running, maybe you could try out for theater. There's the tech crew if you don't want to act. That might be fun to learn lighting and sound."

Elena did one of those slow turns my direction, the straw from her drink lowering from her mouth as she stared at me. "You're telling me to be a theater techie? Do I look like I listen to the *Hamilton* soundtrack on repeat?"

She sounded way more offended than she needed to be. "It's a great soundtrack."

The rest of the group joined us and we filed into the theater. Elena, clearly done talking to me, rushed ahead to walk with Deja. Inside, I found a seat between Christina and an older couple. I was stuck at the end of our row of my teammates and the guys. I couldn't hear anything they said.

It sunk in which movie we'd bought tickets for. The race car one Tala and I made fun of earlier on the phone.

A half hour in, I got up to take a bathroom break, even though I didn't actually need it. I only wanted to see Tala.

I shifted past the old couple and a family at the opposite end of the aisle from my friends. Out in the lobby, I didn't see Tala anywhere. I visited the bathroom, then did a second sweep of the lobby and concession stand. Still no Tala, so I returned to the movie.

I didn't attempt a second sneak-out since leaving became such an ordeal from a middle seat.

After the movie, my phone showed a text from Tala.

Tala: *Sorry if you looked for me. I had to clean a theater. Find me later!*

In the lobby, I still didn't see Tala anywhere.

"We're going to get food," Christina told me. "You're coming, right?"

"Yeah, totally." I'd ridden here with her and the point was to hang out with them. Not look for Tala.

We made our way across the parking lot to a diner-style restaurant with a 1950s retro atmosphere. We came here after meets sometimes for hamburgers and seasoned curly fries.

The guys had taken off, leaving just us girls. Cramming ourselves into a U-shaped booth, it started to feel a little more normal now that no one showed off in front of guys. Everything they'd said and did had apparently been hilarious.

"So, Holli," Christina said from her spot in the middle of the U. "You've been running, right? Hopefully not slacking off."

Leave it to Christina to circle back to running schedules. "Yeah, I've been running. Of course." All chatter around the table quieted. "It's not the same as being here, I know, but I'm trying. I'm actually helping train someone for a 5k."

"Training, as in currently?" Elena asked with an edge in her voice. "So, you're not coming back?"

"Oh, no. I mean, yes. I'm back. I think." I internally winced at my own words, but I didn't want to lie.

The girls exchanged looks.

Christina looked over her menu at me. "I'm sure Coach will let you join our next training run."

A sense of panic rose up. Why would I not be able to run just because I'd been gone a few weeks? Last summer, one of the incoming seniors had taken off on a month-long vacation to her family's cottage in Kentucky. She hadn't been leading the team or anything, but still she hadn't been blocked from practice when she came back.

"She can run if she's not partying like a Grace clone." Elena pointedly looked away from me, though what she said was loud enough for everyone to hear.

Jasmine snickered.

"I'm not my sister." I couldn't help the hurt from showing in my voice.

Elena looked at me now. "I just think if you're going to blow your team responsibilities to party, then you need to face the consequences."

"Elena," Christina said in a warning tone.

"What?" Elena looked at the others. "I'm not saying anything brand new here. We get it. You wanted a taste of your sister's life and you got it. You don't get to have the team too."

An ache hit me square in the chest. "It's not like that." Except I didn't know what to say it was like.

Elena rolled her eyes. "Your sister barely graduated. And what she pulled at the ceremony, dancing on stage in a bikini? Why were you even with her graduation night? Why would you *drive drunk*?" Elena fired off so many questions, the rest of the girls stared with mouths half-opened.

I should try at least, to explain. "I didn't drink at the party. I only—I drove because...it was really chaotic and I wanted to get us out of there. I drove so my sister didn't have to."

Elena's head cocked to the side. "Well, that's not what people are saying. They're saying they saw you drinking too. And your sister hooked up with Kennedy's boyfriend. Then she made Kennedy OD—"

"None of that is true." I let my voice rise. "You weren't there."

"Maybe she's right." Jasmine aligned her menu with the table edge. "Kennedy had those pictures up from the party, but she took them down."

"Well, somebody did after she ended up in the hospital," Elena said. "Anyway, Kennedy is just as messed up as Grace."

I fisted my hands underneath the table. All the covering I'd done for Grace, and where had it gotten me? My own friends treated me like a traitor.

The server showed up, cheerily asking for drink orders. I eyed the red EXIT sign over the door. The server finished the orders and the table grew silent.

"Look, Holli." Christina tore at the edge of her paper napkin. "We're just worried. You're not acting like yourself. Disappearing the way you did after the accident, you left us hanging. We didn't know what to believe since you never told us."

"We're supposed to be a team," Elena added. "*We* share stuff."

Her "we" clearly didn't include me.

The lie was too big. I couldn't control it, and now the team blamed me for abandoning them. I managed an apology, hoping they'd believe I was sincere. I truly was sorry.

The thing was, I knew their hurt didn't source completely from believing I'd been drinking at a party. Elena and Jasmine went to parties too. But being on the team meant sharing about yourself, even the hard stuff, because that was what close friends did. The team constantly dished about break-ups and family issues. Had I gone to Christina right after the party and told her everything, maybe this would have played out differently. Instead, gossip filled in their gaps until they'd formed their own version of what happened.

I'd always worked at distancing myself from what Grace did. Letting that control slip meant the rumors ran as wild as Grace herself.

Deja shot me a sympathetic look, then changed the subject to the movie we just watched. The conversation shifted, but I couldn't make the words mean anything.

I'd let them down. While I'd tried to fix Grace, I'd let my own life break.

A numb, sick feeling troubled my insides. "I think I'm gonna go." I slid from the booth and headed for the door.

"Holli, wait," Christina called after me.

She left the table and followed me to the waiting area by the hostess stand. "I know I was hard on you when I messaged you about needing to talk to Coach. I wanted you to shake off whatever was going on. To get back to the team."

"I know." Except getting back to the team wasn't what I thought it would be.

"Now that your sister graduated, your whole life will be different back at school. You won't have to worry about Grace ruining everything."

An earnest look covered her face. She completely meant it when she said Grace had ruined my life. I'd thought the same myself, but hearing someone else tell me my sister was the problem made me want to defend her more. It was one thing for me to criticize Grace, but anyone else needed to take a step back.

But defending Grace hadn't won me favors. I looked past Christina to the others. They'd probably have a better time eating here without me. I was an intrusion to the group.

"I'm gonna go," I told Christina. "I'm sorry. I really am."

This time, I didn't look back.

Chapter Fifteen

♥

I crossed the parking lot back to the movie theater. The red and yellow theater logo blurred through my tears. I'd have to call home for a ride, and I couldn't handle waiting outside on the curb.

Tala stood behind the concession stand again. Her eyes popped wider when she saw me.

She waved me over. "Hey, I'm so sorry I missed you earlier." Her face fell once I grew closer. "Oh no, are you okay?"

I nodded through watery eyes. I'd been trying really hard to keep it together.

She held up a finger telling me to hold on as she talked to a coworker. Thirty seconds later, she joined me on the other side of the counter. "I'm taking a break. Follow me."

I trailed her around the corner through a door marked Staff Only. We crossed through a hall and to another door leading out to the back of the theater. Dumpsters lined the area at the dead end behind the building and scrubby trees beyond it filled in the view. No one else here.

Tala walked a few paces from the door and turned. "Tell me everything."

I sighed. "They're mad at me for bailing on the team."

"I'm sorry." She gestured to the curb under a patch of shade from a skinny tree. She sat down and I joined her. "Did any of them ask how you're doing after the accident?"

"You mean right after it happened? I got texts."

"I mean now, today. And what about court? Did they ask about that?"

I shrugged. "No. But I don't really want them knowing." It just made me feel guilty.

Guilty of lying to the court. Of lying to my family. To Will. To Tala.

Tension squeezed my shoulders. I pinched at my muscles to loosen the stiffness.

"So, how did it go today at court?"

I told her about the continued service hours and how my grandparents wanted both Grace and me to go back to Deer Cove with them. How freaky it had been sitting in a courtroom hearing my name come out of a judge's mouth. How I'd clammed up, but the lawyer said I'd done okay.

I shook my head. "Christina and them are right to be mad at me. I deserve it. I did abandon them. I didn't explain anything after I left. I just let their texts go unanswered and told Coach I had to leave. They're supposed to be my friends."

"Sometimes friends aren't as close as you think. They seemed more interested in flirting with those guys than talking with you." Tala made a *hmm* sound. I knew she wasn't judging out of jealousy. She wasn't in with the team, but she also had other friends besides me. We protected each other. Tala was the friend I trusted. I didn't have secrets with Tala.

Only I did have a secret. Not only was I not honest with team, but worse, the dishonesty extended to my own best friend.

"I have to tell you something," I said slowly.

"Of course. Anything."

I took a breath. I started with the accident. I told her how Grace had been the one who drove. How I'd panicked at the scene of the accident and took the keys from Grace after we'd both stumbled out of the car to check the damage. I'd told Grace to get in the passenger seat. How a driver stopped to help us and called the police for us.

I kept talking. How I was worried for Grace getting another citation. Then how she'd told me she didn't plan to go to college. I was rambling, but if I stopped, I'd have to face Tala's response.

Finally, I stopped. There was nothing left to say but to apologize. "I'm sorry I kept this from you." My eyes squeezed shut. I couldn't bear seeing her face. "I understand if you're mad at me for lying. I never meant to hurt you."

Tala didn't say anything. Maybe she bolted. I finally opened my eyes.

She stared at me. "Holli. Give me a hug."

"What?"

Her arms circled around me before she gave an answer. She squeezed, then pulled back. "You must have been a wreck. It's like you're taking on the world, every day."

"I thought I was helping. I'm so sorry I lied."

She blew out a breath. "This makes so much more sense. It seemed really weird to me you would offer to drive in a tense moment. You're a stickler for rules. Driving on a learner's permit without an adult? And then being reckless? I just...yeah. Of course it was Grace."

Tala's disappointment in Grace didn't come across as harsh as from my teammates. She understood my protectiveness of my sister, and also knew my sister was more than her bad-girl reputation at school.

"I'm stuck," I said. "I'm stuck and I don't know how to get out."

"I've got your back, beshie."

I smiled weakly at the bestie nickname. "You're not mad?"

"When do I ever get mad at you?" She raised a brow, waiting. "Yeah. I don't. If I'm going to get mad at you for anything it'll be for how you put everyone ahead of yourself. It's not always a good thing. You can be selfish if it means not having to lie to a judge."

Now *that* stung.

"Your story is safe with me. It's not my place to say anything."

"Thanks. Seriously, thanks."

"Why did you tell me? What changed?"

"I didn't want to lie anymore. Not to you." I thought over the past few weeks. I filled her in about volunteering with Will, Piper, and the others, and about helping my grandparents. "Being back home feels weird. Nothing feels the same."

"Are you going to tell anyone else?"

The very thought made me want to curl into a ball and bury myself in a blanket cave. "I don't know."

"Maybe going away wasn't so terrible."

"Maybe." I picked at a weed springing up through a crack in the pavement.

"You miss Will."

Hearing his name from her sent heat rushing to my cheeks. "Okay, one more thing I've been holding back on. We kissed. More than a few times now."

Tala pumped her fist in the air. "*Yes.* I was so hoping that would happen."

"You don't even know him."

"From what you told me, he sounds like a good person." She pressed me for details on our kiss, and of course I had to tell her. Tala grinned. "Okay, so he knows?"

I didn't have to clarify what she meant. Guilt sprang up in me like my own weed. "No. He knows about the accident, but not the truth. Also...a drunk driver killed his brother."

"Oh. Dang, girl."

"Yeah."

Tala stood and offered a hand to help me up. "Well, you know what this means."

"I'm a terrible person?"

"No. You have to go back." Before I could argue, she held up her hand. "You owe him the truth, for one. If he's as open and understanding as you say he is, then you should tell him. Two, your grandparents want to help, right? If Grace is staying here at home, you go back to Deer Cove and let her figure out her own life.

It sounds like you have more waiting for you there than you do here."

"What about my job at the theater? And the team?"

She gave me the same look she used with her younger siblings when she had to tell them news they wouldn't like. "I could pull a string to get you work, but you only wanted it for your college applications anyway. And bonus: me." She flashed a smile. "As far as the team goes, if you're training Will for the race, then you're running. The team will be here when you get back. Remember when that senior went away to France or whatever?"

"Frankfort, but yeah." Tala was being awfully understanding, especially for me lying to her. She really should be more upset.

"Before you ask if I mean it, I completely mean it. Go back to Deer Cove, Holli."

I sighed. "Thanks." This was what it felt like to have a friend who forgave. Who trusted.

We hugged again. Tala checked the time on her phone. "My break's up. Since this is probably goodbye for another few weeks, keep me in the loop." She held up her phone. "And Hol? Give me more credit. I can handle your truth."

I nearly broke down crying a second time. "You're the best, Tala."

I knew Tala could handle my truth. What I didn't know was whether Will could.

·♥·♥·♥·♥·♥·

I called home from the theater parking lot and waited to see which of my parents was unlucky enough to answer. Dad did, and his annoyance was clear. First day back and already I needed a ride.

He'd need to get used to it. I wouldn't be driving for a long while thanks to the court ruling.

Only it wasn't Dad who picked me up. My grandparents' aging minivan creaked to a stop in front of the theater.

I yanked open the sliding back door. "Thank you. I'm sorry you had to come out."

"No problem for me," Grandpop said solo from the front. "I just did a Costco run and your grandmother is visiting with a friend."

Back at the house, elevated voices sounded from the kitchen. Something about the car and curfew.

Grandpop hovered at the door. I stood between him and the rest of the house. The filling in the sandwich between my two worlds.

"Shut up!" Grace screamed unseen from kitchen. "Just shut up, forever!"

It felt like a vacuum sucked the air out of the room.

More banging and shouting sounded from the kitchen. Grandpop shot forward with determined steps.

This was so embarrassing having him see what our lives were really like.

"What's going on in here?" Grandpop stood in the doorway to the kitchen. "Grace, you should be ashamed talking to your mother like that. After all the trouble you caused. You're acting like a spoiled child."

I peeked behind Grandpop. Grace paced between the kitchen counter and the table between it and the family room.

"I'm not spoiled and I'm not a child," Grace spat. "I'll be eighteen in nearly a week. I'll be an adult."

Mom scoffed. "You don't act like an adult. You want everything handed to you. I won't be here as a handhold for you forever."

"Good, because I'm moving out!"

Mom folded her arms. "You don't have any money."

Point to Mom.

Grace narrowed her eyes like she was aiming all her anger in a concentrated dose. "I'm getting a job. I have a place to live. I'll be fine."

Their voices rose again. The front door opened and closed behind us. Grandma appeared. "Oh dear, they're at it again?"

My stomach churned. It was going to be like this until Grace moved out. Whether five days or fifteen or fifty until it happened. Who knew what would play out.

Grandma smoothed my hair. I let her fingers run through the strands, feeling her protection.

When I considered retreating to my room, my cross-country trophies and BTS poster Tala bought for me at their concert weren't what came to mind. Instead, the attic was what called to me. My peek of the lake out the window. The strip of beach and the log I shared with Will.

The pieces fell into place where they'd been edging all along. I didn't belong here. Not right now. I turned to my grandparents, seeing the discomfort on their faces.

"I'd like to go back home now. With you."

Grandma's arms encircled me. "Of course. We'd love to have you."

Grandpop patted me on the back. "How about you go up and pack a new bag. I'm sure you'd like some different clothes to impress those friends of yours."

Chapter Sixteen

♥

I'd figured my parents would tell me I needed to stay in Ginsburg with them. I'd expected it. Dad only sighed when I told him I wanted to go back with my grandparents. He and Mom hadn't even argued. Just nodded in resigned agreement and reminded me of another check-in date with the lawyer.

The Grace effect. She'd worn my parents down so far they no longer had the energy to fight for me to stay. Why did everything always go back to Grace? It was like she'd stolen my parents from me. Maybe she didn't need them anymore, but she hadn't bothered to check if I did.

I hugged Mom and Dad goodbye, but left without a word to Grace.

As my grandparents reversed out of the drive, Grace's face appeared in the upstairs window of her room looking down at us. I pulled back from the van window and took out my phone.

I texted Tala I planned to return to Deer Cove for another...who knew how many weeks. Maybe I'd stay on the coast the whole summer. I only knew my fractured family couldn't handle me and I didn't feel up for practicing with a team who didn't want me either.

My thoughts cycled through what happened the past two days. What a difference between what I'd left in Deer Cove to what I'd come back to in Ginsburg. Except for Tala, nothing felt right back home. I'd grown so used to covering for Grace and playing my part, I had no idea where I fit now that I no longer wanted to do those things.

I blinked, sitting up straighter in my middle row seat in the van. I no longer wanted that version of my life. The one that constantly excused Grace. The one that stayed in my safe zone of school and cross-country with little else.

I'd been missing out on so much. I wanted to go to concerts. To buy a really tight skirt or an over-sized vintage coat—things I'd never normally wear. Just to try them out. Maybe write some poetry. Really bad poetry and then not care that it was bad.

Picking up my phone again, I decided to be proactive and follow up with Christina and Coach. I typed "Sorry for—" and backed over it. I was really over apologizing to people for every little thing. I thought through my words and typed again, promising the team captain I'd keep up my training. For Coach, I followed up with a more detailed training plan and mentioned the 5k race.

Back in my attic that night, the humidity huddled in corners until the crusty old fan blasted it apart. I sat at the window overlooking Lake Michigan. It was too late to walk to the beach. Besides, I was tired down to my bones. And I hadn't even run today.

I sent off a quick text to Will.

Me: *I'm back. For the summer.*
And then I drifted off to sleep.

The creaky attic stairs announced Grandma's entrance. "Knock knock," she said after I groggily sat up. "This letter came for you."

I blinked at the clock. "Why didn't you wake me up? I should have been up by now." I swung my legs over the daybed to the cool wood floor. "Did you just say I got a letter?"

She handed me an envelope with only my name on it. Inside, a folded note.

Meet at the community center at sunset. Bring warm clothes and a towel. Sleeping bag if you have one. Your grandparents are already cool with it. No worries.

-xWillx

My grandparents were *cool with it*?

I looked up.

"Your Grandpop talked to Will this morning. He came by for your run. You were so konked out, we told him you needed the rest."

My heart warmed at the thought of Will coming to the house early for training. And then I'd slept in on him. "Was he annoyed?"

Grandma looked puzzled, then seemed to put together my train of thought. "He's been through a few things with his own family. My guess is he understands what you're going through."

I read the note again, enjoying idea of Will hand writing me a note. It wasn't a love note exactly, but a million times more meaningful than a text.

"You know the drill," Grandma said as she headed back down. "Fix yourself some cereal and get to your chores."

I spent the rest of the morning going through the usual list of room cleaning, towel folding, and washing bedding. We had a full slate of guests again and a lot to catch up on from being gone while the temp filled in.

Grandpop showed off his new electric lawn mower, which he was honestly way too excited about. Only then I realized his enthusiasm had been intentional. His showing off had been a demo. *I* was the one who got to "play" with the new mower.

The humidity sure wasn't shy today, making the air thick and heavy. After a mow of my grandparents' yard and the grass around the inn, I helped Grandpop trim bushes and pull weeds.

I still needed to fit in a run somehow. I cleaned myself up, only to get drenched in sweat for a run early evening. I'd need to start extending these runs to get back in to my longer distances.

After my run and a glorious shower, I returned downstairs to find a pile of camping gear.

Grandpop came into the living room from the kitchen. "You've got a sleeping bag, a pop tent and a mini cooler. I packed it with water, hot dogs, and a treat from your grandmother."

I smiled, feeling the sensation all through my body. "Wow, thanks. This is all great."

"I know you're not your sister, but you just remember we're only a short walk away. We can check up on you kids at any time." He pointed to his eyes and then out across the beach and back again. "We know what kids get up to. We've got eyes everywhere."

Unlike when my parents threatened they'd be watching, I actually believed Grandpop. "These friends don't party like you'd expect." I wondered how much he knew about Will and what happened to his family. They might not know about Will's views against alcohol.

Grandpop squeezed my shoulder. "I believe you, kid. And despite all that's happened, I trust you. Who I don't trust is everyone else." He deepened his stern look. "Boys, is who I mean."

"*Grandpop*." But who was I kidding? Will and I had already kissed. Now I'd be on the beach with him all night. I honestly couldn't believe my grandparents agreed. No wonder he gave me a whole speech about eyes everywhere.

Outside, dusk settled in. "You better head out, kiddo." He quoted a phrase in another language.

"What does that mean?"

"It's a Korean proverb I learned from a friend. It translates to: Don't try to cover the whole sky with the palm of your hand." He'd said this same thing to me before, when I'd left to watch the sunset. "It means the sky is still there, even if you hide from it."

Okay. I wasn't sure I got the meaning entirely, but it sounded pretty.

I gathered the gear and the backpack I'd filled myself and walked the half block to Main Street. The pop-up tent folded small enough into a long narrow bag I slung over my shoulder.

As soon as I turned the corner toward the community center, I spotted a figure in the distance. Black T-shirt and cargo shorts. Black hair and skate shoes.

I ran to him.

It was a slow and a bulky run. Not only was I weighed down by a backpack, sleeping bag, and cooler, but the pop tent swung behind me hitting my back and then out and around to ram into my side. This had to be my least graceful run ever.

But I didn't care.

Ahead of me, Will's grin cracked open. I could see him laughing as he jogged toward me. His own jog slow and clumsy.

We met in front of the laundromat where I dropped the cooler—gently—and ditched the sleeping bag and tent on top of it. I threw my arms around Will.

He smelled like the beach. "Did you miss me?" he asked through my hair.

I pulled back. "Yes." I let my eyes find his. He leaned in, his lips sweet and welcoming, like unwrapping a gift. I clasped my fingers behind his neck. I stole another kiss. And another.

"You really did miss me." Will's cheeks flushed.

"Am I embarrassing you?" This made me giddy. Will was such a cool-with-everything guy, I loved having this effect on him.

"A guy can blush, can't he?" He cleared his throat. "I'm glad you came back."

"Turns out, being home kind of sucked."

He moved a windswept strand of hair from my face. I kissed him again. I couldn't help it.

Will took the cooler by the handle and grabbed the tent bag while I took the sleeping bag. "I did training runs from your schedule. I got shin splints. I had to look up what those were because I thought my legs were falling off."

I winced and walked beside him toward the community center. "Yeah, those are the worst. Did you follow the warm-up routine I gave you?"

"Figured you'd ask. See, that's why I need to train with you. I'm already jumping ahead like I've got this down."

"It happens to the best of us. Don't worry, I'll be training hard the next few weeks."

"Cool, cool. My mom just ordered me running shoes. Those should come in another few days."

I followed Will around the far side of the community center building. The Dragon Wagon was parked at the farthest point of the back parking lot along the sand line. The rear doors opened facing the beach.

"Cool shirt," Antonio said from the back of the van.

I had on my What About Caitlin T-shirt from the concert. "Thanks."

"I noticed too," Will said to me. "But more crucial things were happening at the time. It's not every day a hot girl drops everything to run into your arms."

Antonio made a sucking sound through his teeth. "Ooh you two have got it bad for each other."

Piper ran over with her arm outstretched. "Here." She handed me a thin stick and flicked the end with a lighter. Tiny, yellow-white sparks sprayed outward like a homemade magic wand. "Don't you love sparklers?"

I hadn't even set my stuff down and already I held summer magic.

Drawing a lazy figure eight, I watched the glowing trail catch in the air.

Antonio hopped down from the van and took my sleeping bag and the cooler from Will. Beyond us, a bonfire blazed with familiar faces from the teen group. Chaz and Carmen and several others. A tent large enough for five or six people was set up nearby with windows zipped open.

"So, we really are sleeping on the beach?" It seemed kind of silly being only a few blocks from a real bed. "I can't believe my grandparents agreed to this."

Will gave me a sly grin. "Like I said, everything is cool. I had a nice chat with your Grandpop again today."

"While I was sleeping." I set my backpack down in the sand and kicked off my shoes and socks. "Sorry I wasn't around for our run."

"It's fine." He kindly didn't spill details with so many ears around us. "When I didn't hear back from my texts, I figured as much. I was selfish and thought I'd come see you anyway. Instead, I got to layer another charm base with your family."

I laughed at charm base. "You're lucky they aren't scared off by piercings."

"Oh, I took those out. I wore a shirt made of some space age material for moisture wicking. It's bright yellow."

"You don't have to pretend to be someone else around them."

"It's just a respect thing. I don't know your family well. Besides, the running shirt is the only tolerable—and cheap— shirt I found at the discount store. The moisture wicking makes a huge difference. Who would have thought running gear makes it easier to run."

I shook my head but smiled.

We made our way toward the fire. Will reached for my hand. "I really wanted you here for this."

A comfortable heat spread through me. "This is the best welcome back gift."

The sunset striped salmon pink with splashes of gold. Above us, faintly visible stars emerged. When my sparkler burned down, I found another in a box on a small folding table by the camp chairs around the fire.

A soft boom sounded from south of us, followed by a spray of red and white across the sky.

"Fireworks!" Oh my goodness, I sounded like a five-year-old.

Only when I checked for Will's reaction, he looked just as jazzed. "This is perfect." He slung an arm around me.

Piper crossed the sand to hand me a s'more with the marshmallow toasted just enough to soften the chocolate. "I'm glad you came back, Holli."

"Same. Thanks, Piper."

Will and I sat on a blanket near the fire. The distant fireworks continued beyond the tree line as Piper picked up her guitar and played a song I hadn't heard before.

She paused after the chorus. "An original I'm working on. If anyone has ideas, I'm open."

Piper would probably regret she'd asked, because we all chimed in with ideas. Lyrics, chord progression, making mouth sounds—anything seemed fair game.

Piper took the suggestions in tested some out to hilarious results.

I settled back against Will as we all talked and Piper played more songs. His hand covered mine. The Xes on the back of his hands looked darker and sharper now, like he was newly branded.

I tapped his hand with my thumb. "Did you go to another show?"

"No. Do you mean why do I have Xes on them?"

I nodded, angling to look at his face.

"It's a symbolic thing. It's how you're marked as underage at a show so they know who can't drink. It became a symbol for people who don't drink at all. By choice." He squeezed my hand. "I mean, we're not legally allowed to drink anyway at our age, but this is more an outward identifier that I'm choosing not to."

"Did you explain this to my grandparents? They'd probably let me sleep on the beach every night."

He laughed softly. "It just means a lot to me to live clean. It's important for other people to know it too."

I bristled at the word clean. I knew what he meant, but the opposite of clean was dirty. My sister wasn't *dirty* because she drank. Her drinking caused her to make bad decisions and to lose time blacking out. She was reckless, but I didn't like her being called dirty any more than her flirting with guys got her branded as slutty.

But telling this to Will would bring up other things. *The lie.* I'd barely made it a day back and my secret crept up again like slow-releasing poison.

I had to tell him. Tala told me I should trust Will. She said he'd understand if he was the person I believed him to be. This was why I came back. At least partly why.

It could be as easy as explaining what really happened. Will had told me things he said he didn't talk to his friends about. Personal feelings, and stories about Adam. He would understand. He loved his brother as much as I loved Grace.

Piper stood to take a break from playing. Others got up to replenish snacks and take bathroom breaks inside the community center.

I switched positions to face Will. "Can we talk?"

"Yeah, of course."

It had to be a good sign Will didn't run from those dreaded three words. Grace once told me the phrase was a guaranteed relationship killer.

"Want to walk?" he asked. "We won't go far in case gramps checks in on us."

I laughed through my nervousness. "Did he do the eye thing to you?" I mimicked Grandpop pointing to his eyes, out and back.

He nodded. "Sure did. Plus, small towns have eyes everywhere anyway. The folks who run the bed and breakfast know my aunt and uncle, and the burger place people are friends with my mom."

Both businesses faced out to this strip of the lake not far from the community center.

We walked a few paces out until I couldn't hold it in any longer. "I know I've been acting weird since we met. I wanted to tell you more about what happened."

I took in some air. I couldn't believe I was about to tell Will the bitter, awful truth. He waited for me to speak.

"Holliday." Will stopped walking to take both of my hands in his. His dark hair fell across his eyes, swept aside like a brush stroke. "You don't need to feel guilty anymore. Your sister has her own stuff to work through. Her own journey. Don't feel like a failure just because she's stuck and you're moving forward."

My breath wavered. "It's not that." Well, it was partly that, but not what I needed to tell him.

Will waited.

And still, I couldn't. Cold ice seized in my chest. It could all be over after this.

"You can tell me," Will said. "Whatever it is. I know you're a good person."

Voices from beyond us broke through my silence. "Look who it is, guys. Purity Patrol!" Cackles of laughter followed.

Will tensed beside me.

Antonio walked a few feet from the fire toward our guests. "What's up guys? Toby, right?" He held up his closed fist to bump hands with the taller guy.

"Yeah." Toby wore the same cap he had the night I'd met him partying on the beach. The shorter guy followed behind. Both of them white kids with longish hair dressed in worn hoodies and saggy jeans.

Toby peered around Antonio. "No kegs, huh? This a PG party?"

His friend snickered.

"I think our maturity level is rated higher than you're allowed," Piper spoke up as she approached.

Toby's buddy leered at Piper. "You're pretty hot. Wanna hang out with us?"

"If you're respectful, you can hang with us," Antonio said, attempting to maintain a chill vibe. "We aren't partying your style, but we still have a good time."

The guys looked at each other and cackled. Toby stroked his beard scruff. "I'm not about to get high on God or whatever, but I could be down to pledge some purity, if you know what I'm saying."

"We're not religious," Piper said. "Even if we were, we wouldn't make fun of someone for their beliefs. Again: maturity."

"You girls should come with us." Toby rubbed his hands together. "We'll show you what a real party is like."

Will moved into Toby's face. "Get out of here before I make you."

This only made Toby laugh again and his buddy cackle harder.

But Will, he was shaking. His fists tightened. "Just because I don't kick back with a sixer doesn't mean I can't throw a punch."

"Easy, guys." Antonio held his arms out in either direction. "We're done here. You guys can move along to do your thing, and we'll be here doing ours."

Toby smirked at Will. "Didn't your brother die or something? Is that why you're this anti-drug crusader?"

Will fumed beside me. "Shut up."

"What, did he OD? Did he get so wasted he—"

Will pushed Toby. Hard.

Toby stumbled back, still laughing. "Dude, you are so *triggered*."

Antonio moved between them, his hand at Will's chest to press him back. "Come on, Will. Not worth it."

Toby circled us like an animal stalking prey. "You're such a *loser*. No wonder your brother got himself killed."

I gasped. A horrible, cheap shot.

Will lunged forward and charged him.

Chapter Seventeen

♥

Will landed a solid punch to Toby's face. He swung back, but Will ducked and hammered Toby in the side.

Toby cried out in pain and fell to the sand. Antonio pulled at Will, putting distance between them. Toby scrambled backward in a panicked crab walk.

Voices shouted from the distance and footsteps pounded toward us.

"Come on, Toby." His friend stepped back. "There's too many of them. You can't risk juvie again."

So, this guy already had a record. Or was headed toward one.

Toby hopped to standing and dusted himself off. "You're a freak, dude. We'll see how it is once school starts and your loser squad isn't around to defend you."

"You looking for a fight?" Chaz called over. He pushed up his cardigan sleeves. It would have been funny if I hadn't feared for Chaz's life. Toby and Will were solidly built guys who could hurt someone. Chaz was lean, probably quick, but I wouldn't bet on him in a fist fight.

Carmen moved past Chaz as she cracked her knuckles. "No one told me it's trash day."

"Huh?" Toby looked confused.

Toby's friend tugged at his arm. "She means it's time to take the trash out, dude. You're the trash. Let's get out of here."

Carmen growled and moved closer. I'd bet money on Carmen.

After yelling a string of profanities at the group, Toby turned back the way he'd come with his buddy trailing after him.

"Will, are you okay?" I tried to see his face through the dark. He kept turning, hiding from me.

Toby had known exactly how to hurt Will. He'd found his wound, lined up the knife, and pressed the blade.

Antonio slung an arm across Will's shoulder and talked to him in a low tone. He steered him away from the group.

Carmen kicked at the sand. "Man, I was itching to fight."

Chaz stared at her. "Are you kidding? That guy was huge. I can't believe I threatened him. I must have been fueled by adrenaline. Or by that energy drink. I would have been pulverized."

Carmen patted his back. "Next teen group, I'll show you how to clock a dude."

"Carmen, maybe—" Piper started when Carmen raised a hand.

"I know, I'm sorry. I just get excited to share a skill. I grew up with three brothers and two cousins who formed a fight club for fun."

Chaz looked at Carmen in fascination. "Tell me more."

Piper moved next to me. "Are you okay?"

I rubbed my arms. "I'm fine."

As much as I'd dreaded telling Will my truth, I would have gladly done it over what played out. Will had to be a mess right now.

"Those guys are total d-bags," Piper said. "Come on, folks. Let's get back by the fire. It's cold over here."

We settled back around the fire. Will and Antonio had stayed off a distance talking.

"I wish we all went to the same school," Carmen said. "I'm way out, past the district line."

"But Will has friends, doesn't he? At school?" I couldn't imagine losing his only brother and not having anyone around for support.

"A few," Piper said. "He's got me. Our school is small. Honestly, being friends with Will taught me not to judge so easily."

Antonio and Will returned.

"Sorry you had to see me lose it," Will said to the group. "I let my emotions take over."

"Just name me a day and time and I'm there with my cousins," Carmen said.

Antonio pressed a hand to his forehead.

I wanted to hug Will and tell him everything would be fine. Only I didn't know things would be fine. When summer ended, I'd go home, and Will would still be here. I hated how those jerks would be around waiting to taunt him.

The group talked awhile longer, but the vibe shifted after the fight. Piper and Antonio talked more to themselves while Carmen demonstrated what she called tactical defense moves in front of us on the sand.

As the fire wound down, Piper gathered her blanket. "Sorry to be a bummer, but I'm calling it a night." Antonio moved ahead of her to unzip the large tent door. They both slipped inside.

The rest of us walked to the water's edge, talking about school, family and whatever until my eyes grew heavy. "Am I dork if I'm in bed before midnight?" I'd made it almost that far.

"You wanna sleep out on the beach?" Will asked me.

A clip of wind blew in from the lake. "I'll take a tent."

He moved closer. "I really am sorry for getting angry. I'm embarrassed. I can ask Chaz to walk you home if you're not okay being around me right now."

"I'm good staying," I said. "Besides, I'd feel safer with Carmen than Chaz. She's got some powerful moves."

Will still looked stressed.

"I want to be here," I told him.

"You're not afraid of me?"

"No." He'd been intentionally provoked. He could have chosen not to punch Toby, but at least he seemed remorseful. "Someone once told me it's okay to make mistakes."

He shoved his hands into his pockets. "Sometimes I think that advice is meant for other people. Not me."

His words washed over me. "I understand that feeling more than you know."

Will watched me with that deep sense of looking he tended to do. Then stepped back. "There's room for us in the big tent if you want. The dividers inside zip down to give you your own space. I know you brought your own tent, but if you'd feel safer surrounded by friends…"

"Thanks. Yeah, if there's room, I'd like that." I wanted to say more. I wanted to set right so many things, but tonight just wasn't the night.

We made our way back to the low flickers still remaining in the fire pit. Will squatted and poked at the glowing embers. "I'm gonna stay out a little longer."

Inside the big tent, I put my socks back on and laid out my sleeping bag.

The tent door unzipped again. Chaz and Carmen set up their own sleeping bags on the other end of our divided room apart from Piper and Antonio. The end of Carmen's bag ended up about a foot from my head.

"I'll try not to kick in my sleep," she said. "Hey. I'm glad you joined us. Will seems to really like you."

And I liked Will. A lot.

Even with the layer from my sleeping bag, cold from the sand seeped through the thin tent floor. I pulled another blanket over myself from the pile Antonio brought from the van. Only the chill never quite went away.

I must have finally drifted to sleep, because next thing I knew, rustling and giggling sounded from the other side of the tent. I squinted one eye open to blinding daylight.

Piper emerged from her side with hair tousled. She wore an over-sized sweatshirt and Hello Kitty PJ pants.

"Want s'mores for breakfast?" A bag of marshmallows landed by my head.

"Girl, what time is it?" Carmen moaned. She'd zipped her entire head into her sleeping bag.

Chaz continued to snore softly a sleeping bag's length from her.

I managed to sit upright. I chucked the marshmallows back. "It's too early for sugar."

Piper made a stink-face at me. "How dare you." She took her marshmallows and unzipped the tent's front door. "By the way, Will's in the van. He's dead asleep. Not exactly an early riser."

Right. The whole not wanting to get up at seven to run thing. I wiggled my toes awake, not thinking of much while Piper dragged Antonio out of the tent.

Chaz rolled over. "Did I hear someone say food?"

Carmen had already rolled up her sleeping bag. "I brought breakfast burritos in my cooler. You can have one."

"Are you going to roast it over an open flame?" Chaz asked.

She threw a sock at him. "Do I look like Bobby Flay? I'm eating it cold."

The two of them chattered as they left the tent, leaving me alone to clean myself up.

The tent door unzipped again. "Everyone presentable in here?" Will called out.

I'd slept in my clothes and definitely had pillow creases on my face based on the texture of my skin. "It's just me in here. I'm good."

Will shuffled in with a blanket wrapped around him like a cape. "I thought they'd never leave."

"You were waiting for them to go? And why were you in the van all night? Did I take your spot in the tent?"

He sat at the foot of my sleeping bag. "I'd prefer to keep my limbs intact. I don't want to cross your Grandpop. I slept in the van and there are witnesses."

I tried to imagine Grandpop as a threat. He did have that stare and the uncanny ability to know everything going on in town.

"How'd you sleep?" he asked.

"Fine. I'm groggy. We could go for a run to wake up."

Will pulled the blanket up and over his head in response.

"You need to train. The 5k will be here before you know it."

He peered out from the blanket. "As long as I can finish, I'm all right. I'm never going to score a six-minute mile."

"As your personal trainer, you know I've got to try."

He let out an exaggerated sigh. "Later. We'll run later." He let the blanket fall back to his shoulders. "I've been meaning to ask. How did court go? You didn't text details."

I focused on the blue tent wall. "I said what the lawyer told me to say. Then I listened to a judge talk about zero tolerance laws and responsible decisions. Then we went out to eat. Totally fun day."

"At least your parents took you out for food. After our court hearing, my dad went back to work. My mom locked herself in her room. I was on my own."

Ouch. "I'm sorry."

"Ah, no. I'm sorry. This is about you, not me."

"It wasn't that long ago for you. Anyway, I shouldn't complain."

"Hey, I want to be clear I'm not trying to compare war stories. What you're going through isn't easier just because you and your sister came out all right."

We'd come out alive.

"How's the gallery show coming?" I asked. A safer topic.

"Uh, good," he answered. "We've got more art coming in from another teen group. Really cool photography pieces and some paintings. Here." Will unearthed his phone. He turned the screen toward me.

The first picture showed a painting of a rock formation pushing up from the water near another coastal Michigan town. The sun's setting rays burst from behind. I flipped to the next picture, this one a painting of two young girls kneeling on the beach with sand coating their arms.

"These are great. So much talent." I handed the phone back. "I'm looking forward to the show. Any way I can help."

"You used to want to go back home. Now you're here again." He picked at his leather wrist cuff. "Did you come back for me?"

"Maybe a little."

Also, my best friend said I owed you the truth. And I did. "Things back home felt weird. Grace fights with my parents and then my parents fight with each other. They seemed to think the court case wrapped things up. Like when I'm done with these service hours, everything will be normal again. My grandparents, they could tell... I guess they could just tell I wasn't comfortable staying."

"They seem like great people."

I thought of Grandpop prepping the camping gear for me and how excited he got to show me the lawn mower. Then again, he was probably stoked to have an underling mow for free.

"So, um court," I began. "There's a few things I should tell you."

His face softened. "I get how scary this all must have been. The only time I had to wear a suit was my brother's funeral and to court. It's like impossible to prepare for. With your sister, it seems like this is the first time her drinking had a real effect on her life—and affecting you."

I swallowed. "Except it's not."

"Well, sure her drinking's affected other people. You just thought she was like anybody else, on the beach kicking back a few cans. You didn't know it how bad it could get."

"I did know. She's been like this for a long time." I summoned courage. "Will. It wasn't me who caused the accident. I wasn't the one driving."

Will waited, his expression unchanged.

I plowed ahead. "After the cops broke up the party, we left and Grace just got in and started the car. She was wasted and I knew it, but I panicked and she's...convincing. My sister has always been able to handle anything. I thought she could handle driving home."

I swallowed against the sandpaper in my throat. "I told the police and my family and Miranda the lawyer that I drove because it made more sense. Grace wouldn't have to go to jail or get a DUI. She was supposed to learn from it. She was supposed to get how the bike we crushed could've had a person on it. She was supposed to stop."

Will's focus shifted past me. "Is that why court was so hard? You had to tell the truth to the judge in front of your family? And your sister?"

I could barely get out the rest. If I didn't say it now, I never would, and it would rip me apart from the inside. "I didn't tell them."

The silence may as well have been an entire elephant sitting between us.

His mouth fell open. "But you took the blame for what you didn't do. It wasn't you the whole time?"

I slowly shook my head no. He'd get it, just like Tala had. He just needed a minute or two to let it sink in.

He stared at me, dumbfounded. "*Why?*"

The question I'd struggled with myself so much. "I made it easier."

"You made it easier for *them*. For everyone but yourself. Why?"

"None of it was going to be easy. We would have gotten into trouble no matter what. My sister would have been arrested. Her license suspended. It looked really bad, Will. Saying I drove made more sense, at least at the time. I didn't know it would lead to a court hearing and service hours." Or here, with him. "Something good to come out of this is I came here and met you."

Will tossed back his blanket. He bit at a nail, then yanked his hand away. "I don't get it. It's not just lying to all those other people. I could maybe understand...you said you got panicked, I get it. But you lied to *me*. You lied to me about the whole thing when I told you everything. I told you that you could trust me. *I trusted you.*"

My fears each checked off like one of my to-do lists. "You told me alcohol is poison, and here I have a sister with a drinking problem. You really think I'm going to tell you I covered it up?"

He shook his head. A bitter smile surfaced, then vanished. "You think covering for them will fix it. You can't fix poison."

His words cut into my skin. "I would never let my family be hurt and not do anything. I'm trying to help."

"You can't just *fix* everything."

Heat crept up my neck. "Look, I'm not saying I did the right thing. I'm saying I did what I thought was right at the time." He wasn't seeing anything the way I did. "You know what? Never mind. I thought you would get this." I thought he'd get *me*. I untangled myself from the sleeping bag and stood.

I wobbled on the unsteady ground and reached for the wall. Only my hand slipped against the nylon surface.

Will shot up to steady me. "Don't give up when things get too hard. You know you need to deal with this."

I pulled back from his touch. "I've been dealing with this for years. You have no idea how much I've been *dealing*."

"As long as you're protecting your damaged sister, you're screwing up your life. You're sacrificing for her, and for what? What kind of person is she?"

His words nearly knocked me back. "Don't you dare."

"What?" His severe gaze aimed to the core of me. "What has she done for you besides allow you to take the blame for her mess?"

"She's my *sister*. Don't tell me you wouldn't do the same for your brother."

My words caught Will off guard. "I would do anything for my brother. He deserved it."

And Grace doesn't. No need to say the rest—his accusation came like a swift slap across my face. "Adam's memory deserves your total devotion, but my sister doesn't deserve mine? And what about you? Didn't you say you don't deserve to be here? That the wrong brother died? So, Adam deserves everything, but no one else does?"

"I need to live a life where I help people." He spoke slowly and deliberately. "Adam can't so I have to be that person in his place. But this isn't about me." He kept his voice even. "Your sister is wasting her life. She doesn't want your help. You keep on like this, you're gonna waste right along with her."

"You don't get to tell me what deserves my attention," I fired back.

"Well, I guess I'm not deserving since you've been lying to me all this time."

"I lied so you wouldn't get hurt, okay?" I threw up my hands. "I'm sorry. I'm the worst. Obviously, it didn't work."

"You should have let me decide for myself."

Should have, should have. "And you would have judged me. You're judging me now. You're judging my whole family."

"Maybe your family needs to be judged."

It was like he'd gathered all the hurt from losing his brother and hurled that pain straight at me.

I yanked open the tent door's zipper. "This was a mistake."

A mistake to come back. A mistake to tell him. A mistake to cover for Grace in the first place. A mistake to believe Will would understand.

My life turned out to be one mistake after another.

Chapter Eighteen

♥

I should have trusted my instincts. Telling Will the truth about Grace and the accident ruined everything. He didn't trust me. If he had, he'd have recognized I was trying to do the right thing.

No, maybe this was all my fault. I'd thought we could be together and our pasts wouldn't surface. Stupid wishful thinking. Will's own brother died from a drunk driver. Here I had a sister I'd allowed to drive drunk and then I'd actively covered it up.

I returned to the house through the door to the kitchen, crossing my fingers my grandparents had left to work for the day.

No dice. Grandma stood at the stove. "Did you eat breakfast?" Despite being early, it apparently wasn't so early seeing me came as a surprise.

I opened my mouth to answer and burst into tears.

Grandpop crunched the newspaper page in his grip. "Did that boy try to get fresh?"

I cried harder at Grandpop's outdated phrasing. His protectiveness warmed my heart, but I hated how it felt. I didn't deserve his care right now.

Grandma shut off the burner on the stove. She guided me to the couch in the living room. "Tell me what happened. Are you hurt?"

I pointed to my chest. No, wait. She might mistake my signal for a heart attack. It was only my heart *emotionally* attacked. I fumbled for how to express this through a sob.

Grandpop joined us and sat at the edge of his recliner. If he wasn't reclining, I had his attention. "I will have a strong word with that boy and his father."

I wiped my eyes. "Grandpop, you're being patriarchal. You're just talking about men."

He seemed stumped by this and regrouped. "I'm equal opportunity with my word. The mother will work just fine."

Grandma shooed him off. "We have Becky coming with the handmade soaps in thirty minutes. Go get a check ready."

With Grandpop out of the room, I worked to pull myself together. "Sorry. I don't know why I lost it. Everything's fine."

As if the *everything's fine* line ever worked on her. "How about you get washed up and I'll fix you a plate of eggs."

I did what she said, dreading my return to the kitchen. I didn't know what to tell her. Pure fog clouded my head.

I expected third-degree questioning at the breakfast table, but Grandma only chatted about a family who just checked into the inn. They had a dog, a mountain breed of some type, and she told me how the family trained dogs for a living. I didn't really care, but hearing her talk about a nice family and some dogs made me feel less like stabbing something.

"I have an idea." She swept my empty plate from me and took it to the sink herself. The red carpet treatment. "Come with me today while I run my errands. We can stop at the library and get you some books. It will be good for you to get out."

We headed south to the next nearest town for miscellaneous shopping. She made a point to introduce me to everyone she knew. Grandma had lived here for like forty years and knew everybody.

I couldn't get past how to stay here the rest of the summer if I had to see Will. How would I face him? How would I face him tomorrow for my next slot of service hours?

After a stop at a cute boutique where Grandma let me pick out a pair of earrings and a cute top—surely signs of apocalyptic events to come—we returned to Deer Cove. The sign welcoming us to town looked refreshed with new lettering and a happy bunch of flowers planted beneath it. That or I'd never noticed the sign before.

By the time we pulled into the Sunset Inn lot, I'd almost forgotten this morning's argument. Until Will stood from my grandparents' front steps.

Grandma parked but kept the van running. "Is he here to apologize, or do you owe him an apology?"

I bit the inside of my cheek. "I don't want to talk to him."

"We could go on the lam. I've got a half a tank."

"Wouldn't Grandpop miss us?"

"Eh, we've had a good run."

I wanted to laugh, but Will's somber expression sapped the humor out of everything.

"The boy looks shattered, Holli. Go talk to him."

She turned off the ignition. I could easily walk around the back of the house and ignore Will altogether.

Or I could face my problems.

I managed to get myself out of the van and up the front walk.

"I didn't only come back for you," I blurted when I came within blurting distance. "I'm here to help my grandparents. And to finish my hours at the community center."

Will didn't respond. He just waited on me in case I wasn't finished.

And I wasn't, but somehow the fire in me lost its heat. "I like how the teen group is into stuff that has nothing to do with school sports or grades. I'm not running back home just because you're disappointed in me."

Will removed his hands from his pockets. He had on long pants despite the heat. Nicer material than his usual cargo shorts. Instead of skate shoes, he wore leather boots without scuff marks. "Holli, I'm sorry. I'm so sorry."

My mouth opened to say more, but it closed instead. I expected an argument, not an apology.

"I have this way of reacting," he said. "My gut is to get mad. I used to fight to get what I wanted. I used to get wasted to forget. I don't have those crutches anymore. After you left, I only had me. I only had my thoughts. I hate my thoughts sometimes, Holli."

I hated my thoughts sometimes too. Always trying to make things right or fix other people's problems.

"You were right," he said. "You thought I would judge you, and I did. I never cared about school, but I care about my job and the teen group a ton. I care what happens to that place and they pay me crap. It's not really about the money."

"You work there because it means something."

"I work there because I have to."

"Well, you don't *have* to. You just said they pay crap."

He squinted, thinking something over in his head. "The way I see it is, if I don't do everything I can to make this world positive, then toxic people win. I'm in control of my own life. I make my own destiny. I know it's corny to admit, but for me it's true. I don't want to live a wasted life. I don't want to be numb to block out what's hard. I want to be honest and thing is, I expect that back. It wasn't fair for me to put that on you if you weren't ready to share what happened. That's on me. I'm sorry I pushed you on it."

I hadn't been ready, but maybe I shouldn't have been lying to the people I cared about for all this time. I wanted to hold close the part of Grace I knew was good, that I knew wasn't toxic or destructive. She would always be my sister. I didn't know how to do all those things. To be honest and still protect her.

"I'll stay out of your way," Will said. "You shouldn't have to go back to Ginsburg if you want to be here. I would never want to make things uncomfortable for you."

Will had been through so much—we both had. He'd admitted he didn't have his life together. Neither did I.

"Maybe we could run this out. We've got a few hours until the sun goes down."

Will made a face. "Is running your answer for everything? Because I have an objection."

"Running helps me think. It could help both of us think."

His shoulders softened. He crossed into the soft grass. "Holliday, I'm sorry I acted like a jerk to you."

His apology softened the hard edges inside me. "Thanks. I was afraid to tell you because I expected you to be upset. I made a mistake. A big one. I didn't know how to get the words out."

"I want you to be able to tell me things. Even the hard stuff."

I nodded, my throat too tight to speak.

"I'm sorry I'm no good at running." He lowered to one knee. "I don't deserve it, but will you be my 5k coach again?"

I managed a smile. "I'll be your coach."

He stood, and suddenly we faced each other nearly eye to eye. "If running is your passion, then I want to spend time with you doing what you love."

His words were exactly what I should want to hear. They should have made me happy. They should have weakened my knees. And they did. Only I couldn't help but see a boy who said he was devoted to my passions, but who had already written off someone so much a part of me.

Will and I made plans to meet back for a run. Things still felt weird. Only two people other than Grace knew what really happened.

I liked working at the community center, so the hours wouldn't be a problem. But coming clean to everyone else would only complicate life. So long as Tala and Will knew the truth, the lie didn't feel so big. Or so powerful.

Will and I headed out for our long run and synchronized our pace. Well, as much as our differing skill levels allowed.

Running made me feel like I had a hold on my life again. The one thing I could go back to and find a sense of order. We slowed to walk a few times, but Will never wanted to walk for too long.

"Go again until we reach the next block?" He nodded ahead.

"Sure."

We took off again. Our route wound us through town. With Will now wearing actual running shoes, he relaxed into his stride.

"That's my street there," Will said between breaths. "Want to stop at my house?"

Stopping would cut our run short, but I couldn't pass up the chance. "If we can cool down first, okay."

We slowed to a walk until he angled into the yard of an old house. Farmhouse looking, even though houses lined the block with the town only a few blocks away. A long, covered porch took up the front with a hanging bench swing to one side and the rest of the porch enclosed by windows.

"Home sweet home," Will said, nodding to the house. "This is my aunt and uncle's place, but they're cool with us living here. There's an addition on the back with a family room and two more bedrooms."

Large trees shaded the yard for a perfect place to stretch. I stepped one foot forward to stretch my hip flexor, then my hamstrings.

"Do you think your parents will stay here? Buy a house or rent something?"

Will followed my lead and stretched his legs. "I think so. Mom likes her bank job. Dad seems to be okay with the work he's doing. I thought I'd miss my old friends more, but I don't."

"You've made some pretty great new friends."

"Yeah. It feels kind of like my skate shoes. I love those old shoes. They fit good for the most part, but now that I've got these?" He lifted a foot. "Now I know what a good fit should feel like."

I thought of Tala. She and I would always fit, even if we needed to swap out styles of shoe...or whatever. My teammates, they seemed kind of like what Will described. With distance this summer, I didn't miss them so much. But I needed to go back sometime.

It felt so strange, building one life here in Deer Cove and knowing I had to go back to Ginsburg. Feeling like I belonged here and realizing maybe I'd never belonged back home.

"Want to come inside?" Will asked. "My mom is probably home, but we've got snacks."

"Yeah, sure." I followed him inside, still lost in a cloud of thought.

Inside, a front hall led to a cozy living room with a flowered couch and a heavy wood entertainment center along one wall. We removed our shoes and ended up at the kitchen.

"You seem to be running more comfortably," I told Will as he poured us water from a filtered pitcher.

"Comfortable? Hardly."

"You're doing great!"

He laughed. "You're being nice. I suck. I can't even make a mile without stopping to walk."

"Training builds up endurance. You're right on track."

"The race is next weekend. I'm hopeless." He drained his water glass.

"Just do your best. I wouldn't expect anything else."

Will took out a bag of chips and a cannister of peanut butter-filled pretzel bites. "Now. We feast."

A woman came down the stairs, her hair soft brown and with Will's same eyes and nose. She had on a black Guns N' Roses T-shirt.

"Holli, is that you?" She crossed the kitchen. "I've heard so much about you."

Will rolled his eyes. "Don't lay it on too thick, okay, Mom?"

"Hi," I said to her with a pointed look at Will. "Nice to meet you."

"Call me Jen." She patted me on the back. "And tell me you're staying for dinner."

Chapter Nineteen

Race day. My love for competitive running instantly ignited at the sight of the Summer at the Lakeside Charity 5k Run banner. We'd traveled to a town south of Deer Cove, closer to Muskegon where more hotels and B&Bs catered to a larger crowd of tourists. A town with more than one stoplight and a beach with a pier and a lighthouse.

I fastened my race number to my shirt, which had a lighthouse logo on it. Then pinned Will's for him. "You're going to do great."

He looked a little green. "I should have trained more."

I rubbed his arms to chase away the early chill. "This is why we kicked up the pace this past week. You've done really well."

Will gawked at a group of runners wearing running tights with reflective side panels and high-end shoes. The works.

"Hey." I made Will look at me. "This is a charity run, remember? Even if you walk, it counts."

He gave me a Get Real look. "No way I'm *walking*."

I jogged in place, urging Will to join in to get his blood pumping. Eventually he followed my lead, but his smile never quite caught up. Then again, it *was* early. The race started at nine a.m., and we'd had to drive here from Deer Cove, plus park, and check in.

"Hey, folks." Chaz re-joined us now after finishing his own check-in. He patted Will on the back. "I went to a workshop on how to center your chi. Want me to show you how?"

Will looked up from the stretching I'd advised him to do. "I'll have some chi after the race. They serve that at the coffee place over there, right?"

Chaz didn't miss a beat. "Your chi is an energy force, deep down. Look at me. Look how calm I am." He held up a steady, pale arm. "I should be nervous in this crowd, but I'm not. Chi focus, man."

Since Chaz ran regularly, we talked about other races we'd done while we warmed up. Chaz ran with a meet-up group on lakeshore paths up and down this area of Michigan's coast.

Will had abandoned stretching to check his phone. He seemed distracted, but again, maybe just nerves.

The overhead speakers sparked to life with announcements about the race. We grouped up for our division and waited for the starting bell.

Chaz lightly bounced on the balls of his feet to stay loose. Beside him, Will couldn't have looked more opposite. His shoulders slumped and he still scrolled through his phone.

"Are you all right?" I asked Will.

He slid the phone in a back pocket of his shorts. "Yeah, sorry. I'll wake up in a second."

That's when I noticed the backs of his hands. A wash of gray streaked across where the Xes once existed. Like he'd scrubbed his skin raw.

A sick sensation pitted inside me.

The announcer counted down, and the starting bell blared. *Go!*

The crowd shifted forward, slow at first until space allowed us to start moving ourselves and spread out.

I kept a slow pace at first to stick by Chaz and Will. I planned to race with them and didn't care about scoring an impressive time. Still, it felt great to be in my element again.

Chaz and Will chatted about common friends as they ran. I found myself tuning out and finding the rhythm of my breath.

At the first mile marker we all cheered. A few onlookers outside of the race clapped and rang cowbells.

The runners thinned out a bit, offering more space around each of us. My legs itched to take longer strides. I focused on a woman ahead of me and mentally calculated how many strides it would take to catch up to her. I relaxed into my pace and passed the woman. The next person I targeted wore lime green bike shorts and had on a rainbow jester hat. I pushed further.

Glancing over my shoulder, I didn't see Will or Chaz anywhere.

I slowed and searched for Will's black band shirt and dark hair. Great, I'd left him in the dust when I was supposed to be his support and trainer for his first race.

Okay, well, I'd keep running and watch for him. We all would end up the same place.

Another quarter mile passed, and I still didn't see Will.

I slid my phone from my waistpack and did a quick speech-to-text message to Will.

Me: *Find me at the finish line.*

Will had Chaz with him for support. Funny how Will could have had Chaz as a trainer this summer. I smiled. Will looked for an excuse to hang out with me. And it worked.

Since we'd already separated, I increased my pace and picked off runners. The remaining miles passed by easily. I took in the old in-town houses with over-spilling flower boxes. A few kids sold lemonade on corners. We wound back to the business sector of town. By then, I had a good clip going until I eyed the finish line ahead.

I broke out with all I had and passed three more runners as I crossed.

Yes! Nothing beat the feeling of ending a race strong.

I walked to cool down and keep my muscles from cramping. I checked my phone again, but no return text from Will. Obviously, he had to still be running since I'd left him and Chaz in my dust.

I sent another text describing where I stood and grabbed a banana and water from a big blue tent.

A tap hit my shoulder. "Hey, Holli. We finished!" Chaz held his hand up for a high-five.

I returned the five. "Where's Will?"

Chaz blinked. "He's not with you?"

"Dangit. I knew I shouldn't have run off." Literally. "I got swept up in it."

"I'm sure it's no problem. He told me to run ahead, but I figured he'd find you."

"Well, I texted him where we are, so just look out." I wiped my hairline of sweat. "Is something going on with Will? He was acting weird."

Chaz rubbed the back of his neck. "It's the date. I wondered if he really wanted to do the race today. He swore he'd be cool."

"What do you mean the date? He knew about this race for months."

And then it hit me. Adam. He'd been gone for a year. What if it was *exactly* a year? "His brother?"

Chaz nodded. "It's the anniversary."

"Oh." My heart lurched. Why would Will keep such an important date from me? He'd given me heat about not telling him my birthday. He'd been the one who dumped out his life story the first couple times we talked. Will wasn't one who held back.

Now our blow-up the other day made more sense. No wonder he'd been acting so upset. Beyond me lying to him, the looming anniversary of Adam's death had to set him more on edge.

"Do you think he finished the race?" I asked Chaz.

His brow furrowed as he watched runners exit the race and wander different directions. "I shouldn't have gone ahead. You want to split up and look for him?"

"Look for who?" Will appeared behind Chaz. He took a huge bite of an apple.

My adrenaline spiked. "Where were you? We were *freaked out.*"

He raised his apple-holding hand in a gesture of defense. "I took a detour. No big, okay? I had a side cramp."

"You cool?" Chaz asked Will. Will nodded and they fist bumped. "Well, I'm gonna take off. A few runners from the meet-up are supposed to do an after-run hang out."

Guys.

Chaz hopped off, not seeming the least bit tired after running three miles. I turned to Will. "I didn't know about today. About the date. Chaz told me."

Something flashed behind Will's eyes but disappeared in a blink. "It's just a day."

"Why did you do the race today? You didn't have to. I would have understood."

Will chucked the apple toward a waste bin, but it bounced off the edge and rolled into the path of foot traffic. A kid kicked the core into the grass. "It's just a date on a calendar. It doesn't mean anything. It shouldn't mean anything."

I stepped over the curb, apart from the dispersing crowd. "I'm sorry. I shouldn't push you. If you don't want to talk, it's not my place to ask." I didn't want to agitate Will, especially on such an important day, even if he didn't see it that way. "Come on, let's get out of here."

He looked like he wanted to say something, but the words stuck in his throat.

I moved toward the street name I recognized where we'd parked at a small parking garage. "So—" I stopped. Will hadn't followed.

Will watched me with hands stuffed into his shorts pocket. "That's it then?"

I looked back at him. "That's it what?"

"You're going to stop asking because you don't want to push me?"

"You told me today is a day on the calendar with no meaning. Who am I to tell you otherwise?"

He sauntered over. "I want to know why you're backing off."

"For starters, I'm not going to tell you how to feel about your brother."

"No, but you can push me to question it. Why would you back down? I don't want you to back down."

I let out an exasperated breath. "You pushed me away and now you're mad I listened? You're the one being confusing. I don't know what you want."

"We were having a *discussion*. And then you stopped."

"You were agitated."

"So?"

"So, who wants to talk to someone who's agitated? Especially when it's about something so personal? You're communicating two different things."

Will's expression shifted. Somber, sullen—whatever he felt, I couldn't figure him out. Grace got like this, where she picked at the way I said things, or worse, at what I didn't say. Those conversations reminded me how different we were, and I didn't want my differences with Will constantly brought forward

He sighed. "Look, I know I'm being a huge pain. The truth is, I couldn't finish the race. I left not long after the first mile marker. I suck. But you don't suck. I want you to push me, and to give me crap if I deserve it. I mean, didn't it upset you when I took off in the middle of the race?"

"I didn't know you took off. I thought I'd left you. I ran ahead."

"Because you think the best of people, even when people aren't the best."

"It's not like I think you ditched me. You said the race got to be too much. Knowing the reason, it makes sense."

"Sometimes the way you look at me, it feels like you're afraid of me."

"That's ridiculous." I turned and walked toward the parking garage.

I didn't like upsetting people was all. Maybe before he knew the truth about Grace, I might have acted timid around him. I hated having secrets. But not now. Will knew the truth now.

We walked in silence. When we reached the car, Will headed to the passenger side. He unlocked the door and held it open.

His hands. "Why did you scrub off the Xes?" I asked.

Will leaned an arm over the open door frame. "I almost lost it."

"What?"

"I'm messed up. The date—it's kind of a big deal. I thought it wouldn't be, so I signed up for the race. You know, like create a new memory over a bad one. I don't want to remember the accident. I want to remember Adam."

He turned one hand so the back faced me. "Last night, I hurt so bad I almost called a guy who'd bring me anything I wanted. Anything to dull the pain. I can't stop the guilt sometimes. That I'm here and Adam's not. It's like it presses on my chest so I can't breathe. I'd do anything to get that feeling to go away. Anything to forget."

Guilt, regret, shame. A swirl of ugly hurt I knew myself.

"But I don't," Will said. "I have people I can talk to now. I can do stuff—help people. That makes hiding away in the pain less of an option. That's what the drugs and drinking were for me. A way to hide and not face things."

A memory surfaced. Months earlier when Grace and mom fought about...I couldn't even remember. Grace's grades or how she'd forgotten to fill out college applications, most likely. The usual bickering had escalated to screaming. Even my mom screamed back. Then I'd noticed Grace moving strangely. Her words a little slurred. She was drunk.

Drunk, in our house, fighting with Mom. And if I'd noticed, of course Mom would.

And she had.

The screaming moved to threats. Only the conversation went a strange direction. Mom threatened Grace to clean up her act or she'd tell Dad. Which meant she wasn't telling Dad about Grace being drunk and screaming. Because he'd been working so many hours, Mom hadn't wanted to add to his stress.

When the two noticed me shadowed in the doorway, Mom made me swear to keep quiet. In no way should I stress Dad out with Grace's problems.

And I'd done what I was best at. I did what I was told.

I'd kept it a secret. So well, I'd forgotten that night. Until now.

I wasn't the only one who'd kept Grace's secrets. Mom had too. She'd practically taught me how to ignore Grace's problems and pretend everything was okay.

I wasn't sure what to do with this revelation. Will looked at me with his reliable intensity again, and I found I couldn't handle it. Besides, this was his day to be upset. Not mine.

"You said you almost lost it," I said to get back on track. "What stopped you?"

Will kept his gaze on me. "You."

Chapter Twenty

♥

Piper and I showed up early in the day to the community center to finalize set-up for the night's gallery event.

She adjusted a microphone stand in the corner of the lobby as Antonio arrived. Piper approached him with a sweet kiss to his cheek. "You've got the power strips?"

He winced. "Dangit, I knew I was forgetting something."

Piper let out a dramatic sigh.

Will peeked around the corner from behind the front desk, a walkie-talkie in hand. He wore cargo pants and his Leaf Group shirt. "Do you need something, Piper? I was about to make a run into town."

Town meant the larger town south of Deer Cove.

Will waved me over. "Holli. Want to quest with me?"

I couldn't help grin at his offer to quest. "Sure. Oh—I mean as long as Piper doesn't need me."

Piper shooed me off. "Antonio can help me with the PA and speakers."

I grabbed my bag and followed Will out to the parking lot. I had my hand on the passenger door when Will swept me toward him with one arm. "Have I told you today how crazy I am about you?"

His breath tickled my nose. If I had a mirror, I'm sure I'd see a big, goofy grin across my face. "I'm sorta crazy about you, too."

He landed a sweet kiss on my forehead. My knees shook. From a *forehead kiss*. I was truly a goner if my knees shook from a forehead kiss.

Then his mouth moved lower to my lips and lingered there. My toes nearly curled into a ball.

A little dizziness hit getting into Will's car, but no way would I tell him. I *could* tell him, but then Will would for sure crack jokes about his swoon-worthy effect on me.

We drove toward the turnoff to the highway and headed to a warehouse store south of Deer Cove. Our own little adventure.

I trailed my hand out the open window, feeling ribbons of cool air among pockets of heat. "Is this what skipping school feels like?"

"We're technically still working." He glanced my way. "You've never skipped?"

"Are you kidding? The very idea of skipping school breaks my skin out. What if my parents found out? Or my teachers? They'd never look at me the same."

He laughed. "I never cared what a teacher thought of me. Wait—scratch that. I loved Mrs. Jackson for art. She knew I was terrible at everything artistic except when you glue bits of paper onto something and mash it all together. I was good at that. Nobody deserves to fail art."

I let the sun warm my skin from the open window. "It feels like we can do anything. Even if it's twenty minutes away, no one is looking for us. It's like we've crossed out of where we're supposed to be."

"Usually when I skipped, I was mad about something. There was that moment when I felt the freedom, but then I'd feel crummy again thinking about going back."

"Is school really bad for you now? After moving?"

We slowed as a truck turned off the highway. "It's not so bad. I have a few friends, and I keep my head down. I'm not as depressed as I used to be. You'd think I'd be more out of it since Adam died. It's not really like that, though."

"I've always liked school. I can't imagine dreading it."

"Makes sense why you never skipped, then."

We fetched the needed power strips and other items on the list the community center needed. Afterward, we swung by a fast food place for lunch. Just as we parked, Will's two-way radio squawked.

"Will?" a community center staff questioned. "Can you stop by the state park ranger station? They need a few extra hands at the yurts."

"Roger that," Will said. "Wanna eat and then check on the yurts?" he asked me. "Huh. I never expected to say those words ever in my life."

"Once yurts enter the equation, the conversation becomes unpredictable."

"Once you go yurt—"

"There's no other way to flirt."

He raised a brow. "You think I'm flirting with you?"

"You're not?"

He closed the distance between us in the car and kissed me. This time on the lips.

My brain went to fuzz.

"Holli?"

"Yeah?"

"Did I make you speechless just now?"

His smirk made me want to deny this repeatedly. I shoved him. "Don't get full of yourself."

"Hey. I'm a half-full kind of dude. At least let me get a little close to full."

Will continued to grin and, well, how could I be mad? He reversed out of the parking lot and looped us around to the drive-thru.

Our lunch date turned to eat-on-the-go as we made our way back to Deer Cove and the state park.

Will directed us to the ranger station.

"Power's down at the yurts," the ranger said. He gave us access to a golf cart. "If you can take these supplies to the campers up there." He handed us a box with bags tied off and numbers on each one.

A rumble sounded overhead.

I jumped. "Did I hear thunder?"

The ranger glanced overhead at the peek of blue visible through the trees. Thicker clouds formed to the north. "We're supposed to get rain. The heavier stuff looked like it'll pass us."

Grandpop had grumbled about the weather before I left, but I hadn't paid much attention since I figured I'd be inside at the community center. Now that I thought to notice, the air had a heaviness to it and the wind had picked up.

Will took the driver's seat in the cart and I took the box to rest on my lap.

We reached the first group of yurts. In the grouping of four buildings, two had electricity. These were pretty basic set-ups, so it wasn't like they had flat screens in there. Just a simple overhead light and a couple of power outlets.

We dropped off the supplies. Will chatted easily with a family visiting from Lansing. I hung back and checked the laminated map for where to find the next section of yurts.

Will's walkie perked up. "Looks like the storm is blowing this way after all," the ranger said. "We've got some folks out on the trail. Think you can go up to Trailhead C and call 'em back? Over."

"Got it," Will responded. "Over."

We returned to the cart. We drove farther down the maintenance road and veered left at a fork.

Thunder dropped and rippled with a low grumble. "That doesn't sound so good."

"No, it does not." Will pressed on the gas, but only so much *go* existed in this cart. "Sorry you got dragged into this. Hopefully it won't take long."

We reached a large sign with a map matching the one I held in my lap. Will stopped and got out to inspect. Squiggly lines coded in different colors marked the trails.

We'd stopped at the head of Trail C, which looked to be a long and winding journey. The trail itself disappeared into the woods.

Will tapped his cell phone. A colorful image popped up on the screen. "Check it out." He held up the screen. "Weather radar. A storm really is coming in. Can you drive this? Maybe you should go back while I find the hikers."

"I'm not leaving you. Besides, I have a suspended license."

Will's grin faded before it had time to fully form. "That doesn't really matter for a golf cart."

I tried not to feel dumb at his obvious response. "I'm fast. I can run and catch up to the hikers."

"This is an advanced trail. Running is a bad idea."

The woods stood thick in this part of the park, obscuring any view of Lake Michigan. I checked the map. Trail C headed south and then moved east, inland from the lake.

"Maybe they'll find shelter." I ran my finger along the map version of Trail C and stopped at a grouping of triangles symbolizing the huts. "The other yurts are over there. We could keep driving this way on the maintenance road and see if they're on the other side."

"Good idea." He touched a mid-point on the map where a maintenance road ended. "See the utility box marker? We'll stop there and see if we can catch them. If not, we'll go to those yurts."

We returned to the cart like rangers on a mission. My skin ignited with energy. I should have been a tense ball of stress right now with hives itching to bump themselves into visibility, but I didn't feel stressed at all. Will knew the trails. With Will beside me, I could do anything.

The cart stuttered at the sharpening incline. Will squeezed my hand. "You okay?"

"I'm good." Branches shifted overhead in an almost haunting rhythm. The air felt like it dropped five degrees since the yurts.

"Okay, here's the mid-point." Will reached into a bag in the cart and pulled out binoculars. He walked to the trail. "I don't see anybody."

"Did the ranger say when he last saw the hikers?"

Will radioed the ranger to ask. He reported back it had been an hour. Enough time to get to the yurts for sure.

"The yurts?" I asked. Will noted and returned to the cart.

We drove farther. Thunder hit again, louder and sharper. The wind whistled through the leaves like sound effects from a dark and stormy night in a movie.

A fat, wet drop hit my arm.

Minutes later the rain came steady.

"There should be a rain poncho back there." Will nodded toward the cart-sized truck bed attached to the back holding our supplies.

I dug through a hard plastic bin and found two tightly-folded green rain ponchos. "Jackpot."

I managed the poncho over my head just in time to see a sign with a friendly yurt symbol ahead. The trees parted at a clearing dotted by the round tent structures.

"Whoa." I felt my mouth hang open. The sky beyond the yurts darkened like someone tossed a violet-colored scarf over the sun. Bright bolts of light splintered the clouds.

Will parked and flew out of the cart before I could hand over his poncho. He darted to the trail opening first. I checked the perimeter of the yurts. No coolers or camper chairs by the fire pit like the other area. No signs of life inside the yurts from what I could tell.

The sky finally let go and dumped open. Each drop pelted against my poncho like somebody hurled the rainwater at me. I tried the door on the nearest yurt—locked. I knocked even though it probably wasn't occupied.

I turned. Where was Will?

I ran back to the trail opening. "Will! Hey, Will! Where'd you go?"

The cover of trees shielded some rain, but the ground grew more slick with each step.

"Will! We have to get inside!"

His green leaf tee bobbed up and down ahead of me on the trail. Never mind he told me the trail was too dangerous to run. I sprinted to catch up, leaping over rocks and knotted roots.

Will slowed to walking when I reached him. "I don't see them. I *have* to find them." He breathed hard.

"Will?" the ranger called through the walkie. "Head to shelter if you're by the yurts."

A flash lit up the spaces through the trees. Thunder moaned. "The hikers probably turned back already while we drove around the trail."

"We don't know that." Will walked faster. "I can't leave them. We have to keep going. Keep searching."

More thunder sounded. And it came more frequently. "No one's out here. The ranger said we need to find shelter. Let's go to the yurts until this blows over." I practically had to yell over the sound of rain pelting against the trees and leaves and ground around us.

He turned himself in a circle. "We *need* to find them."

Another round of thunder. Even through the cover of trees, the rain aimed at us. "Will, we need to go."

His drenched black hair stuck to his face. "What if something happens? If we can't find them and someone is hurt? I need to save them."

Save? Of course. I closed my eyes. This couldn't only be about the hikers.

The walkie crackled again. "Will? Confirm receipt. Seek shelter. Over."

Will put the radio to his face. "Got it. Over."

I shook out the poncho, now totally soaked, but at least it would keep the rain from his eyes with the hood. I pulled Will to me, feeling his heartbeat, his breath at my neck. Lifting the poncho up and over him, I settled it around his shoulders and arms.

Will's expression appeared at once grateful and conflicted. He hadn't started walking again, instead standing close but staring past me down the trail at a path camouflaged in greenery and tree trunks.

Suddenly, a high-pitched wail sounded. A siren. A tornado warning siren.

The Deer Cove siren's slow ascent to a shrill blare was enough to send me yurt-bound.

I pulled at Will and he stumbled forward. "Time to go."

"I can't just leave them," Will said, still uncertain about the hikers.

"We don't even know if they're out there. Come on."

Reluctantly, he followed. We reached the clearing to the yurts. Ahead of us, sheets of rain turned the yurts into a watercolor painting. We needed to make a break for it.

"I know you hate running, Will, but this is what you trained for. On the count of three—"

"We're already soaked," Will cut in. "It doesn't really matter."

Still, we ran to the nearest yurt. Will scrambled for a key on the key ring the ranger had given him. He jammed the key into the lock and we tumbled forward into the yurt. The not-quite pleasant scent of dust and moist canvas welcomed us. I shut the door behind us and leaned back against it.

"You okay?" Will slid to the floor onto a woven rug.

"I'm trying to remember what it's like to be dry, but other than that, yeah."

He tapped the walkie. "We're at Overlook Point Camp. Seeking shelter in a yurt. No hikers. Over."

"Stay put until the weather passes," the ranger radioed back. "No funnel clouds spotted, so it could just be severe storms. Too soon to tell. Over."

"Over over," Will repeated like a robot.

It should have been funny, but neither of us laughed.

"You did the best you could."

A cold look filled his eyes. "What if my best is some people are hurt back on the trail? It's an advanced trail. Bears are spotted out here sometimes. There are points where the path narrows and borders drop off. In the rain, somebody could slip."

"And we could have slipped trying to find them."

Will tugged at the poncho sending water flinging out. "I should have tried harder."

"It wasn't up to you to save them." It came out quiet, but needed to be said. "You can't save everyone. But I think maybe this isn't really about everyone."

His brows pinched together in thought. "Look, I'm open about why I need to help people. It's for Adam. That's not a secret."

My own thoughts jumbled together. "What you're doing with the community center and the teen group is good. But to go running off in a severe storm to search for hikers? The rangers are trained for that, not us. Saving people...it sounds like an obsession."

"No." He wiped rainwater from his cheeks. "I'm not obsessed, I'm intentional. That's different."

"It's like you're trying to save your brother over and over. Only you couldn't have saved him, Will. You don't have that kind of power, as much as it hurts to hear."

Rain battered the roof desperate to get in.

Will stared at the floor. My heart thrummed in time with the rain. This was the boldest I'd been with Will. He was the bold one, not me. But he needed to hear this. That he'd believed he needed to save those hikers showed me he'd taken the saving too far.

"You're wrong," Will's voice came barely audible over the rain. "I'm supposed to help people. I'm the one who's still here."

My mind cycled through to something I'd heard on a daytime talk show when I was home sick. People who survived horrific events and felt guilty that they'd lived. To imagine not only losing someone but then feeling bad you survived? That had to be devastating.

It sounded like Will. That he was battling thoughts like that, it hurt my heart.

"Will." I reached to him, my hand on his arm. "I'm so sorry about Adam. You deserve to be here regardless of what happened. You don't owe anything to anyone. Even to Adam. From what you told me about him, he loved you for who you are."

He sat quietly, his own thoughts keeping him busy.

Static woke up the radio. "Will?" the ranger said. "We found 'em. The hikers are at the ranger center. They came back via Trail B. Over."

Will pulled up his knees and let his head slump. He heaved a big sigh. He responded to the message and set the walkie aside.

"They're okay," I said as much for myself as for Will. "I'm glad everyone is where they need to be."

He still had his head down, but he reached for my hand. "Yeah, me too."

We sat in silence. Well, we didn't talk. It was anything but silent with the rain throwing a tantrum out there. I wondered how the rain hit back in town.

"Oh no. My grandparents are probably freaking."

Thankfully, my phone felt only slightly wet in my pocket. And miraculously, I had two bars of connectivity, despite being in a hut in the woods.

I hit the call icon with my grandparents' photo. "Grandma!" I nearly shouted into the phone. "Hi. I'm safe. Me and Will are at the state park—we're in a shelter. Sorry if you've been worried, but I'm safe."

"What are you doing out there? I thought you were down the street at the community center."

I winced. "Sorry. Will got called over here by a ranger and I went with him."

Grandpop said something in the background.

"Are you guys okay?" I asked. "Did the storm hit the inn?"

"We're inside and safe. No tornadoes, just rain and wind." Her tone sounded off. Like she was holding back.

"Are you mad I'm not where I said I'd be?"

"Oh, no. If you're with Will and you say you're safe, I believe you."

My shoulders eased. But still. Something was up. "Are you sure you're okay?"

"Yes, we just...heard some upsetting news. I'll tell you when you come back."

Grandpop's voice grew clearer. "I've got the inn covered if we want to go."

"What? Why do you need the inn covered?"

Grandma sighed and I could imagine her shooing Grandpop away from the phone. "Holli," she said with a tone I couldn't decipher. "It's your sister. She's been arrested."

Chapter Twenty-one

♥

Arrested.

"Your sister is all right," Grandma said over the phone. "When it's safe to come home, I'll tell you the rest."

Rain continued to smack against the yurt's thick canvas walls, urgent and unrelenting. Beside me, Will squeezed my hand, looking concerned by how my own face surely looked concerned.

I couldn't handle waiting to hear the rest. "What happened? She's all right, but what happened?"

The silence on the line told me she debated whether to tell me.

"Please, Grandma. I have to know."

She let out a breath. "There's been an accident. Your sister, with her friend."

"An accident? Was she driving? She can't—"

"Not a car accident. They were at a party." The way she said *party* I knew she didn't mean a community center-sponsored bonfire with a bunch of high-on-life teenagers. "Grace was with Kennedy and your parents brought her to the police. Wait until the storm passes to come home. Don't travel until it's safe."

I stared at the phone where the time showed after the call ended. Grandma and her short goodbyes.

"Holli?" Will asked. "What's going on?"

My mind raced. "An accident. My sister. She's okay, but she...was arrested."

I avoided looking at Will's face. Too much to deal with right now.

I called Dad's cell. "Dad?"

"So, Grandma told you."

"I don't know much. Are you with the police?"

He breathed into the phone. "Your sister was supposed to be at Kennedy's house. They weren't supposed to go anywhere else."

Muffled sounds came across the line. Also, he hadn't answered my question. "Dad? Where's Grace? Why was she with Kennedy? Last I knew, they weren't talking."

"Grace is with the police. Kennedy's at the hospital. We don't know too much either." Voices carried over. "I'm sorry, I have to go. We have things to sort out. But your sister is fine. Drunk but fine." He ended the call.

Thirty seconds. Dad gave me thirty seconds of barely any information. All I knew was my sister was safe but drunk. Again. She'd been with Kennedy, but it obviously hadn't gone well if Kennedy landed in the hospital. My heart ached for Kennedy and her family. For my parents who didn't seem to know what to do.

Will waited beside me. "I don't want to crowd you. If you need me, I'm here."

My eyes blurred with tears. Wasn't I wet enough already? I leaned into Will's embrace. His solid body gave me a sense of comfort. An odd sense of peace when I felt so disjointed. The tears let themselves go and drained across my cheeks.

The rain showered around us as the only sound. If only we could stay here in our safe bubble inside the yurt. As soon we left, we'd face whatever the outside world had in store for us. And I didn't mean bears.

I couldn't sit still. I called Mom. On the second ring, Dad answered. "Holli, I understand you want to know what's going on. We're in the middle of finding out."

I resisted the urge to apologize. "It's too much not knowing. I'm part of this family too."

Dad sighed. "We're all here at the station. Your mother is talking to an officer." His exasperation seemed less impatience with me and more like how he sounded when Grace and Mom got into a screaming match. "Your sister is in real trouble. The police found her in a house littered with empty bottles. And there were pills."

"Pills?"

Dad hesitated again, but I had to know. "Please, Dad. Tell me."

"Prescription pills. One of the bottles had your mom's name on it."

Cold dread sank through me. "What kind of pills?"

"Just something for anxiety. Look, it's not your business, Holli. I've already told you too much."

I felt like I'd been punched in the gut by a block of concrete. I needed to punch something myself. Ideally, not concrete. "Dad. It's not too much. I'm already out here in Nowherestown, USA as a punishment for trying to help Grace. I deserve to know what's happening to our family."

"Young lady, you…" Only Dad couldn't finish his thought.

I'd never spoken to him so harshly. That was Grace's role. In my role, I played the daughter who did as told. Or, most of the time, didn't have to be told at all.

"Kennedy is very sick," he said in a quieter voice. "They're saying it's an overdose."

I gasped. This was the second time she'd been taken to the hospital for taking too many pills. "Does that mean—"

"We think she'll be okay. We're waiting on the doctors."

Kennedy would be okay. A good sign. "And Grace?"

Dad didn't say anything.

Which was almost worse. He probably had no idea what to do about Grace. What to think.

And sadly, neither did I.

My family was falling apart. And here I sat, a hundred miles away in a yurt.

"Holli?" Will's outline formed in front of me.

I didn't have words to summarize what Dad just told me.

"I couldn't hear much with that rain," Will said.

I filled him in. "Kennedy is my sister's best friend. They'd been fighting after the party and after our accident, but it sounds like they made up. Only Kennedy's in the hospital for a prescription drug overdose. Dad made it sound like Grace's fault. Or I don't know. My sister is with the police."

A realization struck. "She's eighteen now."

I'd forgotten her birthday. Hers, only a few weeks after mine, separated by two years. Grace turning eighteen meant charges could be more serious.

"It could've been her," I said through my fog. "She could have been the one in the hospital. Or Kennedy, she could have—" I stopped. The feeling I had on the phone with Dad when he'd said she'd overdosed. I hadn't dared think further, but it was right there.

Kennedy could have died. Grace could have died. Dead. Gone forever.

"Hey." Will knelt in front of me. Rain puddled on the wood floor from our still-wet clothes. "I'll get you back as soon as the rain lets up. You'll be with your family. We'll get you back home."

Home. The last place I wanted to be, but where I needed to go.

First, to my grandparents. The place most like home right now.

Will clasped my hand and said nothing. He didn't even ask for details. Suddenly, the room couldn't hold me. I yanked back my hand.

Will didn't flinch. "It's okay. Take your time."

My vision sharpened. "Stop being nice to me." I hoisted myself from the floor and looked through the door's octagon-shaped window. Rain sliced down like metal blades.

"Holli, look I get that—"

"No, you don't get it." I clenched my fists. "Everything I did—it was for nothing. None of it mattered."

He moved toward me as if approaching a scared animal. "I'm sorry. You've done so much to help her and still, this happened."

I'd helped her lie.

I couldn't stand being stuck in here another second. I tore open the yurt door. Rain or not, I needed to leave. Grabbing the poncho, I walked out to the porch and immediately slipped on the wet wooden slats. I caught the railing to steady myself, then stomped down the stairs and landed my feet into mud soup.

I heard the door lock behind me through the rain and Will's footsteps on the porch. I headed to the golf cart. A deeper puddle than I expected drowned my foot.

"Holli, wait up."

I reached the cart and held out my hand. "Give me the keys."

"But you don't have a driver's license."

"I thought it didn't matter when it's a *golf cart*." I desperately needed to throw something but I only had my phone. "Forget it, I'll walk."

"Sorry. Bad joke about the license. Come on back. You're not walking."

"Stop ordering me around." I headed toward the maintenance road on foot.

Will made a noise of frustration. "Wait, stop." He caught up and took my hand. "Come here." He steered me to the cart and into the driver's seat. The cart had a roof providing some relief, though rainwater already soaked the vinyl seat. "You're freaking out, Holli. It makes sense—this is really serious. Your car accident should have been Grace's wake-up call. Only she didn't learn from it."

I couldn't look at him. I wanted to shove him. To chuck these keys into the forest.

Letting out a grunt of frustration, I swung my leg back and then forward and sent a rock soaring down the trail.

He was right and I hated it. I hated hearing the truth I'd been hiding from all summer spoken out loud. Worse, I hated hearing it from Will.

Grace had slept right through that wake-up call. She hadn't gone through the scare of an arrest because I'd made sure she didn't face those charges. "You're right. The only thing my sister learned is she can get away with anything. Because of *me*."

Heat built in my chest. I'd thought Grace wouldn't have driven if she'd been *too* drunk. That was a thing she'd told me about—the difference of being too drunk versus buzzed. She'd said driving buzzed was no big deal. I'd believed her. I'd believed her because I'd made her into an untouchable hero.

My sister, my hero.

She needed help. The kind of help I couldn't give.

"I let Grace go unchecked." I let the words have their weight. "It was my fault."

And Will believed it too.

Will tried to guide me back to the golf cart. "It's not your fault, Holli. You just said I can't save everyone. And maybe you're right. The same goes for your sister. It's not your job to save her."

"She's my *sister*." I couldn't tell now whether my face was wet with rain or tears.

"And he was my brother," Will said with just as much passion. "What you said back there, I didn't want to hear it, but maybe I've been like, fixated on the town—the community center, running the teen group—so I don't have to face how much I can't control. Going after the hikers might have been a little extreme, sure. It didn't feel that way, but I can see how it might be. But, Holli, you can't save anyone but yourself either. Grace has to face her own stuff. Bailing her out only let her get away with more. Pills now, right?"

A thousand thoughts whirled in my head, each one slipping before I could latch on. "I don't know."

"You're right that I feel like I have to make up for what happened to Adam. But I can't save my brother. He's already gone."

I couldn't say anything else. His brother *was* gone. Grace was not. "Of course, I want to do anything for my sister. It's just...it's never enough."

The rain lightened as thunder rumbled in the distance. Will moved a strand of hair back from my wet face. "The best thing you can do for her is be honest. That's the only way she'll change."

Everything I'd done for my sister made life worse. For all of us.

I didn't need to be right all the time but it really irked me right now that I wasn't.

"I can be here for you," Will said. "I'm not afraid of this."

I looked at Will. His matted black hair, piercings, his soaked T-shirt. I couldn't make sense of him. "Why aren't you running the opposite direction? Well, maybe not *running* since you hate it so much. I'm a mess. I lied to you and I'm lying to my family. I'm not a good person."

My throat tightened on the last word. I gulped back a sob.

"The fact you care so much to protect your sister shows how good you are. It's why I'm so drawn to you, Holli. You see the good in people. That matters. It matters to me."

I sat with those thoughts but still couldn't make sense of it. My brain turned to spaghetti. Very wet spaghetti.

He held up a cautious hand near my cheek. I leaned into his touch and felt my eyes fall closed as his fingers moved into my hair. His body drew close. I let myself fold into his embrace. A comfort I didn't know I needed. One steady thing to hold onto.

I pulled back. "Here." I handed the golf cart keys to Will.

"Are you sure? Maybe you need a sense of control. You want to drive?"

It was a terrible idea and we both knew it.

I put the keys in the ignition. "Let's go."

Chapter Twenty-two

♥

I delivered us to the ranger station without incident. I'd never driven a golf cart. Overall the experience felt less intimidating than driving a car, but less fun than a go-cart.

The strangest realization cropped up. I hadn't been sad about stopping my practice driving hours. I definitely hadn't been counting down the days to when I could apply for a driver's license. Maybe getting behind the wheel scared me more than I'd realized.

I probably needed to talk this out with someone.

For now, we needed to get back to town.

The ranger provided water and clean towels for us at the station. He'd contacted the community center after we'd checked in at the yurt to let them know we'd sought shelter during the storm. I liked knowing people looked out for us.

The rain dwindled to a trickle as Will drove us out of the state park into town. On Main Street, scraps of leaves and tree branch remnants scattered across the road. A garbage bin rolled forward and back, eventually settling into a gutter. Daylight owed us a few more hours, but the sky looked tired.

Will drove past the community center. "I'll take you to your grandparents'."

"What about the gallery show?"

"If you still want to come, you should."

I wasn't sure what I wanted.

He pulled into Sunset Inn's parking lot. A family unloaded their SUV and carried bags into one of the cabin rooms.

My hand froze on the car door handle. "Thanks for everything, Will. I'm sure you've got to get back and all, so thanks again."

"Hey." He leaned across the seat. "Are you leaving?"

He meant back to Ginsburg. "I don't know."

"I can come in with you, if you want. This is more important than an art show."

"But you're the leader. Don't you have to be there?"

"I'm not really the leader, remember? Besides, this show is Piper's dream. She's got it, I'm sure. I'll check in once you're good."

I looked at the house across the lot, then back to the inn's office. My grandparents had to be frantic with worry about Grace. She and I had completely disrupted their summer.

"Go on ahead," I told Will. "I'll call you later."

"You'll call if you're leaving, right? To go home?"

I wanted to tell him this was home, but it didn't feel quite right. I was caught between two worlds where neither locked in tightly enough.

I kissed him. The kiss held hope and sadness and gratitude all at once. "I'll call. I promise."

Inside the house, Grandma shot up from the couch in front of the TV turned to the weather station. "Holli. Come here, my grandbaby."

She pulled me into a hug and squeezed. This squeeze meant more than being safe from the storm. I hugged her back and felt the love down to my toes.

Grandpop came in, wiping his hands against his worn jeans. "Let's talk about how we want to handle this." He sat in his recliner.

Grandma nodded for me to sit beside her on the couch. They told me what they knew about Grace and Kennedy, not knowing I'd filled in some details when I'd called my parents from the yurt.

"I say they handle it on their own and we keep you here," Grandpop said.

Grandma crossed her arms. "I don't want to give up on Grace. If we're needed there, I'd like to go. Our son needs us," she said, meaning my dad.

They talked some more until the room quieted.

"What do you think, Holli?" Grandpop looked at me.

He wanted my opinion about our family? "Why are you asking me?"

Grandpop and Grandma exchanged looks. "You should have a say in what happens. It's your life," Grandma said.

This felt very different than any conversation I'd had with them. Ever. Or even with my parents. I was used to being told what to do or think.

Tears set to work brimming behind my eyes. The lie rested heavy in my chest.

I couldn't let the lie about the accident hurt us more. Grace needed to take responsibility for what happened. I needed to take responsibility for the lie I'd created.

"I have to tell you something. It's important."

I took a breath and told my grandparents everything.

I braced myself for the worst. Yelling, scolding, cold silence. Sentenced to my room without dinner or forbidden from seeing Will.

Instead, my grandparents hung onto every word as I told them I'd let Grace drive us home the night of the party. They asked questions. A lot of questions. I ended up telling them about the time Grace came home drunk and Mom warned me not to say a word to Dad.

I knew what telling them the story meant. I knew the promise I would break. Betraying both Mom and Grace would lead to its own consequences. Revealing I'd lied to Dad even more fallout.

But like Will said, honesty would bring change. Covering up for Grace and lying about what happened would only hurt more people. I wasn't okay with more hurt.

Grandpop's face hardened. He stood from his chair and left for the kitchen. I heard the back door open and shut.

I sank into the cushions.

"Holli," Grandma said. "We aren't upset with you. We feel terrible you suffered through this and felt you couldn't tell us." She wrapped me in another hug.

"You know Grandpop is thinking the same? He seems pretty mad."

"I've been married long enough to know he needs space to think. And I've known him long enough he would never blame you for this. We're glad you told us the truth."

I cried into her shoulder. I didn't understand my own sister, and this made my tears fall harder. The emotions inside me burst out into sobs. "I lied to the lawyer. I lied in court."

"Yes, we'll have to address that."

How she understood me through my sobs proved she was a real pro. She let me cry some more.

"You might not know this Holli, but it's common for people to cover for their loved ones who struggle with substance abuse. You're young yet, and I know you thought you were helping your sister by covering up her behavior. That's called enabling."

"I made it worse." It hurt down to my bones knowing I'd added to our family pain.

"It's not your fault, but you're affected by her substance abuse too. I think we could all use a meeting with a counselor to sort through this. Even your Grandpop and I need to do some talking."

Grandpop returned. I heard him sigh.

I looked up and he placed a hand at my shoulder. "You're a good kid, Holli. You were in over your head." He squeezed, then let go. "Let's call your folks."

My grandparents did the bulk of the talking with Grandpop's cell phone on speaker so we could all hear.

I imagined being back in the tent on the beach burrowed down in my sleeping bag. Then Will's hand in mine. How he said he'd be there for me and didn't fear my messy life. He'd offered to come in with me. He was only a call and a short walk away.

Being with Will sounded much better than listening to Dad yell through the phone.

But he wasn't yelling at me. Dad's hurt focused on Grace's irresponsibility and how my mom hid things from him. Mom shot back that he was as much to blame when he'd been living in the same house when it all went down.

Honestly, life didn't seem all that much better after spilling the truth.

All I'd ever wanted was for my family to be happy. To have my big sister recognize me for something, to let me keep seeing her as the coolest girl I imagined her to be. Even if it wasn't true, I wanted to hang on to that.

"I think we better call the lawyer," Dad said.

Chapter Twenty-three

♥

With my grandparents' permission, I left for the community center. The air outside crackled with post-storm energy. Or maybe that was me. I'd just left my own family's storm, having no idea the real damage I'd caused.

The community center doors stood propped open with balloons tied to the handle. A sandwich board sign faced the street reading Student Art Show - FREE! in colorful loopy writing I imagined belonged to Piper.

Inside, a mix of people mingled in the lobby. Straight ahead, the back doors opened to the view of the wide, endless lake. The electric energy I'd felt walking here pulsed inside too.

Piper appeared in front of me. Bright pink streaked through chunks of her hair matching a pink sundress. She wore hiking boots paired with rainbow-colored knee socks. "Everything okay? Will said you had some family things to deal with. He was super vague about it."

Will hadn't told her my business, even though he could have. That felt good. "I'm fine. I didn't want to miss this."

"Come on. You didn't get to see everything all set up." She led me down the hall where art hung spaced out along the wall. "We had youth groups from three churches send in work plus two other community centers. All artists are eighteen and under."

The teen room itself filled with more families and kids excitedly showing off their work. An impressive turnout. "I can't believe how many people are here after such a big storm."

Piper shrugged. "We get those sirens. Storms can pick up steam real quick from the lake effect. You learn a lot about weather living on the coast."

Further inland, we obviously had storms, but I couldn't remember ever hearing a siren warning. Only the test warnings our city did which I'd asked my parents about. But never a siren from an actual storm. "I thought it was freaky. Will and I were stranded in a yurt."

Her eyes lit up and she sidled closer. "Ooh. Alone time with Will. Sounds promising."

Except it hadn't been all so promising. Figured, a potentially romantic moment was wrecked by family drama.

Will emerged from the crowd. "Hey, Holli." He instantly moved to my side. "Things all right back at the ranch?"

I grinned. "Not really."

"Oh. Then why are you smiling?"

"Because I like you."

A low-pitched squeal emitted from somewhere. The squeal came from Piper. "You two are *so cute*." She looked past us. "Excuse me, I need to greet some guests I invited."

I watched her dash toward the lobby. "She seems to have a handle on everything."

"This is a way bigger turnout than I ever expected." Will leaned closer to let someone pass behind us. "She contacted all those churches on her own. I think my head's been too many places. The running, helping out at the state park, Leaf Group. I think I tried to distract myself from the anniversary of losing Adam."

"Those sound like healthy distractions."

"You're my biggest distraction." His face scrunched. "That sounded bad. I don't mean distraction as a negative. Diversion? Re-direction. You've made this summer better, is what I'm saying."

My heart warmed hearing it. "You've made my summer infinitely better." A thought struck. "I don't know if I'd do the same if I had the chance for a do-over, but at the same time, if life hadn't played out this way, I wouldn't have met you. I might not have done what I had to do tonight."

He angled closer. "What happened?"

"I told my grandparents the truth. And then my parents." I let the sounds of happy people fill in around us. "It was hard hearing how upset my Dad sounded. Grace has to be so mad at me."

Will took my hand. "I'm glad you told them."

I didn't want this night to stay a downer. "Show me your favorite pieces."

"That I can do."

Will guided me through the displays. Chaz and Carmen found us and pointed out their contributions.

"Carmen, this is awesome," I told her. She'd made a paper and mixed materials collage of her family. Abstract layers of blues and greens layered around it looking like the lake and parks. It looked like Deer Cove in art form.

"Thanks." She smoothed her hands over the jersey she wore. "I didn't know I had it in me."

Antonio joined our group. Someone next to him caused Will to flinch beside me. I did a double take myself.

"This is Aaron." Antonio palmed the shoulder of the guy who'd been with Toby, the bully on the beach. "He and I hung out the other day and he really wanted to come."

Aaron shuffled his feet, looking at the ground. "I'm sorry about the night on the beach. I ran into this guy" —he pointed a thumb Antonio— "and he wouldn't let me avoid him. He said we could all be cool if we talked about some stuff. Toby just got busted again for something stupid. I don't want to end up like him."

Will held out a hand for a fist bump. "We'd love to have you hang out sometime. If Toby gets his act together, he can come too."

I shot a look to Will. After Toby said horrible things and taunted him, I could hardly believe he'd be so forgiving. Then again, Will defied my expectations.

"We all make mistakes," Will said, looking at me as he said it. "I know I've made a bunch. If it wasn't for this group" —he looked at Piper, Antonio, Chaz, Carmen, and then back to me— "I'd still be looking for trouble out there. Alone and probably real angry."

"Toby's moving downstate with his uncle," Aaron said. "He won't be around at school this fall to be a problem."

A welcome relief for Will, even if he wouldn't admit it.

My mind wandered to Grace and how people viewed her as a problem. If she disappeared somewhere, life would be easier. For me, for my parents, for my grandparents.

But she was still my sister. If she learned from her mistakes, of course I'd welcome her back with open arms. I'd only felt distanced from her because she'd pushed me away.

Like Will, I could forgive. I had to forgive. If I couldn't forgive Grace, I'd only be left with bitterness and hurt. I didn't want to carry bitter hurt around. Training on sand as runner provided enough challenge.

I excused myself from the group and walked to the back wall of windows facing Lake Michigan. Dusk came early with the overcast sky still lingering after the storm.

"Want to walk?" Will asked, now beside me again.

"I'd like that."

We headed out the community center back door, past the garden plot and flower beds. Beyond the playground and picnic area to where the beach stretched to meet us.

"I'm still dealing with losing Adam," Will said. "Every time I feel like I've moved on, something hits me again. I'll never forget him. But this feeling of not totally having it together hasn't gone away."

"You're doing the best you can."

"I get so angry when people throw their lives away and act so careless. It wasn't fair to put my beliefs on you when you told me about your sister. I know I'm not always the easiest to talk to."

"I'm sorry I lied to you early on. I guess I did what I usually do and tried to make things right, even if it was the worst way possible."

We walked farther toward a familiar spot. The driftwood came into view ahead of us. "What matters is what you do now. You did the hard thing by coming clean when it mattered."

"I lied to a judge. I lied to my grandparents, my parents. Even the group back there doesn't know what's really going on."

"You're not lying anymore. That counts."

"Does it?"

"In my book it does."

"I think I have a lot to work on."

"We should form a club. Plenty to work on over here." He tapped his chest. "You were scared I'd judge you, and then I did. I'm sorry for that."

We stopped walking. Will stood before me, open, real, ready. Someone just as broken trying to mend himself and the lives around him.

"I know you feel really strong about this," I started, "but I don't believe all alcohol is poison. I don't believe it makes people unclean. I think it can be abused, but it's not all or nothing for me. I just need you to know."

Will looked over the lake.

"I want you to keep believing it since it's important to you," I added. "I wouldn't want to change who you are. Not your clothes, your hair, or what you believe."

"Thanks." He rubbed at his wrist. "Holliday, you're all I think about. How determined you are. The way you care about your sister makes me think of Adam in good ways. I want to remember the good. You called me out on my own crap. How I'm trying to save people and stuff. I don't deserve for you to overlook my crap. I don't deserve you, but you better believe I want to."

The distance between us felt too far. I moved closer. "I want us to deserve each other."

"Consider yourself deserved." His breath hovered over me, warm and familiar.

He moved to kiss me, but I held up a finger between us. "There's something else. You might not like it."

Will looked mildly worried, but it could have been from my kiss-block.

"I need to go back," I said. "To Ginsburg. But not because anyone told me I have to. Because I want to." I squeezed my eyes shut to muster the courage I needed. "I'd honestly rather stay here. My grandparents are super supportive and I love the beach and training on the trails and talking with you. Everything in me wants to stay here for the summer, but I think I need to face what's waiting for me back home. I need to face Grace."

Will nodded slowly as he took this in. "That's brave, Holli. You're not doing the easy thing."

"It doesn't mean I won't be back." I couldn't imagine not coming back for more time on the beach with Will.

"I'm gonna hold you to that."

Will wrapped me in his arms in a solid hug. We stayed locked together, just us listening to the waves rolling in. A great moment to seal in place before my next big move.

Chapter Twenty-four

Walking into my house in Ginsburg, I still felt like I didn't fit.

But like I'd told Will, and later my grandparents, I needed to come back and face what waited for me.

My parents scheduled a meeting with Miranda where she'd need to take a statement from me. She planned to come to the house.

My grandparents had come here with me. Both of them. Because of course each of them insisted on coming even though I'd told them not to. They provided support to the point I now felt smothered.

I liked how they smothered me. For now.

Grace wasn't home. After she'd been released from jail, she'd taken off to hide out with friends somewhere. Now being a legal adult, my parents couldn't force her to come back. They couldn't force her to do anything.

Not like that development was anything new.

Kennedy had also been released from the hospital. My parents and Kennedy's made contact. It sounded like a tense situation given Kennedy and Grace had Mom's pills when they'd been busted. I didn't get any more details. Unlike my grandparents who included me in family discussions now, my parents kept their information caged up and secret from me.

The meeting with Miranda went about as expected. Awkward. Uncomfortable.

Not because of Miranda, though. She acted as crisp and collected as her appearance in court. My parents, on the other hand, constantly fidgeted and made side comments.

"I'll submit Holli's community service hours to the judge as served as a show of good faith," Miranda said. "We have a good case here to show Holli was intentionally intimidated and coerced into lying to the court."

My heartbeat sped up. "I wasn't coerced. I lied on my own."

Miranda leveled a look at me. "You're fifteen—"

"Sixteen."

She took one short breath. "You were fifteen at the time of the incident. Your sister has been shown to be highly persuasive, even by your own admission. She intimidated you into attending a party with her, outside of your parents' knowledge, setting you up to lie about your whereabouts from the start. She convinced you she should drive home despite being highly intoxicated. You said she physically pushed you from the driver's seat."

"That's true but—"

"And your parents enabled this behavior," Miranda finished. "Repeatedly."

I glanced to Mom who looked eager for a sinkhole to show up right about now.

"Your grandparents and I had a chat." Miranda crossed her legs. "We filled in a lot of gaps."

I expected Mom to defend herself, but she didn't.

Dad reached his hand to Mom's. "We took for granted Holli's good behavior. We never realized how much Grace influenced her. I assumed things were okay at home while I worked those extra hours. I should have been paying more attention."

"I feel terrible." Mom's eyes blurred with tears. "I tried to hold things together. Grace was so...defiant. All the time. I just didn't know what to do anymore. I stopped doing anything."

If only Grace hadn't acted up. If only Grace hadn't forced me to lie. She wasn't even here to defend herself.

But that was the real problem. *Grace wasn't here.* This meeting, facing all of us—Grace needed to be here. Only Grace chose to run. She chose to hide and not confront her problems.

She didn't choose us.

I swallowed any defensive words for my sister. This needed to happen. I needed to let Grace absorb the blame.

I tuned out parts of the remaining conversation. Not because it bored me, but because Grace kept coming to mind. Like Grandma said, I didn't want to give up on her. I didn't want her to give up on herself. That hope wasn't the same as changing my life for her. She needed to change herself.

After Miranda left, the rest of us reconvened in the kitchen around our island.

"I'm planning to stay." I couldn't look at my grandparents. No, I had to. I needed to look them in the eye.

"Thank you so much for everything. I wish—I want...I know it's best if I stay."

"We'll welcome you back anytime," Grandpop said. "You're a heck of a good toilet bowl scrubber."

Grandma swatted him. "Your friends sure will miss you."

I could change my mind right now. Except I couldn't. I knew to my bones I needed to be here. "I'll come back. Hopefully, soon."

I'd be dependent on my family to drive me there.

"We'll take you out," Dad said, reading my mind. "We'll pick a weekend before summer ends."

Thinking of summer ending made my decision even more bittersweet. My time with Will would have been gone soon anyway regardless of whether I stayed.

I cried when my grandparents drove off. I could hardly believe I wanted to go back to Deer Cove when weeks ago I considered being sent there a jail sentence.

I called Tala to tell her I was back. And then I cried some more.

I texted Christina.

Me: *I'm home. For the rest of the summer. If I can join a training...*

I erased and typed it again. I sounded whiny and desperate. Finally, I sent something short about how I was back and would connect with Coach.

A message popped up on my phone. I squeezed my eyes shut.

Finally, I mustered the courage to look at the screen.

Will: *Thinking of you. Stay strong.*

Sigh. Will. He believed in me.

I knew he did, but it helped to see it written out. As I typed a message back, a new text notification buzzed through.

Christina: *Hope you're ok. Next practice is Tuesday at 8 a.m.*

Christina: *Actually, are you free in an hour? And up for a run?*

I told my parents I wanted to meet Christina for a run. I was no longer grounded, but because I'd lied, I needed to clear things with them to leave the house.

Mom shadowed my bedroom door as I slipped on running socks. "Holli. I owe you an apology."

I didn't feel like talking. We'd done so much stinking talking with Miranda earlier. "Okay."

"I put you in an impossible position. I should have never asked you to lie to your father. I shouldn't have covered for Grace. It's no wonder you did the same in a crisis."

I didn't know what to say, so I didn't say anything.

"I failed to protect you, and I'm sorry. Your father and I have already seen a counselor together. We will do better. We're both so very sorry for everything."

She inched forward like she wanted to hug me but looked too pained to make the first step. I met her at the door and opened my arms.

The hug felt different from Grandma's or Will's. Mom's felt unsure. She pulled back first. "I'm so sorry, Holli."

"I'm sorry too."

Everyone was so darned sorry, it made me even more grateful to get outside. Running with Christina, we would fall into a rhythm where talking wouldn't matter.

We'd agreed to meet at the public park connected to my neighborhood. I jogged the familiar route down my street and past the elementary school until I reached the entry point for the park. I joined the paved path and headed to the parking lot by the picnic pavilion.

Ahead of me, Christina exited her car. Out of the passenger side, Elena.

My stomach dropped. This was a set-up.

"Hey, Holli!" Christina called over as she and Elena walked toward me. "Don't be mad—"

"She made me come," Elena said with arms crossed.

We all stood together on a strip of grass to keep the path clear. "Hey," I said.

Christina pulled her hair back into an elastic band. "I thought you two should talk."

Elena huffed and rolled her eyes. "Okay, *Mom*."

"As *team captain*," Christina stressed the title, "I don't want this tension ruining our team. Let's do this. Get it out."

Elena stared at me. I stared back. I never had anything against her. Having things against anyone wasn't my style. I spent a lot of time trying to be liked.

And look where that had gotten me.

But I'd come home to deal with what needed to be dealt with. I'd ditched my team with barely anything to go on, so they'd filled in the rest from gossip. This was my chance to clear the air.

I took a breath. "I'm sorry—"

"I should start by saying—" Elena said at the same time.

Elena released her arms and stretched them in front of her. "I'm sorry I talked about your sister so harshly. I know she has problems." She let her arms fall to her sides and looked at me directly. "I've been through a few things with my family. I shouldn't judge."

I nodded, taking this in. "Grace is complicated. I'm sorry my family drama took me from the team. We're working on it."

Christina slung an arm over my shoulder and the other over Elena's. "See? Now we're getting somewhere. Holli, we want you on the team. We just want to know you're up for it."

I nodded, but stepped back to gain some space for myself. "I felt guilty the whole summer. For pretty much everything." I wanted them to know the truth, but maybe not as much as Tala and Will knew. "Can I fill you in while we warm up?"

We started with a walk on the park path where I told them more about my family. Elena chimed in with how her parents had divorced when she was young and now she had to adjust to a stepfather. Christina said her cousin was sent to a juvenile detention center this summer and it had shaken up her family. As we graduated to a run, the conversation moved to school and then movies and what music we were into.

I hit my stride and felt what I loved about running. That burst of almost peace-like energy that fueled my steps. I looked over at my friends. Maybe they were part of that feeling too.

We circled the small lake in the park until dusk drew closer, ending our run back by the pavilion and parking lot.

Elena pressed a hand to her lower back as she slowed to a walk. "Remind me again why we do this to our-selves?"

Christina elbowed her. "Because running is the best. *After* you've run."

"And during," I said. "It's kept me sane this summer."

"Is that all?" Elena asked, catching her breath.

"Is that all what?"

"I meant who." She arched a brow. "You were living in a beach town. Tell me you didn't meet somebody while you were there."

"I—"

"You can't because you did," Elena said. "I can tell. Who is it? What are they like?"

I sputtered to come up with a response. Christina dropped her mouth open. "Did you meet someone, Holli? Tell us!"

"I don't know how you could possibly know, but yes. His name is Will."

"Is he older?" Elena asked.

I laughed as she peppered me with more questions. Talking about Will made me miss him and not miss him at the same time.

Since it was growing dark, we said our goodbyes and I headed home through the neighborhood, declining Christina's offer to drive me. I wanted the extra time to think.

Passing by the playground at the school near my house, I stopped dead at the sight in front of me. I squinted to be sure.

Grace, on the swings. A mere block from home.

Before I could dash into someone's yard for escape, Grace looked up. Our eyes met. She didn't move, just looked at me.

I'd come home to face my problems. Not run. Well, I'd also come home to run, literally, with the team. But the figurative run, no. Right now, a very real moment sat in front of me I needed to face.

I jogged in place to keep my muscles from cramping. Now or never.

I made my way across the grass, beyond the brightly colored climbing structure to the swings.

Grace watched me. She had on a navy blue hoodie and shorts showing off long, tanned legs. Her dark hair was swept back in one of those effortless ponytails pretty girls made look easy, the messy strands part of the look.

She pushed back with her feet and swung forward. "Hey, Hol. So, you're back."

"What are you doing here?"

She shrugged. "I'm around. I saw the grans' old van in the driveway."

"Mom and Dad have no idea where you are."

She acted so casual about it. If she hadn't been eighteen, they would have alerted the police for a missing child.

She stuck her feet down and twisted in the swing instead. "I don't think it would help if I showed up. Everyone pretty much hates me."

Did she even know I'd spilled the truth? She had to know by now. "Aren't you mad at me?"

"Come on. How could I be mad? You're an angel. You tried to save me. Have you figured out yet you can't?"

She sounded like she'd been talking to Will. Or spying on our conversations. Seriously, how did she know so much? "I don't understand you."

Grace laughed, but it came out chilled. "It was great while it lasted. Thanks for trying. Now I get to figure out the rest of my life."

Slowly, I paced the length of the swings, itching to stretch my legs. I couldn't focus on my stretches with my impossible sister actively being impossible.

"Is that what you're going to do?" I asked. "Figure out your life?"

"It doesn't come easy for all of us, you know. Not everyone fits the mold of straight-A student, college, and happy career. I'm just trying to get out of this town."

Except she did anything but. If she'd applied to the colleges our parents suggested, that would take her out of town, plus they'd pay for most of it. She could have come with me to Deer Cove. Sure, the town was dinky, but it proved to be a nice change of scenery. And it led to great things for me.

"You don't have to live that life, but you won't get far hiding from all of us."

Grace leaned forward in the swing. "I'm looking at license suspension for at least six months. Fines for the minor in possession, and it's a second offense so they're higher. More fines for those useless prescription pills I *allegedly* took." She rolled her eyes. "Being eighteen means jail time is a possibility. The cops said I'd probably get mandatory substance abuse something or other. As if I haven't been punished enough."

My jaw hung open. "Substance abuse something or other? Grace, *I'm* going to counseling. I just learned about group sessions for family members of alcoholics—"

Grace sputtered a laugh. "I'm *not* an alcoholic. I maybe partied too hard a few times. You're all over reacting."

Anger and frustration bubbled over. "You haven't learned anything. Everything you just said is all about you. Have you even considered how you've hurt other people? How what you did could have seriously injured someone? Even killed them?"

Something flickered in her eye stopping short a snarky response.

"A friend of mine lost their brother to a drunk driver. It changed everything for them and their family. You could have been that driver. Now that you know this, you can't pretend everything is fine. If you do, you risk harming others. You have a problem, and if you ignore it, you become the problem."

Grace chewed at her lip as she studied the wood chips on the ground. "People think Kennedy's overdose is my fault. I would never hurt her."

"What really happened?" I flattened my voice, not intending to accuse, just to know.

Grace seemed to fold into herself on the swing. "We were just doing our thing. I guess she'd had more to drink than I realized and the guys we were with were mixing pills. That's not what I'm into so I wasn't really paying attention." She pressed her lips together and her eyes watered. "It was late and I wanted to go but I couldn't find her. I walked all over the house and found Kennedy in a bedroom passed out on the floor. I couldn't even lift her."

I stilled as her story unfolded. I imagined Grace finding her best friend unconscious. Kennedy—someone I'd known through Grace since early grade school.

"I asked for help to get Kennedy out of the house," Grace went on. "I was really starting to freak out. It was like no one cared, but I couldn't just leave her. I called 9-1-1. The guys, they all got mad at me for narcing on them when an ambulance showed up. I didn't...I didn't know what else to do."

She'd done one right thing at least. "It was good you called for help, Grace. You saved Kennedy's life."

She let out a short laugh. "Not if you ask her parents. They think their precious Kennedy would never have gone to that party if not for me. Just look what I did to my own sister, getting straight-A Holli in trouble with the court." She directed a pointed look at me. "You're always the saint, Holli. No matter what happens."

Her bitter tone erased any sympathy I'd been building up for her. But before I could come up with a response, she spoke again.

"I never would have driven if I knew...I wouldn't hurt you, Hol. You have to know I never would."

But you did. In so many ways.

She'd hurt so many people.

I ran my fingers along the metal swing set pole. "You were so drunk you don't even remember what you said or did getting into the car. That's a problem."

Suddenly, Grace flung herself up from the swing into my space. "What do you want me to do about it, huh? I can't go back in time, okay? Don't you think I would if that was possible?"

Grace couldn't see past herself. She couldn't even step outside her own shadow. "You need help. Mom and Dad will get you help. Our grandparents will get you help. You have to want it. Come back with me, Grace. Come home."

She mumbled about being eighteen and something about freedom, but I was so done with her refusal to take any responsibility. "If you're not mad at me and you don't want to come home, I guess I'll say what I need to say now."

She huffed out a breath. "Okay, fine. I'm listening."

I didn't have a whole speech prepared, but for the past few weeks I'd been going through what I would say to my sister. This had changed over recent days, but the core message remained.

"I love you, Grace. You're my sister and you always will be. I might not ever understand you completely, but I tried. I hope you get help. I don't want to see you lost or hurt or hurting other people. If this wasn't a wake-up call, then I really worry for you. But I can't be on the hook any more to fix you. I won't lie to our parents for you or smooth things over with my friends. Your party barge is your problem."

"Wait, what party barge?"

"Never mind. I'm done, Grace. I'll always love you, but I won't lie for you ever again."

Her expression appeared blank. I hadn't expected much, but secretly hoped for a few tears. Maybe an apology, even if not entirely heartfelt.

Nope. Grace appeared shut off with a distant look in her eye.

So that was that. "Goodbye, Grace."

I headed out of the park. As the sky dimmed, the fireflies woke up. A gentle reminder that life carried on even when it felt like a part of me wouldn't survive. The part that loved my sister dimmed. Just like the fireflies, it flickered again.

"Holli?" Grace called after me.

I slowed but didn't turn.

"Thanks. I love you too."

Chapter Twenty-five

♥

My new normal became daily runs, either on my own or with the cross-country team. I still noticed tension and whispers, but Christina acted as a bridge to the others. I promised myself I'd be honest with them, even if it meant sharing difficult things.

It was too late in the summer to apply at the movie theater with Tala, plus my parents didn't like the idea, so I met with Tala when I could. We set up sleepovers and movie nights.

In between all of this, Will and I texted and talked for long stretches at night. Sometimes on a video chat app, other times just talking.

I made plans to go back to Deer Cove after my next court date. The one where Grace and I were expected to appear together.

Grace. She came home three days after our discussion in the park. At first, I thought it was same as usual with her and Mom already at each other's throats. But then Grace broke down. I'd never seen her cry so openly.

She left again, but ended up back at our house the next day and hadn't left since. In fact, she'd barely left her bedroom at all, so things weren't exactly one hundred over here. But it was a start.

I'd just finished a morning run at the park path when I noticed an unfamiliar car in our driveway. Scratch that. Familiar, but shouldn't be here.

Stickers covered the back of the car and a hot guy leaned against the driver's side door. Dressed all in black even though the temperature would climb to ninety degrees in another few hours.

Will should have looked out of place here. He didn't fit in my life here in Ginsburg. He shouldn't fit, but somehow he stood whole and complete in front of me like he'd always been here.

I ran to him.

Will swung me up and around like a scene from a movie. He set me down and pulled me into a kiss. A deep and wonderful kiss.

We broke apart, but his hands stayed around me. He didn't even complain about my sweaty back.

"You're here," I said.

"I am."

"It's early. You don't like early."

"No, I do not. But I like you. It was worth it to get here now. I was hoping to spend the day together."

I squealed. "You're here to see me? I mean, obviously you are. How did you know I'd be here?"

"I may have done a little recon with your grandparents. I know you've been in touch a lot so I had them check your schedule."

"So that's why they'd asked about my team training camp next week." Crafty grans.

"I couldn't wait until our planned day in Deer Cove. Plus, I wanted to see where you live."

I stepped aside so he could see our two-story house with a well-maintained yard and bright flowers in the window boxes. Not exactly an accurate picture of the inside.

"You'll meet my parents, I guess. Dad's at work, but my mom is here working from her home office."

"Cool. Your grandparents already let them know I was coming."

"Did everyone know but me?"

"Who's the hottie, Holli?" a voice called out a second story window.

I looked up at Grace sitting in the window in her room.

I rolled my eyes. "She knows about you," I said to Will. "I finally had to tell her. Of course, now she'll try to embarrass me with you here."

Will sent a friendly wave toward the window. Grace smirked, then disappeared.

"That's kind of sibling 101, right?" Will asked. "Embarrass your younger sibs."

I moved us from our spot in the middle of the driveway to the shaded front porch. "She's been seeing a therapist and started one of those anonymous groups. Though I guess by telling you, it's no longer anonymous."

"Good to hear. I hope it helps. Maybe I can draw some of these on her hands." He lifted his fists to show off shiny black marker Xes.

I laughed. "She actually might. Grace applied to community college. We'll see how that goes. Which means she'll be living here like old times."

"But not exactly like as old times. Things are different."

They sure were. Will had listened to earful after earful over the phone about what was up at the Hayes house. And here he sat now, not scared away.

Will snapped his fingers. "Remember I told you I'm helping my dad restore my uncle's fishing boat? We took it out on the lake. Not Lake Michigan, but a smaller one. More like a pond, but it's where the fish hang out."

"That's great, Will. I'm glad you've been working with your dad."

"I miss you." He moved aside a strand of my hair plastered to my neck with sweat. Again, not even grossed out. "That's not to make you feel bad about coming back to Ginsburg. Just a fact."

"We're hoping at court I'll be cleared to get my license. It depends on a lot of things." And also depended on whether my parents would allow me to drive anywhere, let alone a longer trip to Deer Cove. "It might be a while yet before I can come see you, but I at least have it to look forward to."

Will jumped up. "I have something for you."

He jogged to his car and unearthed a backpack. Then a larger something flat and square in shape. He returned to me on the porch.

A framed photo collage. Photos of our Leaf Group and pictures from the gallery show with Piper, Antonio, Chaz, and Carmen filled the frame. Bordering the photos, a paper collage in blue and green.

"Carmen did this, didn't she?" I looked at Will.

"We all helped. Well, I got the photos developed at the drugstore. That counts I think." He grinned. "Carmen did the collage and Piper and Chaz took all the pictures since they're better at that sort of thing. Antonio hung around for moral support."

"Sounds about right."

"I've been thinking. It's cool to be part of a group where people are better at stuff than me. Then we each get to contribute something. I'd like to think I'm the guy who brings us all together."

My eyes blurred. "This is really sweet. I'll text everybody thank you."

I hugged Will and stayed there. His arms felt so good. So right.

"I missed you too," I told him. "So, what do you want to do? We have the whole day."

"Anything. So long as I'm with you."

Well, how about I just turn into a puddle right here. "First, I desperately need to change out of these running clothes."

"Maybe into something black?"

"Don't try to change me." I stuck out my tongue. "You wear enough black for the both of us."

"Not true. There's no such thing as too much black."

I pretended to think this over. "Maybe not when it comes to you."

"For real though, I like you just as you are. Sweaty pits and all."

"Ew."

"You're my *ew*." His cheeks colored. "I mean, if you'd like to be. My...what I'm trying to say is... Holli, may I have the honor of being your boyfriend?"

We hadn't put a label on us, but this felt right. "Yes. I accept."

Will stood and held his hand out for me. He pulled me up and wrapped his arms around me again. "I can't wait to see what we can do together. Even with the distance, I don't see that stopping us."

Neither did I. Ahead of me lay a path wide open and wooded, familiar like Deer Cove, but could be anywhere. I could see Will and I fitting where we needed. Ginsburg, Deer Cove, or somewhere else entirely. So long as we had each other.

Epilogue

♥

"Sleeping bags?"

"Check."

"Marshmallows?"

"Check. All other s'mores supplies on deck."

"On deck?" Will peered over the hood of his car to where I stood in the Deer Cove Community Center lot.

"You know, like sailors on the deck. Of a boat." I shrugged. "You know I don't know anything about boats."

Will grinned and walked over. He wrapped me in a bear hug, then growled into my hair. I squealed but didn't push him away.

He pulled back enough to see my face. "I'm glad you came out for our last summer bash. It wouldn't be the same without you."

"You're welcome, by the way," Tala said and twirled the end of her ponytail.

"Thank you, Tala," Will said in a purposely loud, dopey voice, still holding onto me. "Thank you for driving Holli here this weekend."

Tala struck a ballerina-worthy pose. "No problem. After you gave me a heads-up for those pre-sale concert tickets, I feel like I owe you."

Elena and Christina joined our group after grabbing bags from Tala's car. We'd all carpooled with me and Tala to Deer Cove for the weekend. We had the best accommodations in town—Cabin 4 at Sunset Inn. I'd claimed top bunk.

"What I like most is how both your fashion choices are influencing each other," Elena added, looking at me and Will.

I had on a new band shirt. A white shirt, not black, featuring the band with the skull and hearts-for-eyes logo.

Will smoothed his short-sleeved button down shirt which hung over a black T-shirt. "Hey, I've got layers. Literally and metaphorically."

He'd gotten a skate shoe upgrade to a new gray and white pair and his hair had longer lighter roots now that he let the black grow out. He still had dark hair, but dark brown. He said he'd grown tired of buying hair dye. I figured maybe the all-black look no longer fit for him. Sometimes that happened, where what used to fit no longer did.

Another vehicle pulled into the community center lot. The addition our party needed: the Dragon Wagon.

"What's up, fam?" Antonio sauntered over with Piper, Chaz, and Carmen. Coming in on his own from a different direction, Aaron, the group's most recent addition.

The first embers of bonfire flickered to life on the beach. We set up the usual circle of blankets and chairs and coolers by the fire with more supplies in the Dragon Wagon's open rear door. I loved this. Old and new friends mingling together.

I set down my bag on the sand and looked back at Will. "You think you can make the meet next weekend?"

"When you cross the finish line, I want to be the first person you see. I've got my Team Holli T-shirt ready to go."

I covered my face with my hands. "No! Are you trying to destroy me by humiliation?"

"The shirts are real. Ask Piper."

"It's true," Piper called over from nearby. "I have a screen print press and we made them yesterday. Hot pink lettering on a black shirt. I've got spares."

Spares? "For who?"

Antonio unearthed a giant tub of cheezy poofs from the van and cracked it open. "Oh, you know. Us."

Chaz set a cooler on the ground. "I found a great deal on wholesale, American-made pre-shrunk cotton shirts so we ordered an even dozen."

This was so embarrassing. "A *dozen*?

Elena plucked a cheezy poof and crunched. "Ooh, Holli. You have fans."

"Your grandparents wanted shirts," said Will. "They chipped in on the order."

He appeared to be serious. "Are you guys road-tripping with my grandparents to my cross-country meet?"

Antonio gestured toward the van. "If they want to ride in the Dragon Wagon, I'm down."

"We can fit up to eight people," Piper added. "Well, maybe six since we need room for the signs. The Team Holli signs."

"Oh my gosh." I buried my face into Will's shoulder.

We settled into spots around the bonfire as Piper and Carmen added wood and kindling. Christina and Elena stoked the flames to get the fire going.

A round of Campfire Shuffle kicked off the party. Tala and I dominated the game, much to Will's amused frustration. Rookie move to let us get sorted onto the same team.

Elena leaned in toward me. "Your small town friends are pretty cool, Holli. When you told me they were the high-on-life crowd, I had my doubts."

"I heard that." Christina threw a marshmallow at Elena, who caught it mid-air. "We can't all be as cool as your senior friends running Midwest Wild Adventure back home."

Elena tossed the marshmallow back. "Ha. I wish."

The local theme park with water slides (and more!) was notorious for being run by the under-twenty-one crowd. Everybody went at least once over the summer since the prices and proximity beat driving hours to the larger theme parks in neighboring states.

A trip to the water park was yet another experience I'd missed this summer being in Deer Cove. But I wouldn't trade what I'd done here, hanging with decidedly older senior friends at the community center.

The sun lowered and split the sky into competing blues and oranges. Will and I wordlessly rose from the blanket circle. I glanced to Tala. She nodded and scooted closer to the others, grabbing another marshmallow to roast.

Will and I headed for our log. When we reached it, I leaned up to meet his lips with mine. He deepened the kiss and I sent back all I had through our connection.

I nearly melted on the spot.

He made a move to pull back, but I kept him close. Just another second.

"Holding onto summer?" His mouth brushed against mine.

"Holding onto you." I winced at my own words. "Dorky?"

"Not dorky. Even if it was dorky, I'd like it because you said it. Too much?"

"Not too much."

I ground my toes into the cool sand. I wanted to soak up every inch of the beach to last me until my next visit. "I'm hoping to come out here one weekend a month. Then with you coming to see me, we trade off who visits who."

"I'll pencil you in between these morning runs."

"As if you'd wake up early to run on purpose. Are you still running at all?"

"Only to outrun a bear."

I looked around. "So, not much running I take it."

"Nope. Sorry."

"Don't be sorry. You hated it."

"How about, I tried something and moved on."

I grinned. "That's the attitude I know and love. I'm even learning it for myself."

The sinking sun filled in for any words.

I thought back to Grandpa's poetic words about not covering the whole sky with your hand. I'd finally looked up the phrase. One of the meanings meant closing oneself off to truths, or avoiding what's in front of you. The sky would always be there, even if we didn't want to see it.

My sky, my broken little family. My sky, Will, and my feelings for him. My sky, letting what needed to break, break. To live each day, cracks and all.

The sun let go of its hold on the day, and night filled in around us.

"Will?" I looked up at him. He stood half a head taller, but the difference didn't feel so much in bare feet.

"Yeah?"

"I'm glad I'm back, too."

Thank you for reading! Reviews help readers find books. Please consider leaving a review on your favorite retailer.

Next in Series: Big Wild Summer
Read on for chapter 1 of Elena's story!

Big Wild Summer

I never imagined the first day at my dream summer job would involve waiting alone in a supply shack to meet the boy I'd crushed on since seventh grade.

I was truly living the dream.

Hired at the coolest summer job in the vicinity of Ginsburg, Michigan—Midwest Wild Adventure theme park, featuring adventure-themed rides and a pretty dope water park.

Best of all, what Midwest Wild Adventure had was KJ Keene.

My longest-running crush. My now within-reach crush, a recently graduated senior and lifeguard at the water park in Wild Adventure (what everyone called the park, or if you were on staff, just Wild. I was *so* excited to call it Wild).

Not only would I appease my parents by taking on responsibility with a summer job, I could finally make something happen with KJ before he left for college.

Day one on the job and already I had an opportunity for alone time with KJ. All I had to do was wait here in this supply shack and he'd meet me. My friend, Chelsea, from West Ginsburg High arranged everything. She'd even gotten me the job.

It sure was hot in this shed. I lifted my hair and fanned my neck with a stray piece of cardboard. Moments ago, I'd shaken my hair out from a ponytail. Maybe I should put it back up. I wanted to look summer casual for KJ when he arrived.

I'd been watching KJ for years. He was a classic hottie. Tall, dark hair, that olive skin which people mistook him for half a dozen ethnicities—Mexican, Puerto Rican, Spanish. He was biracial Honduran and white and since junior year had a hint of scruff along his jawline. Cute, full lips and a real knee-buckler as far as grins went. His hair naturally curled at the ends in the humidity, something I'd noticed as late spring crawled into the heat of summer.

KJ was the kind of guy who showed up to charity events and looked cool doing it. He would spend the summer shirtless at the wave pool saving children.

I fanned myself some more. Kind of hard to look cute sweating in a shed beside metal racks loaded with tools and boxes. Two folding chairs angled toward each other with an ancient portable stereo on the floor between them. I could sit but nerves kept me standing. A single bulb with a chain pull provided light.

I checked my watch. Any minute now he'd be here. Maybe he had trouble escaping the wave pool. This was my first real shift, but Chelsea promised to cover for me at the Little Adventurer Kid's Zone. She'd told me it was key to get time with KJ before the summer started rolling.

The door to the supply shack creaked open. By instinct, I leaped behind cover of a shelving rack positioned in the middle of the space. I smoothed my hair against my shoulders and my brand new staff T-shirt. I took a breath and stepped out.

A hulking figure stood in the doorway. I squinted as my eyes adjusted from the bright sunlight streaming in.

The person who entered had brown hair that limped against wide shoulders. Arms like cannons nearly burst through the sleeves of a Midwest Wild Adventure Crew T-shirt. A huge dude. Besides the fact he probably wasn't much older than me, he looked like the kind of guy who worked the door at a night club or appeared as back-up to the bad guys in a movie.

He scowled my direction. Definitely not the easy-going KJ smile.

"Oh hey," I said, edging the nervousness from my voice. "I'm, um, waiting for someone."

The guy sighed. "He's not coming."

My heart dropped to my stomach. "What? Where's KJ?"

The guy shrugged. If you could even call it that. It was more of a twitch in his massive shoulder while the rest of his body remained solid and unmoving like a commercial-grade refrigerator.

"I just wanted to talk him," I added, the nervousness spilling out anyway. "I know him. We go to school together."

He seemed to be waiting for me to finish talking. "They're all here. Grab one of those boxes."

Who...what?

The big guy opened the door wider and murmuring voices carried past him. Who was here?

I took a box, the nearest thing to me, and followed him out.

Everything next happened in painful slow motion.

Menacing laughter circled the air. Someone pointed their phone at me and snapped a picture. Applause rippled through the crowd.

"One wild virgin down!" a voice declared.

My jaw dropped. *Wild virgin?*

Okay, first there was nothing wrong with being a virgin. I was and was proud to say it. I had a whole speech about women's autonomy and patriarchal standards of womanhood and I wasn't afraid to use it. My parents were frequently afraid because I was blessed-slashed-cursed with what they termed a naturally sassy mouth. It bought me trouble, and often.

I looked at the huge guy who'd walked out ahead of me. What exactly did they think had happened in this supply shed?

"What's that girl's name?" someone asked above the laughter.

"I think her name is Elena something," came a suggestion full of pre-packaged innocence.

That came from Chelsea, who absolutely knew my name. She even knew my last name, which coincidentally, matched the theme park. De Wilde. It was spelled with an E on the end due to my uber-Dutch heritage, but it sounded the same when spoken.

I gaped at the faces before me, all in Wild Adventure staff shirts. "What is this?" I asked Chelsea.

Chelsea grinned. "You win."

To my horror part two, someone stage left set a pink plastic crown on my head. I yanked at it, but the crown's tiny plastic comb teeth snagged against my hair. The crown was eating my head.

Finally, I tugged the crown free, bringing with it a snarly sample of my dark red hair. The crown featured a middle gemstone with a "V" marked in Sharpie.

Forget my jaw hanging open, my face dropped to the ground. I shot my gaze to the big guy. He just stood there, all large and definitely not in charge. "But we didn't *do* anything."

"Doesn't matter." Chelsea sashayed toward me like a fictional siren. A siren who lured other girls to be pranked, apparently. "You believed KJ would meet you there."

Okay, sure, I wanted some solo time with KJ, but it wasn't like I thought we'd *do* anything. I'd just wanted to finally tell him how I felt since Chelsea...*dangit*.

Chelsea had been feeding me lines how KJ would be perfect for me. For *weeks*.

I was so stupid. So stupidly trusting.

I should have known day one was too soon for KJ to finally stop seeing through me like a freshly Windexed pane of glass.

I'd been set up.

Spotting KJ in the crowd, my pale pre-summer cheeks flamed redder than the fire engine ride in the Little Adventurer Zone. There was no escape. Just eyes and barking, howling laughter.

KJ held a hand over his mouth. He stepped forward, leaning in like he intended to share a secret. "Every year, girls try to hook up with their crush. We see who's gullible enough to go to the Love Hut and wait for their Romeo. I guess that's you."

Oh no. Oh no way no.

"That's not—" I fumbled for words. "Why did you—"

Lie to me. I couldn't complete my thoughts out loud.

Chelsea smirked. "Now you know how it feels."

I had no clue what she was talking about. We were *friends*.

It was like I was being crushed, slowly. The weight of my own humiliation pressed down.

"What's going on?" a voice boomed across the fenced yard. That would be my new boss, Terry.

Terry stood with hands at his hips like a gym teacher fired up for a round of burpees. Not that he'd be doing burpees himself. Terry had a wiry frame and translucent white skin streaked with SPF infinity-strength. "You kids pranking the new blood again?" He shook his head with the wisdom of a seasoned twenty-three-year-old night shift park manager. He held out his hand. "Give me the crown."

I walked two shameful steps toward him. It was stupid to feel any shame when 1.) I hadn't done anything to feel ashamed of, and 2.) I'd been duped by staff who knew better.

I handed Terry the stupid plastic crown.

I cut a glare at Chelsea. Her honey-blonde topknot bobbed up and down as she made a production out of stifling a laugh.

Chatter floated through the group until Terry blew a whistle. He really did channel gym teacher vibes. "Moving on. Where is Elena De Wilde?"

I slowly raised my hand.

He shook his head slowly. "Really turning out an all-star performance your first day, huh? You were supposed to be shadowing your team lead in Lil' Paul Bunyan Square. Can you tell me why you weren't in Lil' Paul Bunyan Square and instead in the Love Hut?"

Well, when he said it that way it sounded really bad. "Do Chelsea and KJ have to answer next? They were involved with this whole Love Hut set-up."

"Oh no she didn't," someone said and snickered.

Terry flipped his sunglasses up onto his sandy-haired buzz cut. "You think this is a joke? You abandoned your post."

An *oooh* chorused through the crowd.

"Can anyone here repeat for Elena what the number one rule is working at Wild Adventure?" Terry asked.

"Never abandon your post," the staff answered at the same time.

"Unless?" Terry asked again.

"Unless you have coverage," the group finished.

Terry looked at me. "You, Elena. Did not secure coverage. If this had been a scenario where you hadn't been shadowing another staff, you'd have left a children's area void of supervision. Do you know what happens when children are left unsupervised?"

"But they weren't—"

Terry cut me off. "Can someone tell me what happens when children are left unsupervised?"

"Lawsuits," the group stated as one.

"Exactly. Lawsuits. Allegations. Bad press." Terry folded his arms. "We have probationary hiring for a reason. We don't want another Cayden Moore situation."

The group chatter dwindled to silence.

I looked around at frozen, somber faces. I thought quickly. Who was Cayden Moore?

Terry paced in front of me. "In case you don't recall, Cayden Moore was a child injured here last summer. A huge media blitz followed, declaring how our park was unsafe. *Not a place for families.* Thankfully, Cayden turned out okay—and the family was incredibly generous with their forgiveness. But we can't afford another hit to our reputation."

The heat of attention shifted from me to the guy next to me. The big guy.

I had so many questions.

The guy stared straight ahead, his eyes deadlocked on absolutely nothing. This guy's eyes pooled with black. Like a very dark lagoon.

A chill ran down my arms and it was still eighty degrees out here.

I was now fighting total social humiliation and a public reprimand from my new boss. I'd disappointed authority once or twice and survived—mouthy girls didn't get away scot-free every time. I knew what I had to do.

Grovel. I had to make this right.

"I'm so sorry," I said to Terry. "It won't happen again."

"You're right it won't happen again." He flipped a paper over on his clipboard.

Great. One day down and I was about to get the chop. My dream job lasted one whole day.

"I'm reassigning you," Terry stated. "You're moving to the old park. You'll be on go-karts with Jonah."

The crowd shifted, this time to look back at me. Their faces, a mixture of shock and pity. One sneer belonging to Chelsea. What was her *deal*? KJ at least had the decency to look a little guilty.

"Who's Jonah?" I asked Terry.

He pointed to the scary dude with the dark eyes. Who now stared daggers at me.

Acknowledgments

♥

Big thanks to everyone who helped get this book to where it is now. Early readers Kelly Garcia, Vanessa M. Knight, J. Leigh Bailey, and Sarah LaPolla. Thank you to Melanie Hooyenga and Liza Street for recent support on publishing. There are honestly countless others who have helped me both directly and without even knowing it. The Pitch Wars community and my Romance Writers of America friends, your support is immeasurable. And to my family and husband who not only cheer me on, but dare me to dream bigger.

Also by Stephanie J. Scott

Young Adult Books
All Last Summer
Sunset Summer
Big Wild Summer
Free Wheeling Summer
All-Star Love
Alterations
Adult Romance
Falling Into Place
OMG Christmas Tree

www.stephaniejscott.com

About the Author

Stephanie J. Scott writes young adult and romance about characters who put their passions first. Her debut ALTERATIONS about a fashion-obsessed loner who reinvents herself was a Romance Writers of America RITA® award finalist. She enjoys dance fitness, everything cats, and has a slight obsession with Instagram. A Midwest girl at heart, she resides outside of Chicago with her tech-of-all-trades husband and fuzzy furbabies.

Photo: Leah Lewis Photography